ECTOSTORM

Book Three of the Stanley Cooper Chronicles

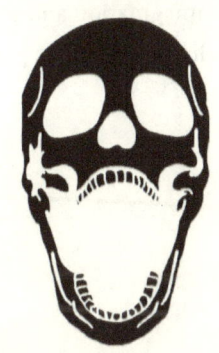

Scott A. Johnson

ISBN-10: 978-0692165270

ISBN-13: 0692165274

Edited by Lily K. Coy-Johnson

Printed in the USA

Second Edition

This book is dedicated to the person who gave me back my life and made me feel like me again. Thank you, Katie. Without you this book wouldn't exist.

THE AUTHOR WOULD LIKE TO THANK

There is an old saying among writers, that the act of writing is a solitary practice and that we, the writers, are most happy when left alone. But the truth is, without a strong support system, without friends and family, without encouragement, these books would never be written. It is, therefore, from the bottom of my heart, that thanks go out to: My wife and children, my parents, my brother, and the rest of my family. To my friends in Evergreen (the real one) and the people of Monroeville, to the Lifeless, and to Professor Emcee Square, Pointy, Stiffy, Helga, Leah, and Fritz. There are also people who I consider my mentors and friends, Gary Braunbeck, Tim Waggoner, and Mike Arnzen, whom I thank for their wit, wisdom, and friendship. To Doctor Pus, the great man behind the Twisted Library Press, and to all my friends, students, colleagues, and fans, without whom I wouldn't have a job. Also, thank you to the "Mean Girls," Nikki, Erica, Venessa, Kristin, Kerri, Jared, Paul and Gia. Thank you to the faculty, students, and alumni of Seton Hill University's WPF program. To all my friends who die in this book, and to the students of ALPHA, whose murder moved me to maniacal laughter. And to Steve, Debi, Nomad, Buzz, and the rest of the Dread Central staff. And finally, thank you to the great state of Pennsylvania, and more specifically, Pittsburgh, for making such a lasting impression on this Texas boy.

EXTRA SPECIAL KICKSTARTER THANKS

This book was something of an experiment. I wanted to see if there was demand from the fans for a third installment, and so I launched a project on Kickstarter.com with a modest goal. The support was overwhelming. So to all my supporters who made this book possible, my most sincere and humble thanks. They are: Paul Grant, Sheena England, Alyssa Boebel, RonGavalik, Julie Schuler, Erica McEachern, Symantha Reagor, Carrie Miller, Jennifer Della'Zanna, Kerri-Leigh Grady, Ron Shannon, Jessica Vann, Michelle, Valerie Anderson, Todd Harlan, Jodie Claes, Irene L. Pynn, Nancy Johnson, Chris Jeane, Jenny Gottsch, Kristina Butke, Venessa Giunta, Alleen Erin, Ann Kopchik, David Day, Fran Van Cleave, Leadie Jo Flowers, Genevieve Eldredge, Mike Brendan, Rebecca and Derrik Smootz, Elsa Carruthers, Calie Voorhis, Troy Bucher, Clint and Heather McCrocklin, Nikki Hopeman, and CJ. You people made this book possible, and any thanks I give will never be enough.

2018 ADDENDUM

How often can we go to the well before it dries up? When this book was first published, I thought this was the end of Stanley Cooper's adventures. In all honesty, I thought it was the end of my time as a writer. This book came out at a time when my life changed forever, and not in the best of ways. To be honest, I quit writing, and I had no intention of going back to it. But then, something extraordinary happened. I met someone who made me feel like me again. Her name is Katie, and it is because of her that I am here, now, writing this. So, more than anyone else, thank you to my Katie. Thank you for giving me back my life.

COMING SOON

BITTEN

Book Four of the Stanley Cooper Chronicles

MOJO

Book Five of the Stanley Cooper Chronicles

1

"We're losing her!"

The child writhed and thrashed her head from side to side. It was all I could do to keep my palm on her forehead. With only one good arm, I couldn't grab hold of anything, but her light faded with every second that ticked by. Darkness bit chunks out of her aura as we tried to purge it from her body.

"Not while I'm still breathing," growled Maggie.

I stole a glance at the other four people in the room. The child's father held one of her arms in place, a priest the other. Two guys built like linebackers, the girl's brothers, held a leg each, which left me in the unenviable position of straddling the girl's midsection while Maggie stood behind the headboard of the bed.

To anyone else, the scene might have looked cruel. A child thrashing on a bed, four grown men holding her down while a fifth sat on her, a woman who wasn't her mother muttering eerie phrases in a forgotten language. But to me, the scene was much worse. No one else saw the black sludge that oozed out of her nostrils and ears and eyes and mouth. No one else saw her beautiful blue and pink aura as it faded and fractured. No one but me.

There were signs visible to anyone. Her eyes, for example, were no longer pale blue, but blazed hot amber. Her sweet voice dropped two octaves and sounded like an old wino who gargled with drain cleaner. Then there were the other things. Subtle things, like dressers that moved across the room and fires that started in the bathtub while it was full of water. Not to mention the indoor tornado in which we currently sat.

Like I said, subtle.

The family did what most others would do, I suppose. They called doctors, shrinks, healers, priests. All of them walked away with shaking heads and shaken faith. As hard as they tried, they couldn't help the little girl. Then, somehow, they found my number, probably through a friend of a friend or some distant acquaintance. As usual, I was their last resort. And for no reasons other than bull-headedness and pride, I wasn't going to let this kid down.

"He's in too deep!" I shouted. "He won't let go!"

Maggie narrowed her eyes.

"Tell me your name!" she commanded.

The thing inside the little girl laughed. The sound turned a giant screw in my stomach.

"Our name is Legion," it growled. "For we are many."

"Oh, come on," I spat. "I've seen that movie, too! How many does it take to hurt one little girl?"

"The girl is shit," said the thing. Its amber eyes locked with mine as a sick grin gashed across her sweet face. "We want you, Stanley Cooper."

It said my name. The damned thing knew my name. Its voice oozed across my name and made it dirty, covered me in filth.

"Don't listen!" shouted Maggie over the wind. "Kayla!

You have to fight!"

The tiny pink and blue light surged for a second, then dimmed. I knew what was coming, and I didn't like it. But I couldn't see another way out either.

Maggie grabbed the child's head and liquid fire raced down her arms, through her fingertips, and into Kayla. Her light grew brighter again with the infusion, but the dark creature would not let go. The more she poured in, the more the thing ate.

"He's not letting go," I shouted. "Get ready."

"Don't you do it!" Maggie's eyes blazed with anger and fear. She knew what was coming, too. Truth to tell, I didn't want to do it either. In theory, I knew it would work, but I'd never tried it before. The chances of doing real damage to myself were high, but I didn't see much of a choice. If Maggie kept pouring power into Kayla's tiny frame, she might kill the creature, sure, but it was likely she'd burn the kid out as well. None of the prayers, spells, begging or asking pretty-please-with-sugar-on-top had any chance of getting it to let go, so the only option was to give it what it wanted.

I leaned over the child and cupped her head with my hand, then I locked eyes with the demon.

"You want me, you son of a bitch? Come get me."

The next thing that hit me was intense pain, like someone stuck two live electric cables to my eyes. The thing in the little girl struck me with enough force to knock me backward off the bed. I hit the floor hard as its cold darkness swam through my system. I felt foul, felt like doing bad things to good people. The scent of the little girl's innocence intoxicated me with the need to tear her flesh from her bones. Her fear dripped from my tongue like rancid honey. In the back of my mind, the awful thing whispered, tempted. And in my mind's eye, I could see it.

"You're kidding," I said.

Far from any "Legion," or even anything impressive, the creature appeared to be a little lump of a thing. For the life of me, it looked like a burnt marshmallow on toothpick legs.

"Do not laugh at me!" it shrieked as it stretched its arms out. Liquid darkness poured from its body into my brain and began sucking the energy out of me. The marshmallow bloated and stretched, the toothpicks swelled. In the physical world, my limbs went limp. I didn't even have enough strength to lift my head. I saw the world the way it saw it, diseased and rotten and ugly.

I wanted to call out to Maggie, but pain lanced through my body and my muscles jerked, my jaw locked as the monster inside me fought for control. But Maggie knew what to do. Warmth flooded me as she took my hand and added her energy to mine. It was just the boost I needed.

"Surprise, asshole," I grunted through clenched teeth.

I felt the thing recoil, felt it tear pieces of my soul as it dug its ethereal fingers in, but as strong as it was, it couldn't match the both of us.

Everyone has a place deep inside where wicked and evil thoughts lurk and try to get out. The little voice that tells people to push the obnoxious kid in front of an oncoming bus lives there, as does the one that tells folks that bonking the hot secretary isn't really cheating if the wife never finds out. Things like hatred and greed, sorrow and pain live there. The darker the person's soul, the bigger the place. I've had some pretty dark days.

In my mind's eye, a big steel door opened, and the darkness behind it howled in rage. The demon's grotesque face twisted, and for a moment I recognized terror. I almost felt sorry for it. It screamed my name as it flew backward, and the door slammed shut behind it.

I gasped for air as my body finally relaxed, and opened

my eyes to find Maggie's worried and angry face staring down at me.

"It worked," I croaked. "Got him."

She shook her head and pushed herself to her feet, then rushed out of the room. Kayla's father went after her, leaving the dumbfounded priest and the other two boys to help me up.

"You okay?" asked one.

"Yeah," I panted. "I think so."

"Did...you just do what I think you did?" The priest stared at me.

"Yeah," I nodded.

"But what about..?"

"How's Kayla?" I didn't need to hear it from him. Since the day I died and came back, priests gave me the same lines and worried looks, asked me if I was concerned for my immortal soul and if I'd prepared for the afterlife. In the end, nothing they said mattered. No amount of kneeling or praying or *Hail Marys* or *Our Fathers* changed what I felt, changed what happened to me.

"She's fine," he said. "But right now I'm more concerned about you."

"This isn't my first rodeo," I said. "I'll live."

"But why would you invite..?"

"It was either her or me," I snapped. "She's got her whole life ahead of her."

"But what about you?"

I snatched my coat off the floor and made for the door.

"Wanna trade places, Father?" His face turned ashen. "Didn't think so."

Pithy comebacks and life-threatening situations don't come naturally to me as one might think. I'm not a hero. I certainly don't look the type. I don't have classic features or a chiseled physique, and I look anything but tough. In fact, I'm short, a little doughy, and while I do have great hair, there's a lot of it. I'm not a hero. I'm just the only guy I know who can do what I do.

I stepped out of the building and sucked in a lungful of cool autumn air. The year was dying, fighting the good fight against the beginning of the dead season, but it was still a few weeks until the first snowfall usually hit Pittsburgh. Stars twinkled in the cloudless sky. Still, the air felt charged, like the buildup to a terrific thunderstorm. I felt good, despite the knowledge that I would be pretty sore in the morning, and that I had an unwelcome boarder imprisoned in me without a single clue how to get him out.

Maggie stared hot daggers at me as she leaned against the hood of her car. "You're going to kill yourself, and you're going to make me watch."

"There was no other way and you know it," I said. "It would've killed her."

"You don't know that," she shouted. "We could've found another way."

"That kid didn't have any other options," I said. "We didn't have time to try to coax it out, and asking it nicely didn't work. What did you want me to do?"

She didn't say anything for a moment.

"So now what?"

"I don't know," I said. "Think you can figure out how to get it out of me?"

"Not while you're alive," she said.

I was going to make a witty comment, something that would make her laugh or at least make her call me a smartass. But my legs wobbled, my vision blurred, and the next thing I knew, the sidewalk reared up and smacked me in the forehead, then the world went black.

2

Weird stuff happens to me more often that it does normal folks. By normal, I mean the average Joe who goes to work, watches the news, drives an import, and goes home to his wife, two-point-five kids and dog, and enjoys watching football. First, I hate football. Baseball doesn't do it for me either. I like hockey, but that's about it as far as organized team sports goes. Second, I don't have kids, and if I had a dog I'm pretty sure Maggie's cat, Bitsy, would tear it apart in record time. Third, I prefer to drive American-made cars. I don't actually own one at the moment, but my last car was a Chrysler. Oh, and I died once and can see ghosts now.

So waking up in my bed surrounded by candles and burning incense didn't really faze me. The fact that I was naked at the time gave me a slight pause, but it wasn't as if it hadn't happened before. What bothered me was that I was alone. Whenever I got hurt in the past, Maggie watched over me. I'd awaken to find her kind and concerned face staring down, chanting, pouring me full of her healing energies. It's one of the perks of having an honest-to-Goddess, spell-slinging witch for a girlfriend.

But today, I woke up without another breathing soul in the room. Not only that, but the air, though warm enough, was still. Either something was wrong, or Maggie was angry with me. Neither scenario filled me with joy.

I got up, found a fresh pair of jeans and a long-sleeved pullover on a chair, and went downstairs.

Maggie and I lived in her apartment above her shop. I owned a place of my own, a two-bedroom apartment with windows that overlooked Pittsburgh's three rivers, but it was more of a storage unit anymore. Not for our things, but for items that needed to be kept safe, away from innocent hands, or from those who might use them for less than savory purposes. I never went there unless I had to.

The stairs groaned and creaked as I made my descent, as did my body. I felt like I'd been mugged by a renegade hockey team. In truth, I might have felt better if the Penguins skated over me and used me for slap shot target practice. I hurt all over, almost as bad as I did when I died. And worse, there was a new pain inside, one that itched and churned and fought its way up.

The demon. That slimy little bastard I pulled out of the girl still had some fight in him.

He knew my name. He said I was the one he wanted. A paranoid person might think such a thing meant he used the little girl, an innocent, to come after me. The thought made me gag.

I stopped on the bottom step, centered myself, and opened the door.

Maggie's shop was, as far as I knew, one of a kind in Pittsburgh. Sure, there were other shops that catered to the witchy-fad kids that bought their weight in fairy statues and patchouli incense, but Maggie's was known as a place for the *real* practitioners. There was no sign on the street proclaiming the name of her shop, no list of services offered in the dark-tinted window. There wasn't even a display to entice passersby into the store. The only mark was on the outside of the door: Two silver crescents with a circle in the center. People who knew what it meant got the message. Those who didn't know, most of the time, didn't care. Sure, she got the odd kid in every now and again who wanted some dusty forgotten tome, but on the whole, her shop carried herbs, teas and lotions that Maggie made herself. She also made candles and other things that I didn't know the name for. I did, however, know that Maggie's wares were one hundred percent real, filled with her own energies and potencies.

And, besides, how many other shops in Pittsburgh were actually *alive*?

The bell jingled over the door as I walked inside. Maggie glanced up from behind the counter, then went back to whatever she was reading. Her long red hair was pulled up in a severe pony-tail, never a good sign. The air around me chilled by a few degrees. Yeah, I was in trouble, and I didn't need to ask why.

"Fourteen hours," she said without looking up. "That's a new record."

"It had to be done," I said as I crossed the floor.

She didn't speak. Bad sign.

"I mean, that thing would've killed the kid before it let go."

Still nothing. The urge to turn around and bolt for the door was strong.

"I can handle..." I wished I could suck the phrase back in.

"Think so?" she snapped. "What about me? Think I can handle watching you *damn* yourself so you can play noble cowboy? I love you, but what you did... "

"It couldn't be helped. Besides, I'm fine," I said, and wished by the fire that blazed in her eyes that I'd remained silent.

"Really?" she shouted. "You know that for a fact? Because *I* sure don't know what happens when someone takes a demon into himself on purpose! What do I know? Hell, let's set up a halfway house for demons, why don't we? We can use what's left of your soul to feed them and that empty space between your ears as living space!"

She slammed her book closed and stormed off to the back of the shop, which left me standing dumbfounded. After a moment or two, during which I rehearsed a wonderful argument in my head, I followed. My plan was to launch into an explanation, remind her of what would happen to people like that little girl if I didn't jump in. I didn't ask for this bizarro "gift," but I had to do something with it, dammit. I passed through the beaded curtain and found her sitting at her workbench with her back to the door. I could tell by the way her body hitched up and down that she was crying. My whole argument evaporated.

"Maggie...?"

"Why?" she sniffled. "Why'd you do it? I mean, look at you. Look what all this has done to you. How many times have you almost died? Look at your arm."

She had a point. Beneath my long sleeve, my withered left arm was a horror to behold. I had a tattoo just at the wrist once, one that protected me from bad energies. But it exploded, burnt my arm from the bone outward. The hand looked okay, just... gimpy. But the arm was grotesque, like melted wax around bone. I couldn't move it, couldn't feel it even. But I couldn't let the doctors amputate it. It was a part of me, and I couldn't let it go. I kept it clean, and there wasn't any real risk of infection. Besides, keeping it allowed me to live with the illusion that it might start working some day, that with enough work and will, it might heal and I might be a whole person again.

Of course, there were other scars, and not just on my

body. I'd lost friends, gained a whole host of new phobias and neuroses, and developed what Maggie liked to call a "death wish." It wasn't true, of course. I had no desire to die. Again. What I saw when I died the first time was enough to make me want to stay firmly planted on *this* side of the hereafter, thanks very much. What I saw was... nothing.

Most people, when they die, if they come back, tell stories of seeing bright lights or tunnels, string music or friends and family. A few talk about a place I can only assume is hell, complete with fire and brimstone. Me? When I died, there was nothing. Like I was a universal afterthought. No choirs, no family to greet me, no floating up above my own body or bright lights. Just nothing. Just dark. And it scared the hell out of me.

"What do you want me to do? I should've let that little girl die?"

"You didn't have to take it into yourself."

"It wasn't going to let go of her," I said. "It would've killed her and jumped into someone else. And you know it."

"But that doesn't mean it has to be *you*. Sure, someone needs to speak for these people. Okay, I get that. But why does that someone always have to be *you*? Haven't you done enough?"

"You're missing something," I said. "It knew my name. It used her to get to me."

"Demons lie," she said. It was the same tone of voice she used when she wanted to convince herself of something she knew was wrong. "Maybe it was just trying to rattle you."

"I don't think so," I said as I moved to put my good arm around her. There was nothing I could say that would make anything better. Despite what she said, she had the same thought. It wanted me. And if it knew my name, chances were good more demons would, too, and they might be on their way. The thought of watching me slowly kill myself was torturing her. But instead of curling up in my grasp, she shrank away, slid off her stool and headed out the back door toward the stairs to her apartment. In her wake, the room got colder.

"I know," I said. "She'll come around."

Most people might think a person who stands in the center of a room talking to himself was crazy. But I wasn't talking to myself. I was talking to the shop, the living, sentient being inside which I stood. She was brought to life a little over a year ago, and she didn't like it when Maggie and I fought.

The chime over the door rang as a man in a dark overcoat and sunglasses stepped inside.

We get all kinds in Maggie's shop, from the straight-laced types to the really flamboyant weirdoes. But the ones that crack me up the most are the ones who act like they don't want to be noticed, like they're afraid to be seen in such a place. Typically, those are the types who are looking for something, and don't know enough about the Craft to know that what they're looking for doesn't exist. Most of them are looking for either get-rich-quick spells or the super-killer love potion that will turn anyone of the opposite sex into a slave for their depraved wills. They all wear dark sunglasses and outfits that make them look like a bad cliché of a secret agent. Just like this guy. If I hadn't seen it a hundred times, it might've been laughable.

I set my resolve, put on my best non-threatening smile, and headed toward the door to greet him.

"Hiya," I said. "Something I can help you find?"

"Not something," he said. "But someone. I'm looking for Stanley Cooper."

It wasn't that he said my name that gave me the urge to giggle. It wasn't even that he was looking for me. It was *how* he said my name that made me want to look for a hidden camera. The guy obviously watched too many old spy movies, and I'm not sure but I could swear I heard a trace of a fake accent that was supposed to be either French or German.

"That so?" I said. "Who wants him?"

The man looked around, as if he thought he was being followed, then lowered his sunglasses. The eyes that peered over the black plastic rims were plain brown, if a bit twitchy.

"I represent a group of like-minded individuals," he whispered. "We would like to meet with you."

He passed a card to me with all the skill of a poorly trained chimpanzee, then he pushed his sunglasses back over his eyes and hurried out the door. I stood there for a few moments, stunned, as I tried to piece together just what in the hell happened.

"Stan, I..." Maggie emerged from the back of the shop. She didn't look contrite, but her anger seemed to have calmed a bit. She stopped halfway across the room and stared at me with a puzzled look. "What?"

"I don't know," I said. "Just had some weirdo come in."

"My customers aren't weirdoes," she said. It was an automatic response. She knew just as well as I did what some of her patrons looked like, but to her, they all deserved dignity and the benefit of the doubt. "What did he want?"

"Me, I think."

I turned the card over in my hand. On one side was an address, today's date, and a time. The other side, in bold black letters, read "SPIRIT."

"What for?"

"I don't know," I said as I tucked the card in my pocket. But I'd already made up my mind to find out.

I spent the rest of the day splitting my time between trying to not look at the card and trying to not look at the clock.

The date on the card was today's, and the address was only a few blocks away. The time, however, was for six o'clock, well before closing time, which meant precious little time to figure out how I was going to get out of the shop without making Maggie suspicious.

It wasn't that I was trying to hide anything from her. More that she was already worried about me, and I didn't want to increase her fears. I figured I'd scope out the weirdoes first, then, if everything seemed on the up-and-up, I'd introduce Maggie.

At three o'clock, the back door opened and happy warmth spread through the shop. I didn't need to look up to see who it was. The shop only reacted that way for three people. Maggie and I were already there, so that meant Andi was home.

Andrea Bedford looked like the average twenty-something, cute, spunky, with tattoos and multicolored hair. This week, it was purple with emerald green that framed her face. The week before, pink and black. Next week, I shuddered to think. I often wondered if she remembered what her natural hair color looked like.

"Hi, sweetheart!" Andi called out as she ran her hand along the shop wall. The air quivered and a wave of happiness rippled through the store. A year ago, Maggie's shop was like any other on the street. But then things got weird and, to make a long story short, Andi accidentally brought the whole building to life. And the odd thing? Bringing the house to life wasn't the weirdest thing that happened that day.

"It's about time you showed up," said Maggie. "We've got packages to ship and a group of beginners due in about an hour."

"Yes, boss," said Andi with mock-exasperation. "Let me get settled and I'll..."

"I can run the packages out," I said. Both of them stopped and stared at me. "What?"

22

"Oh... kay," said Maggie with a sideways glance. "We have about a dozen that need to go to the post office pronto."

"I'm on it," I said. Maybe I was a little too eager, or maybe I was just as terrible at hiding things from Maggie as I'd always been. Whatever the case, she knew something was up.

"Look," I said. "I don't really want to be here for the class. I'd feel out of place and it's not really my thing. I'll go take the packages, then bring the car back and maybe go have a beer or something. Okay?"

"You never go out," said Maggie.

"I'm just trying to help," I said. "If you'd rather, I'll just sit here and let you guys scramble to get everything done..."

"No," she said as she handed me her keys. "Okay. The boxes are by the back door. We should be done by about nine."

"Gotcha," I said as I hurried out.

It took some time to get all the packages loaded into the car. With both arms, I could've done it easily in two trips. But the bum wing made it harder to function. I was glad Maggie's car was an automatic, otherwise driving it would've been a lesson in humility and rising insurance rates.

At the post office, I parked in the handicapped space, one of the few perks to having my arm mangled, and found one of the more helpful postal workers to unload the packages. He brought out a rolling cart, had me sign a few forms, and got me on my way fast.

I checked my watch as I pulled in behind the shop. There were five or six other cars there, with a few more parked on the street. Class was probably in full swing, which suited me just fine. I pocketed the keys and made my way down the sidewalk at a slow pace.

First, a demon called me by name, then some goofball in a trench coat came looking for me. If I believed in coincidences, I might've chalked it up as weird happenstance. But experience taught me that there were no such things as coincidences. Whether there was a grand design or not was still open for debate, but one thing I knew for a fact: Everything was in some way connected.

A group of like-minded individuals.

It wasn't too much of a stretch to figure out he was talking about a club of some kind, and clubs made me nervous. Especially *secret* clubs. The last one I encountered was Evergreen, a group of the most powerful and knowledgeable metaphysical minds in the world. Every religion a person could think of was represented, every creed welcomed. And they managed to get along and work together for the common good. Until, that is, one of their ranks turned psycho on them, used another member to do his dirty work, and in-fighting and mistrust splintered the group. Maggie still kept in contact with a few of them, but their power as a whole was broken, and I wasn't keen on being used by another group for any purpose.

On the other hand, it might not be at all what I thought. For all I knew, this group might be selling timeshares on Lake Erie.

Whatever the case, my curiosity swelled as I rounded the corner and found the address. It was a bookstore.

Evergreen met in a bookstore. My stomach twisted.

It was not, however, one of the big chain bookstores, but a mom-and-pop used book *shop*, with mountains of yellowed paperbacks and no real filing system. I checked my watch. An hour to go.

Across the street, a sandwich shop stood open for business. After a quick realization that maybe it was a lack of food that churned my belly, I hurried across the street and took a table inside, next to a window, so I could keep an eye on the comings and goings of the bookstore while I ate.

Halfway through my French dip, people started to arrive. The first was a blonde woman in a motorized wheelchair. After a few minutes, the goon in the trench coat, who I decided to call Boris, rounded the corner. He kept looking behind him as he entered, as if he were sure he was being followed. Then came a man on a walker, a couple, a mother with her children in tow, a man with a guide dog, and more than a dozen others. It seemed strange to me that many of them were, in some way, handicapped. If they were looking to stage an ambush, I had serious doubts about the possibility of success.

I checked my watch again. Ten minutes until the time listed on the card. Just enough time to pay for my sandwich and get across the street to find out what was going on.

Traffic slowed to sporadic in the strange time I called the "shift change," when the daytime shoppers went home and the nighttime hot-spots hadn't opened yet. It was the only safe time of day to be a pedestrian crossing Carson Street.

The front door of the bookstore was wood, worn with several layers of paint peeking through the forest green that was this year's coating. The scratched gold lettering on the front glass only added to the rustic feel of the out-of-time bookstore. I could almost hear it wheeze its last breaths before the large corporate chains swallowed it whole. I must've passed by a thousand times, but for some reason I never saw it. Or maybe I saw it, but just overlooked it as another old business near Maggie's.

"Excuse me," came a voice behind me. I looked up at its source, a thirtyish woman with long dark hair and glasses. She wore a ringer tee with bellbottom jeans and boots. A small tattoo of an angel stood beside the scar that ran halfway up her arm from the wrist.

"I'm sorry," I said as I stepped out of her way. "I was told there was a meeting..?"

She stopped and stared at me, expressionless.

"I know, Mister Cooper. We were hoping you'd come."

Either her icy demeanor or the tone of her voice made the skin on the back of my neck try to crawl up under my hair. First a demon, then Boris, now this woman.

"Come on," she said as she held the door. "We're at the back of the store."

Of course they were.

She waited for me to enter before she closed and locked the door, pulled the old-fashioned shade down, and flipped the sign over to "closed." Then she gestured toward the back of the shop.

The smell of musty yellow paper and ancient mysteries, romances and adventures tickled my nose as I followed her along the scuffed old floor.

"I'm sorry," I said. "And you are?"

"Through here." She pushed open a door at the back of the shop and gestured for me to enter.

The room was small, about the size of Maggie's back-room workshop. Against the walls, mountains of books threatened to avalanche down in literary disaster, and a few boxes sat beside the back entrance. The people I watched enter stopped talking when I walked in. Those that could, stood from their folding metal chairs. None of them smiled.

"You came," said an older man in a wheel chair. "I didn't think you would."

"Told you," said Boris. "I'm good." I wanted to slap the smug look off his face, but I figured I'd wait to see how everything played out.

"Yeah," I said. "I'm here. Someone want to tell me what's

going on?"

"You didn't tell him?"

Boris shrugged.

The older man sighed and shook his head.

"You'll have to forgive Dennis. He watches too many old spy flicks." He wheeled over to a break in the circle of chairs and gestured. "Please, everyone. Sit. Let's get started."

I took a chair closest to the door, next to the mystery girl, in case I felt the urge to make a hasty retreat.

"Mister Cooper," said the old man. "My name is Randall. Welcome to the Society of People Immediately Returned In spite of Termination. SPIRIT, for short."

"I don't follow." The people in the room seemed to have few, if any, common traits. Sure, many of them were handicapped, but there were also many who weren't, at least as far as I could see. There wasn't any real dominant race, an equal number of men and women, hell, even a couple of children. What they had in common, I couldn't guess. "Terminated? Like what, you guys are job hunters?"

"Terminated," said Mystery Girl with an exasperated roll of her eyes. "As in *dead*. Everyone in this room has died and come back."

I looked from face to face in shock.

"Oh, come now," said Randall. "You didn't really think you were the only one, did you?"

3

Of course I knew I wasn't the only one. I just didn't realize how many of *me* there were.

In movies, when a person discovers they are not, in fact, as rare as he thought, the powers that be assign one of two emotions. The first, the crushing blow that the character is no longer special, or wasn't ever as special as he thought he was, often takes a back seat to the overwhelming relief of the second, that the character isn't actually alone. With both, the character usually thinks the others of his kind have all the answers to life, the universe, and everything concerning their weird existence.

And he's usually disappointed when he finds out how wrong he is.

Which is why, after the startling revelation, I didn't bombard the people of SPIRIT with every question that leaped to my mind, like if they knew why we came back, and just what the hell they saw when they crossed over. I did, however, manage to say something witty and smooth to cover my surprise.

"You're kidding."

"No," said Randall. "We're not. Everyone in this room

has died. Some from accidents, others from... other means. But we all came back. And we managed to find each other."

"Why?"

"Support? Compare notes? I'm not sure, really." Randall rolled his chair a little closer. "Before I had my accident, I could run, walk, play with my grandchildren. But we were hit by a drunk driver. My grandkids died in the accident. So did I, only I didn't stay that way. We've all got similar stories. And it keeps us from feeling lonely. We've been watching, hearing about all the good you've done, and, frankly, you're an inspiration to many of us. We'd consider it an honor if you'd be a part of our little group."

"I don't know what to say."

"Take some time," said Randall. "Think about it. You know where we are. This is my bookstore, so you can find me whenever you like."

It was surreal, to find so many people like myself. And while I should have been overjoyed, or at least relieved, I couldn't help the sense that something wasn't right. Almost no one at the meeting smiled. I learned a few names, found out how a few people died, but everyone seemed guarded, as if they were afraid of me.

When the meeting, which was more of just a mixer, was over, I took a handful of cookies off the back counter and a plastic cup full of punch and waited while people filtered out. Randall rolled over to me.

"So," he said. "What do you think?"

"I think there's something you're not telling me," I said. "Everyone's jumpy."

"Everyone here is wary of strangers," he said. "That's all. Try to remember how you felt when you returned. How people treated you."

He was right. Even my closest buddies dropped me like

30

a bad habit when I tried to tell them about my afterlife. It seemed natural that they might be skittish. Still, it seemed like there was more than just *stranger danger* at work.

"I guess so. Look, I didn't ask before, but that girl who sat next to me…"

"Niccole," he said. "Yeah. She takes some getting used to. Doesn't open up to folks easily."

"The scar on her wrist…"

"It isn't my place," said Randall, "so you didn't hear this from me, but she came back after she tried to kill herself. Got a second chance. She doesn't talk about it much, but what she saw when she died scared her bad. Enough to make her clean and sober for eleven months now. Just give her time. See you in two weeks."

He waved as I headed out the back door.

Carson Street was alive with nightcrawlers. Bars up and down the street blasted their own brand of music, though some of it could only be called such by the loosest of definitions. College kids walked up and down the street looking for their next hookup. In the alleys, predators watched for easy prey. It was just like any other city in the nation, except this one was mine. Of all the places I could've been born, died, and been resurrected, Pittsburgh was mine. But it seemed less so, now, like a huge responsibility was lifted from my shoulders, because I wasn't the only one. I didn't have to be the go-to guy anymore.

At least, I didn't think so. We never got to that all-too-important, "how-many-of-you-go-trying-to-protect-people-from-supernatural-monsters" part of the conversation. Similar experiences or no, I was willing to bet I had them all beat in that area. And I didn't know if any of them could see ghosts.

Again, I'm not the hero type. Despite how it looks to the outside observer, I don't wear a cape or arrive to fanfare to rescue the breathless maiden. The scarred-up arm isn't even so much sexy as it is grotesque. I'm not even particularly brave. I generally try to avoid trouble. It just seems to know where to find me all the time.

But if there were others like me, if I weren't alone, maybe... what? We could form some kind of metaphysical Justice League? Right. And everyone would wear capes.

The front of Maggie's shop was dark, which didn't surprise me. That there were only two cars in the lot behind the shop, did. I glanced at my watch. It was past eleven. I took deep, even breaths as I climbed up the stairs and braced for what was to come.

When I opened the door, I was greeted by Maggie and Andi, both with worried expressions on their faces.

"*There* you are!" shouted Maggie as she rushed over and hugged me. "We were worried!"

"I'm a big boy," I said. "Nothing to worry about."

"Yeah," said Andi. "But you never stay out after ten."

"I was having a good time. So sue me."

It wasn't a lie. I enjoyed meeting people like myself. But I didn't want to bring Maggie and Andi into the group. Not yet. When Maggie brought me to Evergreen, I felt like an outsider. Hell, when she brought Andi to them, *she* felt a bigger connection because of shared beliefs. Me, I was just the guy who talked to ghosts. So I didn't exactly fit in, and I didn't become really friendly or close with any of them.

Except for Bill. Him, I trusted.

But this, the SPIRIT group, they weren't metaphysical marvels or priests or witches or wizards. They were like me. How much like me, I still didn't know, but we shared a common bond. We all knew what it was like to take the big dirt-nap and come back to tell the tale. Maybe, in time, they might loosen up around me and really accept me as one of their own. It bothered me how much I hoped they would.

"Besides," I said. "I didn't want to risk walking in on naked time, or whatever you guys call it."

"These were beginners," said Maggie. "We don't go skyclad until the advanced classes."

"Well, now I know that." I headed into the bedroom. "I'm going to get some sleep. Long day."

I left the two of them with questioning looks as I closed the bedroom door. That last part was truth, plain and simple. I was exhausted, physically and emotionally, but in a good way. The building cooled the air as I took off my clothes and slid between the sheets.

"G'night," I said. The lights dimmed and I drifted into an easy sleep.

"Coming to get you, Cooper..."

I ran. I didn't know from what, or even where I was. But I knew it was behind me, that it wanted me, that if it caught me there was a lot worse than death on the menu. Trouble was, there were no walls, no streets, no surroundings at all. Just darkness everywhere I looked. I didn't even know if I ran the right direction, but I kept moving.

"Closer... Closer..."

Dim outlines appeared ahead of me, shapes of people whose faces I couldn't see. The closer I got, the more I recognized. The man in the wheelchair, the spunky posture of the girl, the slouch of the tall man. Randall. Andi. Taylor. Good God, Taylor. And in front stood Maggie, her arms crossed, eyes blazing. In front of them all lay an inert shape on the ground in a spreading pool of dark liquid. Her face was distorted with a horrific silent scream, but I recognized Niccole all the same.

"Kill them all... Going to get you..."

The little s'more-shaped demon skittered into view.

"Oh," I said. "I'm dreaming. You don't scare me, little man. Get back in your cage."

I reared back to knock it on its doughy behind, but stopped as it bubbled and swelled to monstrous size. Even though I knew it was a dream, and it couldn't really hurt me, I took a step back.

"Think you're tough?" Its voice bubbled like molten cheese. "How tough are you without them?"

My friends collapsed, puppets with their strings cut, eyes open and unfocused.

I woke up with a jerk to find Maggie sitting across the room in a chair, knees drawn up under her chin, eyes locked on me.

"That was some dream," she said.

"Demon. Playing games, that's all. I've got his number now." I wiped the cold sweat from my face.

"You want to talk about it?"

"Nah. Nothing to talk about. Soon as we get him out of me, the better off I'll be."

"Okay," she said. "Who's Niccole?"

Shit.

"Who?"

"Don't lie to me, Stan. Honesty, remember?"

"She's just someone I met tonight," I said. "That's it. I don't think she even likes me. You've got nothing to be jealous over."

"I'm not jealous," she snapped. "You said her name in your sleep, and I wanted to know what other woman was in your dreams, if not me."

"If it makes you feel any better," I said, "you were there too. And you were just as dead as she was."

"Dead?"

"I told you. The demon's fucking with me. Okay?"

She nodded and slid out of the chair. Even in her biggest, baggiest t-shirt-cum-nightgown, she was still the most beautiful creature to my eyes. She left her hair down in a copper cascade when she slept, in which I loved to bury my face. As she climbed into bed next to me, I put my arms around her waist and kissed her cheek.

"There's no woman in the world who holds a candle to you," I said. "I promise."

"Good." She put a hand on my forehead and whispered something in Latin. "Now you should be able to sleep for tonight without any more trouble."

I love my witch.

4

If something seems too good to be true, my father used to say, it means that it is. Dad wasn't school-educated, but he was a pretty smart guy with common sense and practical know-how. Which meant that my father was right most of the time, whether I wanted to admit it or not. He also once said that just when everything was going the right way, someone always came along and changed the road signs. That one I always hated.

Especially when it turned out to be right.

Morning came and I woke up alone again. I lay for a moment and stretched while I tried to put together some sort of agenda for the day. Maggie needed help in the shop, of course, but I also wanted to do something nice for her. It wasn't right to leave her out of all the goings-on last night, so I figured maybe a hot caramel macchiato from Caribou Coffee up the street might serve as a decent peace offering. Or at least the start to one.

A heavy knock at the door was my first clue that the day wasn't going to go according to the Stanley Cooper schedule.

I got up, pulled on a pair of pants and a sweatshirt and hurried to the door. When I opened it, I saw two of my least favorite Yinzer cops, officers Appel and Menold. Neither wore their customary blue uniform, but were instead dressed in slacks and blazers with ties.

"Officers," I said with my most cheerful smile. "Uh... hi."

"Cooper," said Appel. "We need to speak with you. It's official. May we come in?"

I've had plenty of run-ins with the law in the past six years. I've even been arrested a few times. Of course, those charges never stuck, but in the past that was thanks in no small part to a friend. While Taylor was usually the one to get me out, for some reason the two cops at the door were most often the ones who put me in to begin with. Maggie said something about our fates being intertwined. I just called it dumb luck. But the more it happened, the more I started leaning toward Maggie's way of thinking. No matter what kind of trouble I got into, there were Appel and Menold like, well, cops.

"Yeah," I said. "Sure." I took a seat on the overstuffed easy chair while Appel sat on the couch. Menold hovered just inside the door like he was afraid I might turn into a bat and fly around the room.

"So what can I do for you?"

"Where were you last night?" Appel wasn't the kind to mince words, which was one of the reasons I almost liked the guy.

"Um... when? I went to a bookstore about six or seven blocks down, but then I came back here and went to sleep."

"What were you doing at the bookstore?"

"There was a group of people who wanted to meet me," I said. "That's it. Why? What's going on?"

"Was a woman named Niccole Hopeman at that meeting?"

My stomach lurched and tried to climb up my throat.

"There was a woman named Niccole," I said. My mouth

went dry. "I don't know if that was her last name. *Why*?"

Appel looked up toward Menold.

"Why don't you go check his story with Miss Perry downstairs?"

"Gladly," muttered Menold. "Guy gives me the creeps anyway."

Appel waited until the door was shut before he continued.

"Niccole Hopeman was found dead this morning," he said.

And there it was. Traffic turned and wasn't going my way anymore. In fact, it was headed straight for me.

"Am I a suspect?"

"No," said Appel. "Officially, you're a person of interest. But I knew Taylor long enough to know he wouldn't have helped you out if you weren't a good guy. So I'm here to ask you if you know anything."

"I just met her last night," I said. "The group was for people like me, who had near-death experiences. We split up around... maybe ten-thirty? Eleven? I don't know. But I came straight home after."

"Do you remember the names of any of the other members? You mentioned a bookstore down the street."

"I only caught first names, but there was a Dennis, Niccole, Randall... He owns the shop."

Appel took out a notebook and jotted down everything I said.

"So, what? Was it a mugging or something?"

"No." Appel looked down toward his shoes and took a deep breath. "We think she was targeted. Through you."

"What? Why would you..."

"Your name was written on the wall of her apartment, right over her body."

39

Shit. My stomach reversed course and dropped a few feet down.

The human body puts off a field of energy that some people call an aura. Scientists and con-artists hook up all sorts of wires and use special cameras to see that energy and try to interpret what the different colors and intensities mean. They talk about how strong an aura is, or what it tells about the person it surrounds, and they make it all seem very other-worldly and metaphysical. On the other side of the fence are people who don't believe in the whole "human bio-battery" theory and write off all the Kirlian photographs and electrostatic paper as carnival-grade chicanery. They're the same people who don't believe in ghosts, magic, or other such nonsense.

And they're wrong. I know because I don't need fancy equipment or special cameras. I see energy fields just fine without all the gizmos.

Anyone with a decent meter or enough gumption can measure a person's personal energy field. Measuring is the easy part. What they don't tell folks is that the energy the body puts off leaves impressions, afterimages on the things around it. Most people know them by their more common name. Ghosts. Which is why visiting the scene of a person's death is never pleasant.

Menold waited outside the apartment door with a couple of uniforms while Appel walked me inside. The body was long gone, but a huge pool of darkened crimson marked where they found it. The white tape outline, however, looked odd, less human shaped. I couldn't quite put my finger on why for a moment, then it hit me.

"She didn't have a head."

"No," said Appel. "We haven't found it yet. We had her

40

identified by fingerprints and her tattoos."

The angel on her wrist, just above the suicide scar.

The little demon inside me must've caught the scent of death because I felt his hunger.

Little flags dotted the floor, folded plastic numbers and markers around bits of lint, hairs and debris that someone thought would turn out to be evidence. A swath of deep red streaked the wall, arterial spray, and above it in the same sticky mess, the killer wrote my name.

Four times in the past two days, someone I didn't know knew my name. And now one was dead, and my name dripped with her life on a stucco wall.

I closed my eyes and willed my perception to shift. Doors in my mind rattled and swung open, walls slid aside or fell. When I opened my eyes again, the room vibrated in technicolor brilliance. And I Saw her again.

Niccole walked toward the door, opened it, and smiled as someone I couldn't see walked in behind her. Then her expression changed. She went from joking and warm to terrified in the space of a blink. Then he killed her. I couldn't see who it was, but a long gash opened up on Niccole's throat as if cut with a sword. She clutched at the wound as if she could somehow stem the flow of blood, but a second slice split the back of her hand and took her head off. She fell to the carpet. The demon inside me wriggled with delight, gave me the urge to vomit. I looked away before the image started to play again.

On the wall, my name pulsed like neon, but below it was something I didn't expect.

Nice to see you again.

The message was written specifically for me. No one else could see it because, as far as I knew, I was the only one who could see energy patterns and intent, will and life. Beside the words was

41

a symbol, a crude drawing that looked like a Christmas tree. A pine tree.

It was difficult to keep quiet about what I saw. Even more with Appel in the front seat pressing me with questions and Menold giving me the hairy-eyeball from the back seat.

I swear, I felt his gaze on the back of my head like my hair was on fire.

They let me out in front of Maggie's shop with assurances that several of their brothers in blue would keep an eye on us. It didn't make me feel better as I hurried inside.

"What's going on?" demanded Maggie, hands on hips, as I walked in the door.

"Aren't those the two cops that keep arresting you?" Andi mimicked her stance at the cash register.

"Yes," I said. "And they're detectives now. They got promoted."

"Good for them," said Maggie. "What the hell is going on?"

"We need to talk," I said. The door locked behind me and the front window darkened. "Yes, with everyone."

We went to the workshop in the back room where Maggie made all her candles and oils, cast her spells and did other witchy things. She and Andi sat at stools around the table while I stood like I was ready to make a run for it.

I told them about Boris, about the group. I also apologized for not telling them about it. Then I dropped the big bombshell on them.

"Niccole was found murdered," I said. "And the person who did it wrote me a note on the wall. Whoever it was knows me well enough to know how to write something so I'm the only one

42

who'll see it."

"That's horrible," said Maggie.

"It gets worse," I said. I didn't want to tell her, but I had to. If anyone could help me, it was Maggie. "They signed it. With a pine tree."

The color drained from Maggie's face.

"I don't get it," said Andi. "A pine..?"

"An evergreen," I said.

Andi's eyes widened as recognition set in. The most powerful group of metaphysical folks this side of a role-playing game split a year ago when a traitor covered Pittsburgh with zombies. We still kept in contact with a few of the members, but they kept to themselves lately. Besides, cryptic messages written in blood meant the traitor, the one who got away, had his shorts in a knot again. And for some reason, I was his target.

"We need to leave," blurted Andi. "We need to get out of town. Run."

The walls trembled and the temperature plummeted, all the doors locked and the lights went dim.

"No," I said, loud enough for the shop to hear me. The walls stopped shaking. "You two should get out of town, but I'm not going anywhere."

"But..."

"Do you really think leaving town will keep him away from me? It's obvious he wants me, and he's willing to kill people to get me."

"I'm not going anywhere either," said Maggie. "If you're staying, I'm staying."

"That poor girl," said Andi. "Did she have family? Friends?"

"I don't know." It was truth, but even more, I didn't *want* to know. It was hard enough to know she died because someone

43

wanted to get my attention. I couldn't think about grieving parents or siblings. But there were her friends. More to the point, there was the group. Someone needed to tell them, if the police hadn't already.

"I'll be back," I said as I headed toward the door. "I need to talk to Randall."

"I'm going with you." Maggie rose from her stool.

"No," I said. "I need to do this by myself. They don't trust outsiders."

"But..."

"Look, if he wanted me dead, he'd have done it already. This was a message, and I need to find out why." I tried to turn the door handle, but it wouldn't budge.

"I'm coming back," I said. "Don't worry."

"Let him out," said Andi. The door relaxed and opened. I stepped out into the sunlight.

The old bookstore was only a short distance away, and the walk gave me time to figure out what I was going to say to Randall. I didn't really know him. Or Niccole, for that matter. But her death hit me hard, and not just because my name was on her wall. We didn't hit it off very well, and she barely said two words to me for the entirety of the meeting. But she was like me. I didn't know what she saw when she died, but I knew it scared her. Did she see hell? Or did she see the same nothingness I saw? I didn't get the chance to ask her.

Of course, death, to me, lacks the same sense of finality it holds for most people. I've had more than my fair share of conversations with dead folk. Sometimes I can't keep away from them.

The walk also gave me time to think, and a lot of questions

44

popped up. By the time I made it to the bookstore, I had a first-class case of anger brewing, and it didn't show any signs of going away.

The bell over the door chimed as I walked in.

"Randall?"

"Back here!" The voice came from the back room where the meeting took place. I wove my way through the stacks and shelves. Randall rolled into view behind the counter.

"Mister Cooper!" he beamed. "Back so soon?"

"Have the police been by here yet?"

A look of genuine confusion crossed his face. Either he really didn't know what was going on, or he was one hell of an actor.

"Why would the police..?"

"Niccole Hopeman was murdered last night. I'm sorry." I let my words fall flat.

If he wasn't already sitting in a wheelchair, the impact of the statement would've knocked him down. Randall stared at me like he hoped I'd shout "punked" or something, mouth agape. But when he recognized how serious I was, he broke into tears.

"But... but she was here last night. I just spoke to her..."

"They found her this morning. Police think she died sometime around midnight last night." I tried to be gentle, but a fluffy way to tell him his friend was dead just wouldn't come to mind. I did decide to leave out the more gruesome details to spare him that horror, but there was one I couldn't ignore.

"The killer wrote on the wall," I said. "My name. And a message that only I could see."

"What do you mean, 'only you?'"

"Did any of you come back with... special abilities?"

Randall considered for a moment.

"Most of us were disabled in our accidents," he said. "But

45

a few of us did gain some kind of compensatory abilities."

"Speak English."

"Well, Arthur, the blind fellow. He lost his eyesight, but he gained a kind of radar sense. He doesn't even need the cane. And the boys..."

"Wait," I said. "The *kids*? I thought their mother was the one..."

"Heavens, no," said Randall. "But she comes to learn how to cope with them. They're quite precocious. They were electrocuted, both at the same time. When they came back, they didn't have to speak to know what the other was thinking. It's really remarkable..."

"Can anyone else see ghosts?"

"Well... no, not that I know of," he said. "Why? Are you telling me you can?"

"Yeah," I said. "And more."

I closed my eyes and lowered the walls in my mind. When I opened them again, I saw pretty much what I expected to see.

"Have you lost any members in the last few months?"

"Yes, we have," he said. "But they were accidents, except for Niccole. Why?"

"Because they're all here, and I'm not sure they were accidents."

When a person dies, it isn't like it is in the movies. Some of them come back as ghosts, sure, but they don't come back wearing long flowing robes or with perfect hair and makeup, and they're rarely smiling. They look exactly like they did when they died. Down to every last drop of blood, every last burned hair, every tear that streaked their faces. To see one is, forgive the expression, haunting.

Behind Randall stood a translucent horror show. There

46

was a man with his head at an impossible angle, a woman whose skin flaked and chipped with black embers. Another man looked like he'd just stepped from a swimming pool, and a fourth stared at me from eyeless sockets. Niccole stood beside them, her head still attached, but only just. She looked angrier than the others, and it seemed to be directed at me.

Randall, on the other hand, sat surrounded by shades of white and blue with swaths of brown cut through where grief touched him.

"I'll find out who did this," I said. Their images shimmered and faded, except for Niccole.

"Coming for you." Her voice sounded like bubbling steam from a pipe. "You can't save us. Save yourself." Then she was gone too.

I closed the doors in my mind and the world faded back to dull, muted colors.

"They... they were here?"

"Yeah," I said. "You need to call the others. They should hear about Niccole from you, not me. Not on the news."

He nodded and wheeled over to his telephone as I turned and left. The tinkling bell over the door rang on my way out, and for the life of me it sounded like Niccole.

Coming for you.

Story of my life.

As I walked back toward the shop, I couldn't help but replay Niccole's death in my head. I didn't want to, but it just wouldn't go away like a hideous song or a joke with a terrible punchline. I couldn't make it stop. I didn't even know her, not really, but her death hit me hard.

Just before I got to the shop, Appel's big brown sedan pulled up and he rolled down the window.

"Cooper."

47

"Come on," I said. "You just let me out, what, an hour ago? What do want now?"

"We got another call," he said. "And I want you to take a look."

"I don't really have time..."

"I'm not asking," said Appel. Menold glared from the passenger seat. I had no doubt that, if I said no, he'd climb out and stuff me in the trunk.

"Can I at least tell Maggie where I'm going?"

"Gotta check in with the missus?" snorted Menold. "Hurry up."

"Where are we going?"

"Homewood," said Appel.

Homewood Cemetery is not the typical old bone-yard resting grounds. In fact, it's one of the more unique places of its kind I've been to. Sure, every cemetery tries hard to look peaceful, and they all have their share of impressive monuments, but Homewood is one of the only ones I've seen with a jogging track and picnic tables. Sure, most of them have benches so people can maintain the illusion of being able to sit and talk to their dead loved ones. But Homewood takes the notion of celebrating the life of the deceased to a whole new level.

It's also one of the few cemeteries where the dead actually do hang around. While many people think of cemeteries as haunted, it just isn't true. Most dead folks don't like being reminded of what they are, and it's kind of hard not to notice a giant stone grave marker. But at Homewood, there's a different vibe to the air, something peaceful that no other cemetery has. At Homewood, the old woman on the bench just might be talking to her dead husband because he might actually be there.

What didn't belong, however, were the long strings of police tape that flapped in the breeze. Officers tried their best to keep gawking rubberneckers and reporters out of the crime scene, but it was like trying to stop folks from looking through cheesecloth.

Appel flashed his badge and a uniform let us through.

The section of cemetery was one I knew, marked by a replica Egyptian pyramid that some rich eccentric had commissioned as his mausoleum. In front of it, on one of the few areas not dotted with headstones, sat the corpse, or what was left of it. The scent of burned flesh still hung in the air, despite the breeze. What skin was left on the thing was charred black. It sat upright on the ground, arms to its side, head thrown back in what I took to be a final scream of agony. Around it were five scorch marks on the earth.

"A ritual," I said. "Gone bad."

"No shit," said Menold.

"So why am I here?"

"That," said Appel. He pointed behind me. On the side of the pyramid, photographers snapped pictures of a word written in blood. Cooper. My name. The little demon in me giggled.

As I moved closer for a better look, I shifted my perception. The world leaped into a montage of grief and peace, mourners and families, partings and reunions. It also showed me something I didn't expect. The ground glowed, green and gold, as did all the trees. They pulsed with life, and I understood why the dead hung around Homewood more than other cemeteries. It was a place of power, where the veil between the living and the dead was thinnest.

As I came to the wall, more words appeared.

He was not strong enough. Beside it, the same crude pine tree.

I turned back toward the still steaming corpse, and the whole thing played out before my eyes. I saw him as he was. It was Boris, the wannabe secret agent clown who brought me to SPIRIT in the first place. But he wasn't afraid. He smiled, nodded, and held his hands out. Then his body jerked in spasms, and the smile became a look of abject terror, then a grimace of agony. Energies rushed into his body. I could only watch as first his clothes, then his hair, and finally his flesh ignited. His expression went from pain to shock, then blank as he fell to his knees, head back, and burned to the crispy corpse that sat on the ground.

My stomach rolled and lurched, and I gave up whatever was left in my stomach beside the pyramid.

"That's just great," shouted Menold. "Someone tag that so we know where it came from."

"Did you know him?" Appel knelt beside me.

"Yeah," I said. "I think his name was Dennis. He's the one who introduced me to SPIRIT."

"How would you know who he was?" said Menold as he stalked closer. "There's not enough left to make a positive identification."

"I know," I said. "Trust me."

What else could I say?

"Maybe you were the one who burned him." Menold glowered behind his sunglasses.

I couldn't think of any kind of response that wouldn't get me tackled and shot with a taser, but Appel stepped between us.

"That's bullshit and you know it," he said. "Go cool your jets."

Menold looked about to say something, but thought better of it and walked away, grumbling with every step.

"Thank you," I said.

"Don't mind him. He just hates dealing with weird shit

like this. So, Dennis, eh? Got a last name?" He flipped open his notebook.

"No," I said. "I'm not even really sure if that's his first name. But he was at the meeting with Niccole."

"Hopeman?" His eyebrows rose. "So they're connected by more than just your name on the wall?"

"Yeah," I said. "Looks like it."

"There's something you're not telling me," he said.

Of course there was. There were about a million things I wasn't telling him. But nothing concrete, nothing that wouldn't point to Maggie, or me, as a suspect, or endanger the other former members of Evergreen. Much as I wanted to try to point him in the right direction, I needed answers first. And I didn't know where to even begin to get them.

Based on what I told him, Appel and Menold dropped me off at Maggie's shop and went in search of Dennis' home. I didn't know how they could find it with only a first name and a charred corpse, but Appel seemed confident. Menold seemed confident that I was the one who burned Dennis, though he wasn't sure how. The only confidence I had was that things were serious and I didn't have a clue of what to do about it. *Not strong enough*? What was that supposed to mean?

In the scene I saw, Dennis smiled, stood where his killer wanted him, and seemed pretty eager to get on with it. He wasn't a victim. He wasn't an innocent bystander. He was a casualty. He knew what he was doing, or thought he did, and got himself killed for it. But the question remained: Just what the hell was he doing? Moreover, why couldn't I see the other person involved? The scenes played out, but just like with Niccole, I couldn't see the person responsible. It was almost as if the person knew I'd come, and didn't want to be seen. But who would know how to hide themselves from me?

I walked into the shop and found Maggie and Andi waiting. Both of them looked more than a little apprehensive, and I guessed it had quite a bit to do with the box by the back door.

"She wouldn't let us bring it in," said Andi as she pointed up, indicating the shop.

"It's okay," I said. "I'll handle it."

The box by the back door looked like one of those flat-rate shipping boxes from the post office, only there were no marks on it except for my name, written with a marker.

"What is it?"

I turned to see Maggie and Andi at the back door, both straining to see while remaining inside the safety of the shop.

I had my suspicions. The notes on the wall and the pyramid were calls for my attention, of course. And there was only one thing I could think of that would guarantee I stayed good and undivided about the subject. I just hoped I was wrong.

You don't want to do that, teased the little demon.

"Only one way to find out," I said. I lifted one of the box flaps and discovered I wasn't wrong. And I hated being right.

Niccole's head was in the box, lain on a bed of red tissue paper. The demon giggled as my stomach lurched.

"Don't look," I called to Maggie and Andi. "Andi, get those detectives back here. They need to see this."

"What is it?" Maggie's voice sounded closer.

"Remember what I said about that girl they found murdered? I found her head."

I was about to push the flaps closed when Niccole's eyes opened and locked with mine.

"You upset my plans," said the head. "You cost me my servant. Now you must replace him. You must give yourself over, or more people will die."

"Fat chance," I said. "Why don't you show yourself?"

"In time." The voice wasn't Niccole's. For one thing, her vocal cords were severed, so the voice I heard had to come from somewhere else. Tricks and black magic.

"Make no mistake," said the traitor. "Her death was your fault. And the longer you resist, the more blood will be on your hands."

The eyes closed.

"They're on their way," said Andi. "What's in the... Oh Gods."

"I told you not to look," I said. I pushed the flaps closed and went back inside to wait for the police. Again.

5

The police came, took the head and our statements, and told us to stay available for more questioning. Appel listened to what I had to say while Menold continued to give me the hairy eyeball. When they were gone, Maggie and I decided we needed help of a different kind. Someone who might be able to shed some light on what was going on.

I sat in the passenger seat, my dead arm in my lap, as Maggie piloted her car across the 10th Street Bridge. It took us a half-hour to persuade Andi to stay in the shop. In the end, it was the seizure-inducing flashing lights and rumbling walls that convinced her. The shop was scared, and with good reason.

We turned right just across the bridge and found our way onto the main highway, headed east toward Monroeville. There were only a handful of people who knew what a message signed with a pine tree meant. And of those, even fewer that I trusted. I didn't know where they lived, and neither did Maggie, but she knew a few phone numbers, made a few calls, and we agreed on a meeting place.

Monroeville wasn't very different from any of a dozen

suburbs of Pittsburgh. In fact, it looked a little boring. Thirty years ago, a filmmaker used the mall to make a famous zombie flick. A year ago, someone tried to make life imitate art, but he used real zombies.

We pulled into the parking lot in front of a large bookstore. Shoe-polish lettering in the dark windows told a tale of broken spirits and ruptured economic times. We killed the motor and got out to wait.

"Damned shame." The voice came from behind us. I turned to see Bill, the head hoochie-coochie man of what used to be Evergreen. Odd that we didn't notice him when we pulled in. It was almost as if he just materialized out of nowhere.

"What is?"

"The bookstore," he said. "And a little bit like poetic justice. All but killed the independent bookstores, then got so bloated they couldn't stay afloat."

"I wonder when it closed," said Maggie.

"A couple of weeks ago," said Bill. "This one was the last. The corporation put eleven thousand people in the unemployment line. I'm going to miss this place."

"Yeah," I said. "Look, we need your help. Someone murdered a girl yesterday. Wrote my name on the wall. Signed it with an evergreen." I decided to leave out the part about the talking head in a box. The old man had enough on his mind without such an image taking up space in his thoughts.

Bill's expression sank.

"Who was she?"

"Someone like me," I said. "Someone who died and came back. Turns out, there's a whole bunch of us."

He looked surprised.

"How many?"

"I don't know," I said. "More than a dozen? There've

been a few who died. I don't think those were accidents either. And there was another one. Burned to a crisp in the middle of Homewood Cemetery."

"You're on dangerous ground," said Bill. "I didn't know there were so many like you. Seems almost to defy the odds."

The thought never occurred to me. Coming back to life after death was a big enough long shot to make any bookie drool. For there to be more than one of us in an area the size of Pittsburgh, while not impossible, seemed unlikely. For there to be as many as showed up at Randall's shop, and all closeby, told me the odds were skewed. Almost like we were being created on purpose. But such a notion was ridiculous. I hoped.

"Neither did I," I said. "But now that I know, I feel a little protective of them."

"Understandable," said Bill. "And what about the..." His voice trailed off, his expression unreadable.

"The what?"

"Well, is that a demon inside you, or are you just happy to see me?"

Of course he could see it. I shouldn't have been surprised.

"It's a demon, alright," said Maggie. She didn't bother to try to mask the irritation from her voice. "He sucked it into himself trying to protect a kid."

"Noble," said Bill. "If ill-advised."

"Any ideas on how to get it out?"

He shook his head and offered me a sad little smile. I knew the look. It meant I was hosed, and in a big way.

"Great," said Maggie. "We'll keep trying."

"In the meantime, did you ever find out who the traitor in Evergreen was?"

"I'm afraid not," said Bill. "As far as anyone is concerned, there is no Evergreen anymore. Brea and I have washed our hands of it. I can tell you how to find some of the other members, but that could put you in serious danger."

Again, story of my life.

There was something off about Bill. Not that he'd crossed over to the dark side or anything like that. But he didn't stand as straight as he usually did. His smile didn't seem as warm or bright. He didn't have the same spring in his step.

"Are you okay?" It wasn't any of my business, but the man trusted me when he had no reason, protected me when it would've been easier to walk away. Out of anyone from Evergreen, Bill was a friend.

"You mean you haven't looked?" For a moment I glimpsed the old Bill in the wry smile, but it faded.

"It seemed rude."

He nodded. "I'll be fine," he said. "We all deal with grief in our own ways. I thought of Evergreen as my family. It's hard to let them go."

"How can I find them?"

Bill was no help. As much as I wanted to press the issue, I couldn't. He knew where most of the members of Evergreen lived, or could find out. But he didn't want to help us for some reason. Maybe he didn't want us putting ourselves in danger. Or maybe he just couldn't bring himself to hand over his friends, no matter how twisted one of them might be. Either way, our meeting left me with more questions than answers.

We didn't head back into Pittsburgh straight away. Even if Bill really didn't know where to find all the other members of Evergreen, I knew where at least one was. And, if we were lucky, maybe he would help us.

For most folks, where they live is more dependent on

where they work than where they grew up. Time was, people felt a sense of pride for their hometown, and for many, the only thing that could get them to leave was death. Come Hell, high water, blizzards or locusts, the people of Pitcairn just couldn't give up on their little patches of dirt. The little town showed signs of dying for years, yet the few who remained stood proud by their crumbling streets and abandoned storefronts.

We turned up the main street and passed by a couple of bars and churches until we found the street we wanted, then turned toward a mammoth crumbling structure. In its day, the church must've been an impressive sight to behold, able to inspire the awe and reverence that built it. Now it inspired a different kind of awe. The kind a person felt when he was sure a building watched him.

The street in front of the church was bare. Cars sat parked all along the street, but not in front of the church, as if someone put up cones to keep them away. Maggie took advantage and parked right in front of the church. As we got out, I realized why no one parked there.

"Can you feel that?" She raised a hand and felt the air.

"Yeah," I said. "It's strong." The energy that flowed from the building extended further than it did last time we were there. Last time, it engulfed the yard as far as the chain-link fence that surrounded the church. Now it stretched out, tendrils of power like taproots as it sought new sources of nourishment.

Maggie reached into her purse and pulled out a broken piece of wood. The person we were here to see gave us each a piece of the church to act kind of like a key. Maggie kept hers with her at all times, just in case she needed to talk. Mine sat on a shelf in my apartment, next to a supposedly haunted doll and big thick book, in a room so covered in wards that nothing could get in or out. I hoped.

"You don't have yours, do you?" She shook her head and let out a sigh. "Take my hand. Follow close."

We made our way to the back door of the church. The first time we came, I used my shifted perception to get a glimpse of the life energy of the church. Years of faithful parishioners poured out their own lives and dreams into the building. Those energies accumulated, and gave the structure a life of its own. Through my altered Sight, the building's aura resembled a sheath of gold electricity that kept out all the bad things. This time, I didn't need to look. I knew the threshold would part like an electric curtain when we approached, that it would let us through, because we held the piece of the altar.

Maggie took my hand at the back door and stepped over the threshold. As I tried to follow, my skin itched and tingled. Then my gut clenched and a wave of nausea washed over me. Before I could take a step over the threshold, something pushed me backward. To be honest, it felt more like something hit me with a battering ram. I landed on my butt in the yard about a dozen or so feet away, out of breath and unsure if I could move.

"What the hell was that?" Maggie's concerned face was the first thing I saw when I opened my eyes.

"I'm not sure," I grunted. My head swam and every muscle in my body ached like they'd been through one long extended cramp. But I was alive, which was something. I winced as I pushed myself to sitting up and closed my eyes.

As I willed the doorways in my mind to open, I caught glimpses of the little demon as he dodged back and forth between my perception barriers. He didn't look happy. Actually, he looked terrified.

Don't go in! it wailed. *It hurts us! It wants to kill us!*

"What a coincidence," I said. Once the last of the walls fell, I opened my eyes and Saw more or less what I expected. The

60

golden sheath of pure life force still surrounded the church, but was stronger than before. Brighter, more intense. It pulsed and crackled, the electric heartbeat of the old building. By the door, the threshold stood protected by the curtain of energy, but there was something different about it. The rest of the building had a steady rhythm, but over the threshold that rhythm was a punk-rock drumbeat.

"Walk through it again," I said. "I want to watch you go through."

Maggie nodded and stood, then marched over to the door. When she reached the threshold, the curtain of energy parted and let her through, easy as could be.

I struggled to my feet and followed. When I was about three feet away from the door, the curtain sparked and jumped, glowed brighter and hummed a little more. I didn't have to think too hard to guess why. But, just like when I was a kid and my father told me not to stick my finger in a light bulb socket, I did it anyway. With similar results. But the light socket just made my unruly hair stand on end. The jolt from the doorway launched me through the air again. I landed on my butt, skidded a few feet, then fell flat on my back.

"That was dumb," called Maggie from the doorway. "You want to try running at it really fast?"

"It was the demon," I said without getting up. Somehow the effort just didn't seem worth the trouble. "The church doesn't want to let it in."

"Huh. So taking a demon into your own body *wasn't* such a good idea? Who knew?"

Maggie loved to be right, almost as much as I hated to be wrong. The trouble was, usually, she was right.

I pushed myself to my feet and took a mental inventory to make sure nothing was broken, then I hobbled to the doorway.

"Toss me the key," I said. "Might be weak for two-"

"Or three."

"-*or three* people. But with just me, I might be able to get through."

She pitched the little block of wood through the door.

"And you," I said to the demon. "Make yourself as small as possible or I'll hum Barry Manilow until you beg for mercy. Got it?"

With the block in my hand, I moved forward. The energies surrounding the threshold licked over my skin, raised the hair on my arms. It tickled at first, then itched. By the time I made it to the threshold, it burned. They pushed against me, like a wall of rubber. But the tiny piece of the altar I held passed right through without a problem. It was all the opening I needed.

"Grab it!" I yelled. Maggie took my hand and pulled hard against the curtain. My muscles contracted and convulsed as the church tried to expel me again, but Maggie was stronger.

In my life, I've known plenty of women. The ones I always found most attractive were strong personalities, sure of themselves and their abilities. Confidence was, to me, an aphrodisiac, the ultimate turn-on. Maggie took her confidence to a whole different level, and could stare down a stone cat, I'd wager. That confidence manifested itself in a variety of ways. It made her hold her head up when she walked, gave her the strength to stand up for herself and what she knew was right, and made anyone who met her take notice. It also made her magic remarkably powerful. Like most magic, hers was a projection of will. And Maggie's will was strong.

"Push!" she grunted as she pulled on my arm. Blue and white tendrils of her will snaked down her arms and across mine, hooked into the opening made by the block, and wedged it open. Another ribbon of energy wrapped around my body and pulled me toward the opening.

As the threshold caught hold, it fixed me in place like a spider web. I pushed through, but it caught on something, held tight like it wanted to pull my spine out. The little demon inside me screamed in agony as the energies tried to drag him through my flesh. Then, with a final push, I was through. Maggie and I toppled into an undignified heap in the floor.

After a moment, during which we assured one another that we were physically intact, we crept down the hall in search of the only human alive in the old church.

Robert Lardin was, once upon a time, a priest. He was considered by many to be a pious man, but generous with his time and one of the few priests who weren't judgmental toward other religions. He grew disillusioned with the dogma of the church, with the hate-filled lies spread by the corrupt in higher power, so he left it behind. When I met him, he was a member of Evergreen. He still held fast to his beliefs, but they were far removed from the dogma that condemned homosexuals and other religions. He was the living embodiment of a good man, and one who embodied the teachings the higher-ups professed to love, all the while shitting on.

Then Trevor turned on Evergreen and unleashed zombies on the Burgh. The infighting was enough to make him return to his parish and try to make amends with his One-True-God. Those of us who knew him called him "Neighbor Bob."

"Bob?" Maggie's voice echoed off the walls and headed off into the darkness. "Are you here?"

"Always." The voice was Bob's, but it came from all around us, from the walls, the ceiling, even the floor. As if his voice were amplified by the building itself.

"We need to talk to you," I said. "It's about Evergreen."

"Come forward," said the voice. "To the main sanctuary.

I'll help if I can."

The hallway brightened a bit, enough to light our way through the musty darkness. The hallway opened up to a large room with ceilings so high they couldn't be seen through the darkness. Stained glass covered the windows in a colorful mosaic of scenes of the passions of saints and good men, the fall of demons, the general triumph of good over evil. The demon inside me squirmed.

"Bob?"

"Here."

The last time I came to the church, the spot behind the pulpit was blank, a lighter spot where a crucifix once hung. Now the space was occupied. Bob's outstretched arms filled in the lighter gaps, his feet off the ground. It was almost as if he'd been nailed to the wall. But instead of nails, the wall seemed to open and recess a place for him. The blinding white of the church's energies intertwined with his until they wove around one another like electric eels.

"How can I help you?" His voice was calm, as if being stuck on a wall like a living crucifix was the most natural thing in the world.

"What... happened to you?" Maggie stared wide-eyed as the wall shuddered like liquid and let Bob glide gently down until his bare feet rested on the worn carpet.

"Nothing I didn't want," he smiled. "The old church and I, we're old friends. We've grown together over the past year. Bonded, you might say."

He seemed serene, too much so for my sensibilities. The smile he wore was a little too placid, and the way he moved, more of a glide than a walk. There was almost nothing left of the Neighbor Bob I knew. The man who stood before us, tethered to the church with some unseen bond, was something new. And more than a little creepy.

His smile faltered when his eyes met mine.

"You are unclean," he said. "I see it inside you like a cancer. How could you? How dare you bring that filth into this house of God?"

The serenity was gone, replaced by abject rage. And to tell the truth, I found it a lot less creepy than the whole Quaalude-cocktail act. At least the anger showed he was still human.

Before I could reply, Bob threw his hands wide. With my perception shifted, I Saw his will, his faith, explode outward in liquid flame. Wherever it touched, the boards of the church floor warped and twisted. The church responded in kind. One moment I stood on solid ground, the next the floor opened beneath me like a hungry mouth. The worn carpets on the floors whipped like ancient moth-eaten tongues. I fell backward and caught myself with my only good hand, but there was no way I could hold myself up. My fingers slipped a fraction of an inch, and cold fear raced through my extremities.

"Bob!" screamed Maggie. "What the hell are you doing? Stop it!"

"There is a monster inside of him!" shouted Bob. "And I will wipe it from existence!"

She gestured and raw willpower raced through her fingertips toward me. It snaked around my waist and took my weight.

Faith is an interesting phenomena, remarkable to behold and impossible to understand for those who don't have it. People like me have knowledge, which isn't the same. The power of faith, no matter in what, can lift cars, move mountains, heal the sick or split a sea. There are no limits to what can be done with faith. Knowledge has limits, empirical evidence of what can and can't happen. When I see someone in the throes of faith, the body glows like a star. That energy builds until it reaches a critical mass, then pours out to affect the world. Magic works the same way, just with a different name.

Maggie and Bob fought with their own faiths, his in the righteous power of what he called God, hers in the power that she'd spent a lifetime learning and honing, until she'd become one of the most powerful witches I'd ever met. Which meant I was the rag in the middle of the tug-of-war rope.

"I had to!" I screamed. "I pulled it out of a child!"

"You're lying!"

"He is not!" Maggie's voice was low, guttural, more a growl than her usually pleasant tones. "He damned himself to save an innocent!"

The light around Bob faltered, dimmed just a tiny bit. It was the opening Maggie needed.

"*Concusso!*" she barked, and a wall of solid intent fired out of her core and knocked Bob on his backside. The church howled in rage.

"No!" cried Bob as he struggled to his feet. "No! It's alright! I'm... I was wrong. Please... forgive me. I forget sometimes about gray lines."

Maggie helped me through the opening, which closed behind me. As I sat panting on the floor, Bob took a few tentative steps toward us.

"You... really sacrificed yourself to save a child?"

"Yeah," I nodded. "Seemed like a good idea at the time. Now I'm not so sure."

"I'm so sorry," he said. "I had no idea..."

"And you didn't bother to ask," spat Maggie. "Just condemned him on the spot."

"I'm truly sorry," said Bob, his head bowed. "I get no visitors here. I feel I may be losing my balance. I can try to exorcise the demon..."

"No, thanks," I said. "He's dug in like a tick. Won't come out till I'm dead or he is."

"Your arm..."

"That happened a while back," I said. "Remember? When things went sour with you and Evergreen?"

He nodded.

"Sometimes I miss them."

"Yeah," I said. "Well, about that. We need your help finding some of them."

It took me the better part of an hour to explain what was going on. When I came to the part about the messages on the walls, Bob shivered.

"The thing I don't get," I said, "is how there can be so many of us, and I never knew about it. I mean, you'd think someone might've mentioned a support group for people like me."

"There is no one like you," said Bob with a sad smile. "You're one of a kind. But I think I may know why there are so many others who've survived death. Have you ever looked at the rivers?"

The question struck me as odd. I lived in Pittsburgh my whole life. Of course I'd seen the rivers. The Monongahela and Allegheny rivers met at a single point to create the Ohio River, right outside Heinz Stadium.

"Rivers used to be revered as powerful," he said. "Pagans and the like still feel that rivers carry the life force of the earth from place to place. Maybe it has something to do with so many of your brethren returning from the grave."

Maybe, but at that moment I was more concerned with how to keep those people who came back on *this* side of the great whatsit.

"I know where a few live. Kevin, Reneau... I have a few old addresses for some of the other members, and I think I remember where Blossom works, if she's still there."

"Anything you give us will help," I said.

"Please," he said. "Be careful. If it truly is an Evergreen who wants you, you're walking into the lion's den. Without the grace of God to protect you."

"That's why I have her," I said, and winked at Maggie.

We pass people every day, talk to them, serve them coffee, drive alongside them and trust them to not run over us, yet we never really get to know them. The relationship between strangers who just happen to walk next to each other in public is one taken for granted by almost everyone. We trust them not to push us off the curb into oncoming traffic. We trust them to not lace our food with poison, or to not go on a vicious killing spree, and for the most part, our trust is rewarded. And we don't know them at all.

On the other hand, there are the people we call our friends, who come to our homes, dine with us, and who we feel we know better than anyone. But, no matter the length of time, no matter what the circumstance, I believe we can never truly know them. Even among roommates, siblings, lovers, there are still little parts hidden from each other. Private thoughts that, for some, would startle, and for others, horrify.

So it was with no small amount of surprise that we pulled up in front of the Pittsburgh Playhouse. The sign outside read "Uncle Tinky's Puppet Show."

"You're kidding me," I said. "No way he's here."

"The address matches," said Maggie. "Maybe Bob got it wrong."

I closed my eyes and lowered the walls of my perception. If he was inside, I might be able to find him.

Theaters and churches are very similar to people like me. Some would argue that they're similar in every way. But for me, they both take on a sort of life force all their own. The passion of the performers on both sides help to give them power, but the lion's share of the energy comes from the audience. Every theater is rumored to have a "ghost." Most of the time it's just superstition, sort of a good luck charm. Once in a great while, the ghost is real, the stories not just urban legend. The rest of the time, the "ghost" is nothing more or less than the love poured onto the stage by the performers and the response of the audience.

The Pittsburgh Playhouse, however, was a little different. Its ghosts were very real, all five of them. There were three that were run-of-the-mill people who died in one manner or another, a woman and her daughter who died in a fire, and a man, an actor who used to perform on the playhouse stage. Then there was the one that was missing half his face. That one liked to sneak up behind people and scare the beejeezus out of them. But the fifth one, I worried about. As far as I could figure, the red leaping bastard wasn't a ghost because he'd never really been alive. Which, in my mind, made him something far more dangerous. A demon, summoned by accident by a bunch of know-nothing kids.

When I opened my eyes, the building shone as I expected. But there was something wrong with it, dark spots in its aura.

"Stick close," I said. "And be ready to make with the mojo. And if you happen to see any ghosts, don't be shy about letting me know."

I didn't have to look. My skin prickled and the hairs on

70

my good arm stood up as Maggie drew energy into herself. If there was a fight to be had, I pitied the person on the other side of it.

On the glass door was a poster for "Uncle Tinky," with a banner slapped across that read "Free Admission." I shrugged and walked in.

"He probably works here," said Maggie. "We need to speak to the janitor or the handyman or something."

"Or we could just wait for Uncle Tinky to get done with his show."

Roars of children's laughter billowed from the open auditorium doors. Maggie followed my gaze until she saw what I saw. Center stage sat a man in clown makeup, his bald head slathered in white, his clothes hideous in color, and a smile painted all the way across his face. In his lap, a fuzzy purple puppet mouthed off with a squeaky voice that brought peals of laughter from the packed audience house.

"That's the end of our show!" said Uncle Tinky in a nasal hoot. "We hope you enjoyed yourselves! Remember kids, what do me and Pickles say?"

The whole room broke into a rousing chorus of "Why Can't We Be Friends."

"I'm never letting him live this down," I said.

"Cut it out," said Maggie with a giggle and a shove. "He's entertaining children."

"Right," I said. "And who ever thought we'd see that?"

Uncle Tinky skipped and pranced off stage. Maggie and I made our way to the backstage area.

"You're kidding, right?"

Uncle Tinky spun like he'd been stung by something.

"I mean, really, Kevin. This goes against that whole 'I'm-gonna-whip-your-ass' persona that you've got going."

"Cooper," he growled.

"I'm sorry," I snorted. "I can't take you seriously in that getup. You want to wash that off? Maybe you have an oversized hanky or something?"

"What do you want?"

"We need to talk," said Maggie.

Kevin looked toward the open stage, where a few hands swept and reset for the next show.

"C'mon," he said. "Follow me."

From the outside, the Pittsburgh Playhouse may have looked like a small, white stone building with ornate columns and ample parking. But inside was the only way to get an idea of just how big or old the building was. The stairs Kevin took lead to a hallway that seemed to go on forever. We passed rows of racks of costumes, shelves piled high with props from bygone shows. It became obvious that we were not just in the basement, but we were beneath the street, in a building through which the city's life pumped and pulsed. As we walked, Scats shifted and darted through the shadows, unnoticed by normal folks. But then, I hadn't been normal for a long time.

"Dressing room's down here," said Kevin. "I can't use the others."

"Why not?" Maggie's voice sounded far away. I reached for her hand and found it, but the darkness pressed in around us, tried to separate us.

"Because of *him*," said Kevin. The exasperation in his voice was even funnier to me because of the giant floppy shoes and enormous polka-dotted bow tie. I almost didn't notice when he nodded toward the ceiling. The red man crouched in the beams, stared down at us with angry eyes. "*He* doesn't like me very much, and I'm not inclined to endanger anyone else just to have a pissing contest with *him*."

72

The demon stared down at us, at me. Recognition crossed his face, but he stayed put.

The space Kevin used as a dressing room turned out to be a storage closet with a broken mirror and a bare bulb. His clothes sat on a moth-eaten couch while his makeup took up most of the space on a rickety old table. One of the legs, I noticed, was made up of old books.

"Fancy," I said.

"What do you want?" said Kevin as he huffed down into a chair and wiped makeup off his face.

"A woman died last night," I said. "Someone like me."

"Irritating?"

"Near-death experience," said Maggie. "Killer wrote Stan's name on the wall."

"And so did another one," I said. "Burned. Wrote my name by that one too."

"What's that got to do with me?"

"You ever hear of a group called SPIRIT? Made up of people who've died and come back?"

"Yeah," said Kevin. "They run ads in the Penny-Saver every so often. Why?" Cold cream and a towel revealed the Kevin I knew, the one with eyes that could burn through steel. The clothes didn't match the head, but there was something else different about him. He seemed tired.

"They were both members," I said. His reflection locked eyes with me.

"Again, this is my problem how?"

"The killer wrote my name on both scenes," I said. "Signed it with an evergreen."

For a moment it looked like his face was still covered in greasepaint. The color drained out as he stared at me in the mirror. Then he turned.

73

"Walk away," he said. "I'm telling you now. Walk away. I never figured out who stabbed us in the back, but I know it wasn't me. If it was Reneau, or Blossom, or even Bob... you won't win this."

"Aww... is that a little caring I see?"

"I'm trying to save your life!" He stood as he roared and sent the chair skittering across the room. "If not you, then think of her!" He gestured toward Maggie. "Or that other one... Whatshername... You really think they're going to walk away from this?"

"We can take care of ourselves," said Maggie. She bristled, and the air around her crackled with angry energy.

"You think?" Kevin chuckled and threw himself down in his chair again. "You're an idiot. You think you know what you're dealing with? Whoever it is will use you to get to him."

"And how would you know that?"

"Because it's what I would do!" He slammed his fists down on the table. The impact resonated through the floor in a shockwave. "See, this is why I don't like you! You've barely scratched the surface of your potential! Your power didn't take years to master! You just woke up with it and now you don't do shit with it!"

"But why would they want me?"

"Aha!" He stuck a finger into the air like he'd just found the lost treasure of the King of Clowns. "See? That's the *first* intelligent question you've asked since you came in here! I don't know, but that's what you should be looking for! If I were you, the *last* thing I'd be doing is walking up to people who may or may not be homicidal maniacs! Are you really that stupid? Fuck!"

He turned his back to us and resumed wiping the makeup from his face. It was the first time I'd ever seen anyone *angrily* remove clown makeup.

74

"Why wouldn't they just take me? Why go through all the trouble?"

"Don't know," said Kevin without turning. "Good question. Good luck with it. Now piss off."

"Kevin..." Maggie put a hand on his shoulder. It may have been my imagination, but it looked like he slumped a little.

"Be careful," he said, his voice gentle and quiet. "Please. Just be careful."

"C'mon," I said.

We left Uncle Tinky to his greasepaint and headed back through the dark maze of corridors. When we were far enough from his little closet, I stopped and looked up at the ceiling.

"For the life of me," I said. "I don't know why that guy hates me so much."

"He doesn't," said Maggie. "You just... rub him the wrong way, I think. Why are we stopped? What are you looking for?"

"Him."

I didn't need to shift my perception to see the red demon. Not only was he still in the same place we last saw him, but he *wanted* to be seen.

"You got something you want to say to me?" I called. "Come on down and say it."

It takes either a supreme amount of confidence or an epic level of stupidity to engage a demon. I like to think of myself more of the first type of person than the second, but opinions vary.

The red man's face twisted in anger, then rippled to a chuckle as he leapt from his perch. He landed on his heels and bounced for a moment as if he were made of rubber, then came to a rest.

"Save the theatrics," I said. Behind me, Maggie drew in power, ready to fight. "What do you want?"

"I was wondering how long you were going to hold my little kinsman as your prisoner," it said.

"If you've got some idea how to get him out of me..."

"Well..."

"*While I'm still alive*, I'm all ears. Otherwise, get stuffed."

"Really brave, aren't you, Cooper?"

I bristled.

To know a demon's name is to command him. For him to know mine made me feel violated.

"Nice. I can do that too, Ukobak!"

At his name, the demon flinched.

"Or would you rather I just call you what everyone else calls you? What is it, the Bouncing Red Meanie?"

"I don't answer to that name," he said. He managed to sound insulted. "How do you know me?"

"There aren't that many of your kind that can be summoned the way you were," I shrugged.

"So," he said. "You know my name. What do you want?"

"Answers. Question one. How come all of you know who I am?"

His body faded a little as his shoulders slumped and he let out a heavy sigh.

"No wishes? No flying? I'm just a stoolie for you now? Fine. There's a bounty on you. I don't know who put it there, so don't ask, but it was someone major in our world. Every demon in Pittsburgh is gunning for you."

"So why not just come get me?"

"Because there's another player," he said. "Someone who wants you alive."

The traitor.

"So why doesn't *he* just come and get me?"

He looked toward Maggie. "He's not too bright, is

76

he? Okay. It doesn't do any good for a soul to be beaten into submission. You have to willingly give yourself over."

Like Dennis.

"That won't happen," said Maggie.

"Oh? We'll see."

"Why do they want me?"

"That, I don't know. I just know that someone wants you in a really bad way. And with the amount of juice they're throwing around, my advice would be to dig a hole and hide. Deep. Or kill yourself so whoever it is can't use you. Because they *will* find you. You can't hide from this."

"Why're you here?" I asked. "You looking to cash in?"

"Me? Please. I'm here because I like it here." His glow intensified. "I got summoned, but, well there's just something about a theater, isn't there? The smell of the greasepaint, the roar of the crowd..."

"The taste of the young who would sell their soul for a lead role?" Maggie cocked an eyebrow at him.

"I'm out of that game now," said the demon with a dismissive wave. "Now they treat me like the patron saint of this theater. Can you imagine? *Me*? A *saint*? To think of what I used to do... I'd be insane to leave."

"What about the other souls trapped here?"

"Trapped?" he scoffed. "Try to get them to leave. Just try. Especially that half-faced bastard. No, we're more than ghosts and demons here. We're patrons of the arts!"

"Whatever," I said. "If you hear anything else, you tell Kevin. Make sure he gets the message to me. Understand?"

"Fine," said the demon. "Anything else, *master*?"

"Yeah, now that you mention it. Leave Kevin alone. He's... a friend."

"Right," said the demon. "I'm not stupid, y'know. I can

hear. You two don't like each other."

"That's not any of your concern, *Ukobak.*" I let the statement hang for a moment. "You do as you're told. Got it?"

"Whatever," he said. Then he pulled his body inward and bounced out of the room like a crimson kangaroo.

7

We didn't learn anything from Kevin, Bob, or even Bill. Bob and Kevin I expected, but Bill usually had some kind of insight to share. Maybe he just didn't want to talk. But he'd always been forthright with us before. It wasn't like him to hold back information.

As Maggie angled the car around a corner toward Carson Street, I stared out the window at nothing in particular. Pittsburgh was my home. My frozen-in-the-winter, construction-clogged-in-the-summer home. Sure, we were famous for lots of things, but to me, Steel City had a special hold. Most people felt a certain affection for the place they were born. But for me, it was more than that. Sure, I was born here, but I also died here, and came back. That kind of gave a new meaning to the whole "my hometown" argument.

And for a moment, I really thought about leaving.

You have to willingly give yourself over.

Fat chance of that. A lot of things I might be, but a martyr isn't one of them. My sense of self-preservation is a little too high. But I'm also not a coward. At least, I don't like to think of myself as one.

We turned another corner onto Carson. It was a strange little street, where a person could find anything, if he knew where to look or knew the right questions to ask. We passed by clubs and restaurants on our way to our end, where the more interesting shops waited.

Every city has its weird districts, but none of them are quite like ours.

It wasn't the shops that gave the place its flavor, but the people who owned them. An old hippy owned Rock Rags, where a person could buy pre-torn t-shirts and bongs. Down the street was a shop that sold soup, and the chef stared at his customers until they finished the first bite so he could gauge their reaction. The old fellow who ran the music shop told stories of touring with Chuck Berry and Carlos Santana, even though we all knew he was full of crap. And the guy who ran the antique toy shop never sold anything because he couldn't stand to part with any piece of his collection.

Every shop had a story, a personality of its own, Maggie's more than the others on account of it actually being alive, but even before that, there was something distinctly *her* about the shop.

Which is why my stomach dropped when I saw a police car in front of the old bookstore where SPIRIT met, lights a-blazing.

"Stop!" I didn't wait. The car was still moving, albeit slower, when I jumped out and ran to the edge of the yellow tape that marked the area as a crime scene. "Randall!"

"Please, sir. Step back." The young uniform didn't know me from Adam, which was a pleasant change of pace. He looked young, fresh from the academy.

"I know the guy who owns the shop!" The officer didn't

look impressed. "Is he okay? What happened? Goddamn it, answer me!"

"Calm down, Cooper." The familiar voice hit me hard because I knew what it meant. If Appel was there, Menold couldn't be far behind, which meant someone was dead. And I didn't need three guesses to figure out who. "Go home. We're going to need to talk to you anyway."

"Why not now?"

"Procedure," growled Menold. "Now go home and wait for us."

"Just tell me one thing..."

"Yes," said Appel. "It's the owner of the shop. And your name was on the wall again."

My legs went weak. A pair of strong but gentle arms slid around my waist and held me up. Maggie hugged me tight.

"It wasn't your fault," she whispered in my ear. "You didn't do this."

I wanted so badly to believe her. But the proof of my blame was on the wall, just like at Niccole's apartment. Someone had it out for me, and all I could figure was that, somehow, I was to blame.

Death is random. People die every day in accidents or from things out of their control. Murder is deliberate in most cases. People die in the throes of passion, to settle a score, or for something as arbitrary as money or wearing the wrong color t-shirt. But to target someone by killing another, to leave his name on a wall, that takes a serious amount of hate. And all I could do was wonder what I did to earn so much.

The next three hours passed in a haze. Maggie drove me back to the shop and I made a beeline for the apartment upstairs, where I sat and waited. Maggie knew me well enough to hug me, kiss me, then leave me the hell alone. Andi learned from Maggie's example. The shop, on the other hand, kept trying to make me feel better. On the fourth cup of hot tea that appeared from out of nowhere, I felt like breaking something.

"No, thank you," I said. "I don't drink tea."

The walls shuddered, then went still. All the feelings of warmth or happiness went out of the room and, for the first time in a year, I was alone. I slumped down on the couch and propped my withered arm up. My shoulder ached from lack of use. I didn't see much sense in moving it from the shoulder if it couldn't do anything productive once it got there, so the muscles withered just like the rest of the arm. I leaned back on the couch and covered my eyes with my good arm.

There had to be something else we could do, besides walking up to old members of Evergreen and asking "was it you?" The obvious problem was if one of them did kill those people, they weren't likely to admit it. The less obvious problem was we were likely to die for being nosy. If I gave myself up, it might save people from dying, but somehow, I doubted it. Whoever he was, the traitor proved he had no reservations about killing innocents.

I thought, not for the first time, about Trevor. He got caught up in the lies and promise of power, and when it was all said and done, where was he? At Mercy Hospital, hooked up to breathing tubes without so much as a flicker of consciousness. The bastard turned his brains into tapioca, which left us with more questions and quite a few corpses that needed peace.

A sharp rap at the door made me jump, and sent a pencil skittering across the floor. It took me a second to realize that it fell out of my hand. My left hand. The one that was, as far as the doctors were concerned, dead.

Another rap at the door.

Where my hand sat was a notepad covered in scribbles. I snatched it up and stared for a second. The lines almost looked like words. Another knock and I stuffed it into my back pocket.

"Yeah!" I shouted. When I opened the door, Detective Appel nodded while Menold glared.

"I'm sorry," said Appel. "But we need to talk."

As they entered the apartment, a small streak of black zipped out of the back room and wound itself around Menold's legs.

"What the fuck..?"

Bitsy. The diminutive feline was no ordinary cat. To hear Maggie tell it, behind her emerald eyes lurked an intelligence that put most humans squarely in the "stupid" category. Though, to my mind, Maggie had it wrong. Compared to the cat, most folks skipped "stupid" and went straight to "drooling moron." She turned her face toward me and meowed.

"I think she likes you."

"I'm allergic to cats!" snorted Menold.

"Maybe you should wait outside," said Appel.

"You're goddamned right!" shouted Menold between sniffs. He slammed the door behind him. When he was gone, Bitsy turned toward me. The silver crescent between her eyes wrinkled up, and if I didn't know any better, I'd swear she giggled. When she was sure he was gone, she padded over to me and hopped up in my lap, turned twice, then lay down.

"Smart cat," said Appel.

Randall was found dead in his shop by a customer, an older lady who regularly raided the place for bodice-rippers. According to Appel, she found him in the back room, out of his wheelchair, with his skull caved in with some kind of blunt instrument. Appel guessed a ball-peen hammer.

Like the last time, my name appeared on the wall in his

blood. Like the last time, they wanted to know if I had any insight about who or what could've done such a thing. And like the last time, I had nothing to give.

"There's a couple of things," he said. He took a large manila envelope marked "EVIDENCE" from out of his coat and dropped it on the table. "We found this in his desk drawer. It's a list of everyone in his little club. Your name isn't on the list."

"I only went to one meeting," I said. "I don't think they thought of me as one of their own."

"Fair to say. But there are a lot of names on this list. And it looks like he was copying it."

"So?"

"For you. It was on an envelope with your name on it. Any idea why?"

"No. What did the message on the wall say?"

"Just like the last one. Your name. Nothing else."

If it really was like the last one, my name wasn't all that was there. I needed to get in to see what new love note the killer left.

"Can I..?"

"No," he said. "I got in enough trouble for bringing you in on the last one. I'm not doing that again." He reached into his pocket. "I can show you pictures of the crime scene..."

Appel tossed a handful of Polaroids onto the table.

"...And that's pushing it. Anyone asks, you didn't see these, got it?"

I nodded. "Your partner doesn't like me very much, does he?"

"Mark doesn't like anyone much," said Appel. "Don't take it personally. He just thinks you're... spooky."

"I get that a lot. Did you find anything about Dennis?"

"Nothing yet," he said. "We found out his last name was

84

Mersch, and that he was an accountant. That was it. Nothing significant in his apartment, no signs of struggle."

Of course there weren't. He was willing.

The photos on the table showed the brutality of the crime. The room was the one we used for the SPIRIT meeting, minus all the chairs. Randall's wheelchair lay on its side in a corner, the back torn out, one wheel missing. Several shelves lay on their sides, and his backstock of books looked in tatters. Across the walls, crimson slashes and streaks marked the killer's stroke. Slumped in another corner was an amorphous shape, a blanket, from which protruded a pair of slipper-clad feet.

The second and third images showed more of the same, closer for detail, but horror upon horror. The fourth was the one I needed to see. My name, smeared in blood, on the wall. Beside it, a little tree.

"I need to see the scene," I said.

"No way," said Appel with a shake of his head. "I can't take you in there. That would mean my ass and yours too."

"But I need to see..."

"You're not listening. *I* can't *take* you in there. And if you were *caught* breaking in by someone, it would be really bad for you. I mean, patrol cars will go by there every fifteen or twenty minutes, so even if you did get inside, you'd have to work fast."

"Thanks," I nodded.

"For what?" He didn't smile or offer his hand as he got up and walked out the door. But he did leave the envelope with the list inside.

"Maggie!" I ran down the stairs as quickly as I could without my weight taking over and hurtling me like a meteor to the bottom. My gimpy arm flopped, useless but funny-looking, as

I hit each step.

Except it might not have been as useless as I thought.

I burst through the door. Andi squeaked and jumped and sent a strange purple liquid streaming through the air.

"What's your problem?" she yelled. "I've been working on that essential oil for an hour! Now I have to start over!"

"Where's Maggie?"

"Out front. Why?"

I didn't bother to wait. There wasn't time. I ran through the beaded curtain and found Maggie embroiled in a conversation about the ritual use of sex with two boys who were obviously a couple.

"...building energy, but one has to be the chalice and the other..."

"'Scuse me," I said as I grabbed her by the arm. "I really need her just now."

She offered a sheepish smile as I dragged her toward the back of the shop.

"What is your problem?"

"Look." I pulled the notepad out of my pocket and held it out.

"Scribbles. So?"

"I did this."

"Congratulations," she said. "You can draw like a kindergartener."

"With my left hand."

There was silence for a moment while the gravity of the statement sunk in, then she snatched the pad from my hand.

"How?"

"I don't know," I said. "I didn't even know I did it. But I got up, a pencil fell out of my hand and there was all this."

"There are words here," she said, eyes wide.

"Excuse me." It was one of the two boys. "We'd like to pay for our purchases."

"Andrea!" shouted Maggie without looking up. "She'll be right out to help you." I followed her through the beaded curtain as Andi came through the opposite direction. She looked annoyed.

The notepad was covered in pencil marks, squiggles mostly. But a few of the lines twisted into what could've passed for words. One word that was very clear stood out among the others.

Soul.

8

In movies, guys break into crime scenes all the time. They stand in the shadows and watch as the police cars go by, then they saunter across the deserted street, jimmy the lock, and walk in, cool as a cucumber. Just goes to show how full of crap movies can be.

I figured nighttime would be best to get into the bookstore, but one thing I didn't count on was the amount of pedestrian traffic on Carson Street. Even after midnight, people walked up and down the sidewalk in search of the next great hookup or the next easy score. And, for the record, Appel was either wrong or just lied outright. The police didn't cruise by every twenty minutes or so, they sat stationed right by the front door and watched the street for people so drunk they couldn't walk.

I wound up walking three blocks down, one block over, and then backtracking the three blocks so I could come up on the backside of the shop. Just when I thought it might be that simple, I realized that the back door was actually situated between two buildings, which meant I had to walk down an alley in the middle of the night and pray the police didn't see me. Or, if the alley was like so many others in Pittsburgh, that they could hear me when I started screaming bloody murder about being mugged. Either way, my plans looked more screwed by the second.

I shifted my perception until the nighttime world leaped into blazing colors. With my Sight engaged, nothing could hide from me. If there were someone, or something, in the shadows, I'd See it and act accordingly. If it was a person, I could try to bluff my way through. If it was something else, I could turn and run, screaming all the way home.

Lady Luck was on my side, however, and the alley was empty. Filthy, maybe, but empty. I hurried to the tape-covered back door, which turned out to be locked.

What was that I said about Lady Luck? She's a fickle bitch.

With my sight shifted, the threshold shimmered without any sign of being forced. Which meant Randall knew the killer. He let him in, and paid for it. I glanced behind me and almost toppled off the stoop in surprise. Randall stood behind me, his misshapen head a grotesque reminder that he was dead. Beside him stood Niccole, who looked just as pissed-off as ever, and the smoking charred image of Dennis. They were joined by more than a dozen others, every one mutilated in some way.

"I don't suppose you could tell me how to get in," I whispered.

The wraiths flickered and vanished.

"I guess not."

The door looked flimsy, but I wasn't sure about kicking it in. Sure, there was the noise to worry about, but on a more practical level, I wasn't sure it would move for me. More than once, I've hit something that didn't look solid only to discover it was painted to *look* flimsy. I kept looking.

There was a window by the door, conspicuous in that it was the only one on the building without bars. I gave it gentle push and found it unlocked. Anyone else would've suspected a trap. I mean, really, cryptic messages, dead people, and a single open window? The whole thing screamed set-up.

I ignored the little voice that screamed in the back of my head and climbed through the window, which proved difficult with only one working arm. I ended up half on my face, half on my stomach on the floor, but I made it inside, my only injuries to my dignity.

With my perception shifted, Randall's death played back just like Niccole's. He rolled to the door, smiled, then looked surprised as someone I couldn't see struck him. He tried to defend himself, but the attacker pounded him without mercy. The chair skittered to the other side of the room, and Randall crawled backward, one hand in front of his face as he pleaded for his life. Then I watched as invisible blows broke the bones around his eye, shattered his nose and knocked out his teeth. First one side of his head dented, then the other, as the monster beat him to death. It made me sick to watch, but I couldn't turn away. I felt every blow, followed every tear from his disbelieving eyes. With every strike, the demon locked inside of me jumped and twittered like a happy squirrel. And when the monster was done, Randall lay in a heap in the corner, his head a pulpy mess, his lifeless legs at impossible angles.

Tears stung my eyes as I managed to look away. It was one thing to know he was dead, to know how he died, but to sit and watch was a bigger perversion that I imagined. Worse than the quick death Niccole suffered. Randall died slow, in agony, afraid and confused. The person who killed him was someone he knew, that much was clear.

I faced the wall where my name was written. All the

signs of forensic investigation were on the wall. Powders, marks with grease pencils, little flags and markers. They didn't provide the cops with a single clue. But the clues weren't meant for them. They were meant for me.

Below my name, in the same words of intent on Niccole's wall, the killer left another message.

We are close. Give yourself over. A storm is coming to cleanse the streets.

The message didn't tell me anything more than I already knew. But beside the little pine tree, he drew another symbol that made my stomach do cartwheels. Two crescents with a circle in between. The symbol of the Goddess. And the symbol on the door of Maggie's shop.

I wriggled back out the window and ran as fast as my out-of-shape body would allow back to the shop. By the time I got back and up the stairs, my lungs felt like they would burst, and I couldn't stop sobbing from watching Randall die. I threw the door open to find Maggie and Andi waiting on the couch.

"What?" she shouted. "What's the matter?"

I tried to answer, but couldn't. Instead, I staggered to the kitchen, followed by Maggie and Andi, where I gulped down several glasses of water.

"He's... coming... after... you... " I said between wheezes.

Andi's face turned ashen, Maggie's hard as stone. They followed me back to the couch where I slumped down and tried to catch my breath.

After a few minutes, during which they said nothing, but watched me like I might crumble into dust, I calmed down enough to tell them what I saw. While Andi's expression grew more and more horrified, Maggie's grew darker.

"I think I know what happened with the note and your hand," she said when I was done. "Automatic writing. Your hand is dead, but you're alive. Someone used you to leave a message."

"Great. So, what? I'm a human answering machine?"

"Yeah," she said. "Pretty much. We managed to pull a few words out of the scribble. 'Help,' 'soul,' and 'storm.' That's about all we could decipher from that chicken-scratch."

"Okay," I said. "That's not much help."

Maggie and Andi looked at each other. I knew the expressions. There was something else, and they just didn't know how to tell me.

"What?" I said. "Out with it."

Maggie took the envelope left by Appel from the table.

"Have you looked at this?"

"No," I said. "Why?"

"There are a few names on this list that you might find interesting."

9

I said before, I don't believe in coincidence. Not really. Everything in the world is, in some way, connected. Sure, it can be freaky when a person discovers that a girl he's dating knows his sister, but never realized the relationship, but it's not just random chance. It happens all the time, and those little meetings are things that connect everything like a puzzle. At least, that's what I like to tell myself.

Still, the list provided me with names and addresses of most of the members of SPIRIT, as well as notes as to how a few of them met their untimely, and non-permanent, demise. Niccole's attempted suicide was noted, as was the heart attack that killed Dennis, and the accident that temporarily killed Randall. But there were a few other names on the list that I recognized, along with notations I couldn't ignore.

"Kevin!"

My voice echoed off the stone walls and rafters beneath the Pittsburgh Playhouse.

The red demon just watched as I stormed by, a smug look on his face, Maggie close at my heels. By the time I got to the little closet he called a dressing room, I a pretty good mad going.

"Why didn't you tell me?" I threw the list on the table next to him.

His name was there, along with the notation that he'd committed suicide. "Pills," it said.

"Because it's none of your business," he said. "That's why."

"You knew them. How could you..?"

"What?" he roared as he shot out of his chair. "How could I want to look for their killer myself instead of trusting a moron like you to handle it? How could I choose to not share the worst time in my life with you? How could I try to *protect* your silly ass from whoever's killing people?"

"What is your problem with Stanley?" shouted Maggie. I was too stunned to speak. First time for everything, I suppose.

Kevin rounded on her, his face full of hatred and rage. But his anger faded and his expression slid to one of despair.

"What makes him so special?" he asked as he slumped into a chair. "Why? Why'd you come back able to commune with the dead? Why not me? Shit, that's what I was *trying* to do. How 'bout you?"

"It was an accident," I said.

"Yeah." He let out a soft chuckle. "Of course it was. I spent *years* trying to develop my skills, and you do it with pure luck. That's just fucking rich!"

"So, what? You killed yourself trying to..."

"Don't be stupid!" He glared at me. "I wasn't trying to die. I made a mistake. The overdose was an accident."

Maggie looked ready to strangle him, but I stepped in front of her.

"What did you see?" I tried to make my voice as soothing as possible. "When you died, what did you see?"

"Elysium," he said. "Hades. I saw it all. I saw everyone

who ever died, and everyone I ever loved. And every one of them grabbed for me and tried to drag me into the afterlife. I had to fight to come back. And when I did, the world was exactly the way I left it. Flat, superficial, boring. For someone who's seen Heaven, the mortal world is kind of shitty, you know?"

"I didn't mean to die," I said. "I didn't ask to be given this weirdo power. I didn't even ask to come back. As far as I knew, I fell and then woke up in the hospital. I didn't even realize how much time went by."

"And I guess you saw unicorns and rainbows, right?"

"No." I stood up and took Maggie by the hand. "I didn't see anything. No Heaven or Hell, no dead relatives, nothing. As far as I know, the only thing waiting for me on the other side is more nothing. So excuse me if I don't feel sorry for you, and forgive me if your little experiment didn't work. Don't take it out on me."

We turned to leave.

"Wait." His voice sounded broken, defeated. "I want to help. They were my friends too."

I turned to face him and shifted my perception. When I opened my eyes again, Kevin looked very different than what I expected. To me, he was full of rage, always a bubbling cauldron of fury ready to explode out like a kid's science fair project gone horribly awry. I always assumed his aura would be full of reds and other colors of anger and malice. But the person in front of me sat sheathed in blue and white, with enormous swaths of brown. Sorrow, regret, shame, all the worst of the negative emotions without being actually evil. Inside, he was a good person, but sadness touched him to his core, and made him into something else.

"He's not our guy," I said to Maggie.

"Please," he said. "Let me help."

97

In the time I knew Kevin, he never spoke a civil word to me. Every statement he ever made dripped with sarcasm or condemnation. And now I knew why. For all his meanness and his harsh demeanor, Kevin was jealous. And it wasn't something I tried for, which made his jealousy all the more pathetic. The guy didn't really hate *me* per se. He just wanted what I had so bad, and if I had my way, I'd give it to him. To ask in an almost humble tone must've damned near killed him.

Maggie nudged my withered arm and I caught her look of sympathy. I was going to suggest he come along anyway, but her look made me not give him such a hard time about it. But, boy, was I tempted.

"Why not?" I said after a moment. "We can use an extra set of eyes. Do you drive?"

A person's car says a lot about him. And on the other side, certain people just seem to fit with certain types of cars. Take Andi, for example. As modern and punk as she is, there's a real streak of "hipster" in her. For her, the perfect car is an old Karmann Ghia, which happens to be the very car she drives. It's beat up, covered in house paint, and I'm not sure what year it is, or even how it continues to pass inspection, but it fits her. My car, on the other hand, used to be a Chrysler PT Cruiser.

I say "used to" because last year, a bunch of zombies turned it into the world's largest paperweight, and my insurance company, masters of empathy that they were, saw the damage, suffered an aneurysm, and dropped my policy. I've been carless ever since.

Given my initial impressions of Kevin, I pictured his car to be a weird cross between a tank and a race car. Something like the Batmobile, but with more armor and a worse attitude. But when he clicked his key fob, the car that chirped was anything but. It was an import, the kind that was likely made out of recycled beer cans and sounded like it ran on gumbands and hamsters. If he weren't already miserable, I might've laughed out loud. But my sensitive side took over and I left him as much dignity as he could have while sitting behind the wheel of what amounted to an aluminum-covered roller skate.

We made our way through stop-and-start traffic back to Carson Street. The whole way, I couldn't shake a terrible feeling. It was the same feeling I got when I drank too much coffee, a strange frantic feeling that combined manic behavior with the feeling that my skin wanted to crawl off my body. The hairs on my good arm prickled in a way reserved for high levels of energy or for a high note by certain female pop stars. As we drove, I scanned the road and side streets for anything unusual, anyone following, anything that seemed out of place. But there was nothing visible to my unaltered perception.

I didn't want to alarm Maggie, so I didn't say anything as I closed my eyes and shifted. When the doors opened and walls fell, I Saw my city in a way only a privileged few had. For years, musicians sang about cities' heartbeats, but I really got to See Pittsburgh's. Steel City's pulse ran through her streets, collected through her suburbs, and ran out in all directions, a sentient being that fed her citizens and was nourished by them. Every building was alive with the crackling energy that showed life, every street a vein, every highway an artery. If ever there was a doubt in my mind as to whether or not Pittsburgh was a living city, one glance with my perception shifted made me a believer.

But there was something different about it. Not wrong, exactly, but just odd. It might've been a slight shift in the color of the air, or maybe the pulse was a little slower or faster. I couldn't put my finger on it, but something in Steel City wasn't right.

Then I looked up.

Before I shifted, the sky was clear blue, dotted with puffs of white, but nothing that hinted of so much as a drop of rain. But now, the sky looked sick, almost angry. The blue sky took on a hint of orange, while the clouds doubled in number and size, the little cottony puffs replaced with shades of black and green.

A storm is coming.

The demon inside me wriggled. I couldn't tell if it was because it was excited, or afraid.

"We're home!"

The lights in the shop brightened, and the scent of lavender floated to us on a cool breeze. Bitsy lifted her head from the windowsill, blinked and yawned, then went back to sleep. Andi came through the beaded curtain at almost a run.

"What happened? What did you find out? Was it him? Is he the guy?"

"Breathe," said Maggie. "Nothing happened. And he's not our guy."

"Um..." The voice came from the doorway, where Kevin stood with a perplexed look on his face. "Why can't I get through the door?"

"What's *he* doing here?" Andi glared. The last time they met, Kevin said a few not-so-nice things about her abilities. Andi would never admit it, but it still stung. No matter what she said or did, her memory was usually flawless, and she could hold a grudge like almost no one else.

"Let him in," I said. "He's here to help."

She hesitated, then, with a scowl and a sigh, she gave in.

"I'm inviting you in," she said. "But be nice."

The threshold gave a little, but still wouldn't let him in. It didn't seem possible, but he managed to look even more confused than before.

"Threshold," I said. "Keeps out the no-goodnicks. Which, up until just now, included you."

"I don't understand."

"This is Kevin," I said to the shop. "He's a friend."

A blast of warm air ruffled my hair.

"Andi?"

She looked sullen, even pouty, but she crossed her arms and sighed.

"Let him in," she said.

The invisible curtain of keep-out wavered, then parted. Kevin took a few tenuous steps, then hurried through.

"How did you do that?" The look of bewildered surprise never left his face.

"Shop's alive," I said. "I don't think she likes you."

"I never imagined." He moved to shake Maggie's hand, but she waved him off.

"Wasn't me," she said, then pointed at Andi, who stood with arms crossed and murder in her eyes.

"Not bad for a–what was that you called me? Sidekick?"

His expression fell.

"I'm sorry," he said. "I had no idea."

"Whatever," said Andi as she stormed out of the storeroom and into the main part of the shop.

"She's got more power than anyone I've ever seen," said Maggie. "She brought the whole building to life by accident, and she hasn't even begun to tap her potential."

"Amazing," said Kevin.

"Yeah," I said. "Brilliant. Shiny happy people. Can we focus here? You wanted to help. Tell us what you know about SPIRIT."

10

There are moments in all people's lives that make them into who they are. Most everyone has horrible memories of childhood. In my opinion, most folks need a healthy dose of therapy and post-traumatic-stress-disorder treatment after the rigors of high school. But what most people fail to realize is that every bad thing that ever happened to them made them into who and what they are. Every burn, every cut, every harsh word or public humiliation, they all come together in a big ball of neuroses to create the person we see when we look in the mirror every day. And while those experiences do shape us into our permanent selves, they also can be dangerous. The really bad experiences, and even a few good ones, can make anyone go a little mad. A person who wins the lottery, but doesn't have the wisdom of age to know what to do with it, goes a little crazy buying up everything he sees and helping out buddies. Before long, there's nothing left, and he wonders where it all went. On the other end of the spectrum, there are tragedies. I don't mean someone's dog getting hit by a car, I mean something that is *really* tragic.

When I died, I admit, I went a little crazy, especially after all my so-called friends abandoned me. For a while, I thought maybe they were right, that everything I saw was just a figment of my damaged brain. There were spans of weeks during which I wouldn't go out of my apartment for anything other than groceries. And even then, I hurried, almost ran, because I thought I could hear people laughing at me and whispering behind my back. But I got over it. Maggie helped.

Everyone should have a friend like Maggie.

There was a reason Kevin wanted to talk to the dead, why he tried a ritual with mind-altering substances, and why he was so careless as to overdose. He lost his daughter. It wasn't some horrific car crash, or a fall out a window or anything like that. She just... died. One night, she went to bed, smiles and pigtails. The next morning, she just wouldn't wake up. He called the paramedics, and they declared her dead at the scene. No foul play, no discernable reason, just some sadistic higher power having a laugh at Kevin's expense.

The whole "Uncle Tinky" thing made sense, and I just couldn't bring myself to make fun of him for it anymore. In fact, it seemed kind of sad and noble, two things I didn't want to feel about Kevin. It made it harder for me to dislike the guy.

"So when I was revived," said Kevin, "and they decided I wasn't suicidal, they turned me loose. And I found SPIRIT. I didn't stick around long. Maybe a half-dozen meetings. Everyone had such a great outlook, or treated their near-deaths as positive learning experience or something. All I saw was that I couldn't talk to my little girl, and that my life was empty without her."

"What was her name?" Maggie put her hand over his.

"Emily." His voice wavered. Almost a decade later, and he still wore his sorrow like an old coat. It was a wonder the patches of brown didn't deepen to red. I couldn't imagine the kind of pain he'd been through.

"That's how I met Trevor," he said.

The name made an auger in my gut turn.

"I'm the one who brought him to Evergreen to begin with. He was all kinds of messed up when I met him. He really wanted to die."

"What about other members? Anyone else in Evergreen part of SPIRIT too?"

"Several," he said with a nod. "Actually, that's how we met Bill. He and Brea came in to talk to the group one evening. What they said made sense, so I went to an Evergreen meeting."

Interesting, if not particularly useful. I handed the list of names to Kevin.

"We need to warn the rest," I said. "If someone's name is on this list, they've got a target on them."

"Where do we start?" Kevin glanced over the names. There were more than two dozen.

"You take a page," I said. "Give us a page. We'll split up and try to get to them all before something else does."

He nodded, tore off the top page, then headed out the door, a look of grim determination on his face. In the past, I might've mistaken it for hatred or anger, but now I knew better. The man only wanted to protect those people. And, dammit, I had to respect him for it.

"Stay here," I said to Andi.

She bristled. It wasn't that I thought she wasn't capable of protecting herself. I *knew* she wasn't. She was powerful, sure, but still lacked control. The last time she let loose, she brought a storefront to life. I shuddered to think what might happen next time. Besides, Maggie and I had some talking to do, and we didn't need Andi's ears around.

"Please," said Maggie. "We need you here in case the police come by, and we'll work faster knowing you're safe."

"But I can help! Really!"

"Yes," said Maggie. "By staying here."

"But..."

"Shop!" I said. "She doesn't leave. Get me?"

I'm not sure what I expected. It wasn't as if a huge building made of brick and mortar could nod. But one thing I didn't expect was the bell over the door to ring, which it did. I almost took it as a "yes."

"Hello?" A voice came from the front of the shop.

"What am I supposed to do here?" shot Andi.

"Your job," said Maggie. "Tend the shop."

She rolled her eyes in a way that only a twenty-something could, then hurried though the beaded curtain. Her anger radiated off her in waves of heat. She was so angry that the scent of singed hair hung in her wake.

"That went well," said Maggie.

"She'll get over it. She'll understand..."

"When? I swear, Stan, you treat her like a child."

"She is a child!"

"Ahem."

We looked up to find Andi, red-faced and angry, in the doorway, arms crossed and murderous intent in her eyes. There were only three people in the world whose looks gave me that particular brand of cowardly crawlies down my spine. My mother and Maggie were top of the list. But Andi nipped at the rung right below them.

"If you grown-ups are done arguing," she said in a saccharine-sweet voice, "the lady out front wants Stanley."

"Can't you take a message?"

"I'm sowwy," she said. "Widdle kids wike me can't take care of big grown-up business." She stormed to the toilet in the back of the shop and slammed the door.

Fury of hell, woman scorned. One of these days I'd get it right. Maybe.

"See what you can do with her," I said to Maggie as I went through the curtain.

The woman in the center of the room clutched her purse tight and stared around the room as if she were afraid the shelves would blink and eat her. Everything from her dark-blue canvas Keds to her capri jeans and oversized t-shirt screamed "soccer mom." Not the kind of person who frequented Maggie's shop. A smile flickered when she saw me, but was gone before it could catch hold.

"Mister Cooper?" she asked.

"Stan," I said. I stuck my hand out. She didn't shake it. She looked too scared.

"Mister Cooper, I..." She glanced around the room, then back at me. "I need your help."

I don't know what it is about me. Maybe it's a chivalrous attitude. Maybe I'm the living embodiment of a "Good Samaritan." Maybe I'm just a schmuck. Whatever the case, I can't hear the words "I need your help" without an overwhelming urge to leap into action. Like I'm Errol God-Damned Flynn or something. The way I see it, a person who comes to me has to be at the end of their rope. They've probably already tried priests, doctors, shrinks and saints. For them to come to me, to go through the effort it takes to track me down, then to summon up the guts to tell a story that no sane person would believe, they've got to be a short cab-ride away from cracking up.

It would be fine if people came to me to fix a television or rewire their toaster. If I had a shop where they could pull their car in and I could give them a brake job, that would be dandy. But there are very few reasons people seek out someone like me. Someone who can talk to the dead, who can see ghosts. And none of those reasons are very happy.

I spend a lot of time wiping tears off my shoulders.

"What can I do for you, Ms..?"

"Dearbourne. I need... It's my son. He..."

Tears streaked down her face as she fought to keep control.

"Ms. Dearbourne," I said. I tried to make my voice as soft and gentle as possible. "Just tell me what's going on."

"Don't patronize me!" she shouted. "I don't believe in all this mumbo jumbo! I'm a good, Christian woman!"

"Then go pray to your God to help you." Maggie's voice cut across the room like a razor. "If we're not good enough, then get the hell out."

I did my best to flash a cross look at her, but I couldn't. She was right. How many times did people come to me, ask Maggie for help, and turn their nose up at us, all the while taking our assistance? I couldn't count that high. For Maggie, I bet the number was higher, and it stung a hundred times as bad.

"Ma'am," I said with forced patience. "The least you could do is be civil if you want our help."

"*I* don't want your help," bawled the woman. "But my son asked for you by name! He told me where to find you!"

"Has he been in here before?"

She looked horrified at the accusation.

"He's six years old!"

11

Certain things get my goat worse than any other. People who burn my coffee, for instance, piss me off beyond the capability for rational thought. I don't go all ape-crazy over it, but it is duly noted as I dump my seven-dollar mocha in the garbage. People who drive while talking on their cellphones is another one that makes me want to commit an act of road rage. As if people aren't bad enough behind the wheel, it seems like the road is littered with idiots who are just begging to turn their imports into their coffins. But nothing gives me a serious case of righteous indignation like some metaphysical bully picking on a kid. Which is why, if someone calls me and mentions that the person in need is a child, I drop everything and burn rubber.

I gave Maggie a page out of the list and told her to be careful. As much as the thought of her going it alone worried me, we couldn't wait. If someone was to get killed, I wanted it to be while we tried to stop it, not while we stood around and waited for me to do a good deed.

And speaking of good deeds...

Missus Dearbourne sped down the highway toward

Churchill, radio tuned to Christian rock. It seemed as if Maggie's admonishment gave her the need to retreat into the comfortable cocoon of faith. Despite her bad taste in music, I envied her a little.

Faith can move mountains, boil seas and heal the sick. Maybe not, but it can do some amazing things. The power of faith can help someone lift a car to rescue a trapped loved one. It can send cancer into remission. It can even keep bad things like demons and monsters at bay. The trick is to realize that it doesn't matter in what a person believes, so long as they believe in something. Call it God, the Great Spirit, the Force, or any number of other things, it all boils down to the same thing. Human nature dictates that we need to have at least some belief in a power greater than us. That belief grows inside us and radiates out in living energy. The more faith a person has, the stronger the energy field. It's why some people feel an electric jolt when touched by a real faith healer. And it's also why people like me are at a decided disadvantage when dealing with matters of faith.

I don't have any. Instead, I have knowledge. I don't just believe in the energies of the world, I know they're there. I've seen them. It isn't as powerful as faith because it works on the scales of yes and no, as opposed to the sliding gray area of maybe. Faith is maybe. Faith is undefined. And I wish I didn't know the things I do.

"So, Mister Cooper," she said after a few minutes of uncomfortable silence. "How long have you been a... What exactly do you do?"

A crossroads popped up, the kind that most folks don't get but a few times in their lives. On one path, I could try to rationally explain what I did and hope she understood. On the other, I could lay on the bullshit and black magic thick and really try to weird her out. The latter was tempting.

"I see things from a unique perspective," I said, ignoring the little devil on my shoulder. "I had an accident a little while ago. I died. When they brought me back, I could see dead people."

"I see," she said. "Is that what happened to your arm?"

"No," I said with a chuckle. "Different accident."

"Oh. You have a lot of those?"

"A few." I left out the part where it happened saving the city from a psychotic mage with more power than sense. Somehow I thought my descriptions of zombies in Pittsburgh might put her off.

We rode the rest of the way without a word, which suited me just fine. The less I said to her, the smaller my chances of saying something offensive. Not that I cared what she thought. I didn't give a damn what her religious stance was, or whether or not she thought I was going to hell. What mattered to me was the six-year-old boy. No matter his mother's opinions, he was innocent, and needed protecting.

Cue fanfare and hand me my cape.

We pulled up in front of an average-sized house with gingerbread cut-outs adorning the eaves and shutters. The front flower bed was awash with color from seasonal flowers, the kind that folks planted, let die, then planted more the next year. It told me two things: First, she had the kind of money that let her plant disposable flowers. Second, she was very concerned with outward appearances, but didn't want to do any actual work. Easier to just let them die than try to grow something that needed to be maintained. I shuddered for the kid inside, and wondered if she treated parenthood the same way.

She killed the engine and sat for a moment while she stared at the steering wheel.

"I want you to understand something," she said. "I don't believe in witchcraft, or ghosts, or voodoo, or whatever the hell you do. You're here for my son. Just do whatever you do, and get out."

I should've refused. I should've told her exactly what I thought of her bigotry, wished her luck with her problem, and walked home. And if the victim were anyone but a child, I would have. But it was, and I couldn't. So I bit my tongue and climbed out of her minivan and marched toward the house. It was telling that she didn't follow, just stayed in the driver's seat and waited, watched as I, a complete stranger, walked through her front door to deal with her child.

What was she like with her kid's teachers?

"What's the kid's name?" I called from the door.

"Dylan," she said. She sounded irritated that I would dare ask.

The inside of the house told much more about her than I cared to know. The front room was clearly more for display than use, full of antiques and things so fragile I expected to see velvet ropes around them. With white carpet. No one was meant to set foot among the finery, especially not a six-year-old boy. Further in the house was the "family room," which I had a hard time believing ever lived up to its name. Scats ran about, which was a sign of at least a somewhat healthy household, but they ran one direction, away from the hallway. Whatever had them spooked, I figured, was the reason I was there.

There's a certain look and feel that most people expect when a haunted house or a house with a possession in it comes to mind. That's Hollywood's fault. They fill the screens and imaginations with creaking doors and floorboards, flickering lights, and general filth to accompany the unclean spirit. But that sort of thing never frightens me. To tell the truth, the more frightening places are, to me, the ones that look normal, where the invading spirit is more devious, where the malignancy hides just below the surface, and could be living next door undetected for years.

The temperature dropped a few degrees for every slow and cautious step I took. By the time I reached the boy's room, my muscles ached and my joints were stiff and sore. I didn't bother knocking, but took a deep breath and pushed the door open.

Dylan was there. He sat cross-legged in the center of his bed, dressed in choo-choo train pajamas, with wide eyes and a vicious smile.

"So glad you accepted my invitation." The voice that came out of him was older by at least a thousand years, and meaner by a thousand times that many degrees. The demon inside me wriggled at the sound of his voice. I shifted my perception with a blink.

Dylan's aura glowed blue, a bright layer beneath oily black and red that all but snuffed his out. It pulsed as the kid fought for control.

Good kid. Keep fighting.

"Okay," I said. "You called. What do you want?"

"I want to chat," it said. The boy patted the bed. I took a chair instead. "Don't want to be friends? That's rude."

"Cut the bullshit," I said. "What do you want?"

"Why do you defend them?" The boy's expression remained unchanged. "That woman. Why are you helping her? She clearly doesn't like you. So why help them?"

"I've got my reasons."

"Tell me."

"Get fucked."

The boy's expression changed. His aura intensified, then grew very weak. Tears rolled down from his terrified eyes, and a tiny squeal of pain escaped.

"You'll tell me," the demon snarled. "You'll tell me

113

anything I want to know or I'll tear this child apart from the inside out."

"Because he doesn't deserve it," I snapped. "He's just a kid."

"But you're helping his mother."

"I'm helping the kid. Now what's it going to take to get you out of there? Why don't you come into me?"

"And wind up trapped like my little brother there?" He laughed, a sick wet sound that made the demon inside me dance and my bladder flutter. "I don't think so. If I'm to tell the truth, I came to warn you."

"Yeah, right."

"We tell the truth more often than you would think," snapped the creature. "Especially when it serves our purpose. Someone you know, someone close, is dancing close to the edge."

"Who?"

"Like I know," it chuckled. "You all look alike to me, except when you're naked, and then it's just a pathetic sight. I'll tell you this much, though. What they're trying to do will upset the natural order. And we like things just the way they are."

"Tell me something I don't know," I said. "I figured out all of that on my own."

"You're the linchpin." It smiled. "Betcha didn't know that."

"Me? How?"

The thing chuckled.

"Tell me!"

"You're going to have to figure that one out on your own," it said. "But I'll tell you two things for free. First, you're going to want to give yourself to it, and you mustn't. Second, the demon inside you will come out when it has another vessel to move into."

"Like, what? Someone else has to willfully take it?"

"Not quite," it smiled. "Be seeing you, Cooper."

The oily black peeled away and dissipated from around the boy's light. His eyes closed, and he keeled over, exhausted but otherwise alive. His aura glowed blue and strong. The demon didn't feed on him, just needed some way to talk to me. But why him? Why this kid above any other? Why drive me forty-five minutes away from..?

Oh, dammit.

I rushed through the house and out the front door. Dylan's mother still sat in her minivan, her expression neither worried nor matronly. In fact, that she'd left him alone in the house with me, someone she'd only just met, and was about to drive away and leave him alone after his ordeal, told me all I needed to know.

"It's gone," I said as I climbed into the minivan and slammed the door.

"Good," she said, threw the car into reverse, and backed out of the driveway.

"Don't you want to know what happened?"

"No," she said. "It's done, and as far as I'm concerned, I'm not going to speak of it again."

"Your kid was possessed by a demon, and you don't want to know why? You're not even going to go check on him?"

"You said he's fine," she said. "What do you want me to do?"

"Don't you want to know why?"

"Fine," she said with an exasperated sigh. "Why don't you tell me, Mister Cooper?"

"Because you're a piss-poor mother," I said. She slammed on the brakes and glared at me, mouth agape like a fish out of water. "If you spent any time with the kid, maybe he' would have enough love in his life to protect him from things like that."

"I am a single parent!" she shouted. "I have to work!"

"Single and absentee aren't the same thing," I said. "Do you know what I saw in that house? No love. It wasn't a home. It was just a pile of shit with a cover on it, and that kid needs someone to watch out for him. Not just someone, his mother."

"I raise him in the tradition of the church..!"

"Do you know why you couldn't force the demon out of him? Because for you, it's all a sham. You have no faith. You think that because you go to church and give money, that gives you a pass. But guess what? If you don't really believe it, you're just going through the motions. And your son paid for it today."

"Get out!"

I opened the car door and slid out. "I can't stand the stink of hypocrisy in your car anyway."

As I watched her drive away, it occurred to me that maybe I should've waited until we were closer to home before I let her have it with both barrels. Still, it felt good to tell her off. I dug in my pocket for the cellphone that Maggie insisted I keep on me.

Cellphones are marvelous inventions, for people that can't see the energy that they put off. In my eyes, the things look like glowing bricks of living cancer just trying to climb into users' brains. For the same reason, I don't like hybrid cars, computers, or microwave ovens. Microwaves, however, I tolerate because I'm a sucker for French bread pizza.

I flipped the little red phone open and punched the button to turn it on, then started walking. There wasn't much of a point, but the longer I stayed in Missus Dearbourne's neighborhood, the dirtier and less healthy I felt.

When the phone buzzed and chirped to life, the screen told me I'd missed three calls. One from Kevin, one from Andi, and one from Maggie. Kevin and Andi left messages. I dialed

Maggie first. She picked up on the second ring.

"How'd it go?"

"'Bout like you'd expect."

"So where do I need to pick you up?" she sighed.

"I'm in Chapel Hill," I said. "Take the 130 exit. I'll be on the corner of 130 and McCrady."

"Fine. You really need to learn to either say no or keep your mouth shut."

"Just come get me," I said. "And hurry. The demon wanted me out of the way for a while."

"Why?"

"Who knows, but I'm betting so it could do something nasty. How quickly can you get here?"

"I'm ten minutes out," she said.

"Hurry," I said again. "This place gives me the creeps."

"Why?"

"Too... Normal. Ugh."

She snorted as she hung up. I dialed my voicemail box and listened. The first, the computerized voice told me, was from the shop's number. But there was no message, no voice, just background noise and static. I let it play all the way through, almost a full minute, before the automated system cut it off and switched to Kevin's message.

"Cooper." His voice shook. Something had him spooked. "You gotta come to... oh, Gods. You... It was a school. Shit. Penn Hills. Hurry. Oh, fuck me."

The line clicked and the mechanical voice told me the call came less than two minutes ago. I called Maggie back and begged her to break a few speed limit laws.

12

What should've taken her ten minutes took her five, and she barely slowed down enough for me to get into the passenger seat before her car lurched into gear and sped off toward Penn Hills. Kevin called her right after he did me, but because she was on the phone with me at the time, she got the same broken, half-sobbed message I did. All we knew was something bad happened, and that it happened at a school. The trouble was, we didn't know which one. We decided to start at the high school and move down.

The police cars in the high school parking lot told us we had the right place. Kevin sat on a curb, his head in his hands. The vomit stains on his shirt told me he was the one who found whatever it was, and that it wasn't pretty. Two uniformed policemen walked away, shaking their heads.

We pulled up and parked, then hurried over to Kevin.

"What happened?" Maggie put an arm around him, but he didn't move.

"They were kids," he murmured. "Just kids. Just kids."

We took it as our cue to get him away from the crime

scene. As he was in no condition to drive, I took the back seat of Maggie's car and helped her strap him in the front. Then Maggie went to talk to the officers, to let them know he was leaving and that we'd be leaving his car there. A few nods later and she slid into the driver's seat and started the car.

"It's going to be okay," she said. "We'll get you back to the shop. Nice cup of tea will do you good."

It was unnerving, the way he sat and stared for the whole ride. I always considered Kevin to be a mean bastard. Intense with a heart of stone and iron will. I'm not sure why, though. I never really knew him, but that was the impression I got. But the man in the front seat of the car, who rocked and muttered "they were just kids" over and over again, was anything but. Another crack in the wall he put between himself and others, and the man beneath it was someone I felt I might like to know.

When we pulled up behind the shop, Maggie got out and ran around to support him. There wasn't much I could do with my withered arm, but I wedged my other side under him and supported his weight. He looked like he needed it, like the weight of what he'd seen would crush him if someone didn't hold him up. We hurried through the back door, greeted by a wave of panic that came from the walls.

"I need my relaxation tea," said Maggie. The shop responded. One moment the counter was bare. I blinked and the little wooden tea box just appeared. I made a mental note to quit blinking.

"Andi?" I pushed through the beaded curtain. The shop was empty. Weird. It wasn't like her to just leave, and leave the back door unlocked. "Where's Andi?"

The panic in the air increased. That Andi wasn't around was enough for alarm. That the shop threw off such strong emotions was far worse.

"Andi's not here," I said as I returned from the main room. "Did she say she was going somewhere?"

"It's after closing time," said Maggie. "She probably just went home. I'll call her in a minute."

My instinct, not to mention the shop, told me otherwise, but Kevin had Maggie's attention just then, and I needed to find out what he saw. The largest part of me didn't want to know, but I needed to. I had to know if the demon in the Dearbourne kid was telling the truth. I had to know if my name was written on the wall.

Maggie made a cup of tea and pressed it into Kevin's trembling hands. He didn't seem to notice until she gently guided the cup to his lips, then he took a sip. The taste seemed to bring him out of whatever fugue he was in little by little.

"They were kids." He locked eyes with me when he said it. "High school kids. They were there for an after-school creative writing program."

"What happened?"

"Butchered," he said. "Twenty kids, one teacher, and a dog. All because of you."

"How is any of this my fault?"

"It's all because of you!" Kevin sprang from the chair and hit me square at the waist. I landed on the floor hard on my good arm. The damaged one flopped useless at my side. Kevin drew back with real hatred in his eyes like he had every intention of driving his fist through my skull, through the floor, and into the basement below.

The windows around us shook and the lights flickered. How he noticed through his haze of rage, I didn't know, but I was happy he did. The confusion on his face gave way to fear. He probably thought the whole place would cave in on him. And I couldn't swear it wouldn't.

"Better not," I croaked. "She gets pissed when you hit her favorite uncle."

Maggie pulled him off me and heaved him into a chair. It took me a moment to go through my mental inventory to make sure nothing more than my pride and ego was broken, but I managed to get back to my feet with little difficulty. Kevin sat in the chair, head down, hands pressed to his eyes. His breath and body hitched in choked sobs.

"What is your problem?" I roared. "I didn't do anything! This isn't my fault!"

"I know," he said between gulps of air. "I'm sorry. I can't... who would do something like that? *Why*?"

"That's what we have to find out," said Maggie. "Before anyone else dies. Then maybe we can stop them."

"Was my name written on the walls?" Kevin's head snapped up to the question. "Was there a message of any kind?"

"No," he said. "Not that I saw. Why?"

It didn't seem right. Whoever it was left messages for me before, like he wanted me to see something. But this time he didn't? Not likely. Chances were good that he left something there for me to see, or that *only* I could see. Which meant another late-night trespass into a crime scene.

"I have to go back," I said.

"There'll be cops everywhere," said Kevin. "You'll be arrested. And if someone did find your name somewhere, they'll lock you up until doomsday."

"Doomsday is what's coming if I don't stop this." I told them about the demon at the Dearbourne house, what it told me, and everything it *didn't* say. I left out the part about the kid's mother being such a ray of freaking sunshine.

"So, wait," said Kevin. "This thing said you're the lynchpin. Right? So without you, the whole thing doesn't work.

122

You could leave."

"Look around," I said. "All the people being killed. That won't stop if I leave. It'll get worse. I'm not going anywhere."

Kevin needed to get his car back from the crime scene, and I needed to have a look. It made sense for me to drive him over. Not good sense, but practical sense. It was just after two in the morning when we parked a few blocks away. No need to alert the authorities.

Most folks avoid the dark. Call it fear or respect, but the dark is just the place to put someone to see his true face. It's easy to be brave or flippant about weird noises or things that brush against the skin in bold daylight. But put someone in the dark, without a sliver or moonlight or streetlamps, where there are no sounds of cars to mask the strange noises the trees make, and that person shows his true personality. It's a primal thing, I think, left over from when nocturnal predators roamed the darkness in search of the bottom of the food chain, which, for some time, was us. We have predators of a different sort today, but they, for the most part, won't eat us.

Some will do much worse.

So, for the most part, folks tend to avoid a long, or even a short, walk down a dark, poorly lit street. Especially if they know there's blood at the end of their walk. But then, I'm not most people.

I shifted my perception and the night leapt into vivid color. Before, the street looked like a pitch-black tunnel into spookiness. But to me, the trees hummed and glowed green, the grass shimmered, the air hummed with millions of electric motes. The animals that hid from people stood out in stark relief to me with their own life forces.

123

Better than night vision or thermal goggles.

I chanced a glance back at Kevin. His aura stood out, but the patches of brown were larger, more pronounced. Fresh. Whatever he saw in the school hurt him deep.

The cop that guarded the crime scene stood out too. Not that he tried to hide. On the contrary, he sat right in front of the school doors, bold as brass, in his car. Asleep.

"Go grab your car," I said. "I'll meet you back at the shop later."

"No way," said Kevin. "I'm going with you."

"Forget it." Not for nothing, but I didn't like having people with me when I confronted the dead. Apart from it being an incredibly personal thing, I also never knew how I would react. Sometimes I went cold and walked through, clinical as a mortician. Other times, I crumpled into a corner and sobbed as tragic images played out in front of me over and over again. But every time, if someone stood with me, watched my reactions, I had to be the one who explained. And every time, it tore a little piece of me apart. I didn't like sharing that part of my life with anyone. Let alone someone who hated me as much as Kevin did.

"It's not a choice," he said. "I'm going with you, or I'm waking up the cop and letting you explain yourself."

The thought of jail didn't appeal to me any more than having unwelcome company. But I didn't need any more run-ins with the police. My last infraction was about eight months ago, when Maggie and I were arrested for attacking an orderly in a hospital. Even though he deserved a beating, it wasn't our finest moment.

"Fine," I said.

The school radiated with the energies and passions of more than a decade of teenaged hormones and angst, artistic discovery and detention. Every broken heart, every discovery of puppy love, every fight and harsh word translated into the school's soul. It sent a tremor of memory of every shitty day in high school through my mind, and for a moment I was a pimple-faced teenager again. I shook the feeling off with a deep breath by the door.

Police tape fluttered in the light breeze like bandages over unlocked doors. I pushed one open and slipped inside, followed by Kevin.

"Where?"

He pointed down the hall.

With my perception altered, the hallway became a surreal spookhouse. Afterimages of every child who ever went to school there still walked the halls. The clashing fashions did nothing to keep the same stories from repeating with different faces.

I was about to ask Kevin for directions again when I saw the room I wanted. It stood out against the rest of the hallway, where healthy energies glowed and the cinderblock walls vibrated with good intent. The doorway was wreathed in black. Whatever happened had scarred the room, created a hole in the positive nature of the school, and created a place that would be whispered about by every student who stepped on campus for years to come. Maybe even forever. And with every story told, more fear would add to the darkness until the room became more than just a place where tragedy happened. It would become a place that attracted tragedy. One could say it caused it, even.

Haunted was too mild a word.

I took a deep breath, tried to make myself calm, and pushed the door open into hell.

There were twenty students, one teacher, and a dog. For a moment, I wondered about the dog's presence, but there were more pressing things to occupy my attention. In front of me, the twenty students worked away, wrote in their journals, while the teacher stood in front of the dry-erase board and soundlessly delivered her lecture. The board read "Alpha Young Writers." They had dreams. They were there to learn to be creative, to use their imaginations, not to be murdered in cold blood.

In the space of two blinks, the teacher turned and said hello to someone I couldn't see. The students, all smiles, looked up, acknowledged whoever it was, then went back to work. Then the teacher's face shifted, her welcoming smile turned to confusion, then abject terror. The dog let out a noiseless bark, and the heads of the students snapped up in time to watch their teacher's face split across the mouth in vicious smile.

The blade again. A sword, maybe? A machete?

She clawed at the air as her throat opened in a spray of arterial blood and she fell twitching to the floor. For a moment, the crimson mist from her jugular formed a figure I almost recognized as a human form, but it was gone. Then the children shrank back in unison.

"No," I said as I watched, unaware that I'd given the thought voice. Why didn't they attack? Fight for their lives? Kick, scream, claw and bite against whoever it was?

The dog barked and lunged, and I watched in horror as his gut split and his insides spilled across the floor. One of the children ran for the door, but it slammed shut in front of her, and she was the first of the students to die.

When it was over, they all lay dead, broken and bloody. The killer scooped up their lifeless forms and put them back in their chairs. It was strange to watch them move as if carried, like strange marionette puppets, by someone I couldn't see. He made sure their eyes were open so that whoever found them, Kevin, would be haunted by their faces for the rest of his life. It was only after he was done that I recognized the boys from the SPIRIT meeting. I wondered if they spoke in each other's heads as he killed them, if they felt each other die.

My jaw ached from clenching as I watched. My eyes stung and burned with hatred and hot tears. Then the words appeared.

Cooper. Written on the board, in writing only I could see, there was my name, again, filthy from his using it. *Their blood is on your head. They wrote their own epitaphs. You caused them to die.*

The son of a bitch signed it again with an evergreen.

"He's taunting me!" I slammed my good fist into the board. Let the cop outside wake up and arrest me. Let everyone for miles hear my rage. The children didn't deserve to die. No one deserved to die, especially over me, but the children never even got a proper chance to live. The boys from SPIRIT, I could almost understand. But what did the others do? They didn't know me, had no connection to me. So why? Why'd they have to die?

I turned to face Kevin and stopped cold. Kevin's rage equaled my own, sure, but that wasn't what stopped me. They stood around him, all the dead children, plus their teacher. Plus the damned dog. Every one of them bloody. Every one of them butchered. None of them at rest. They stared at me, silent, questioning.

"I'm going to stop this," I said.

"You'd better," said Kevin.

"Shut up! I wasn't talking to you! I was talking to them!"

He looked confused.

"You said you wanted to be able to see ghosts? Well, let me tell you what you're missing. They don't wear white, they don't forgive you, they don't blow kisses and tell you where the will is buried. They show up exactly how they died. Bloody, broken, ruined. They show up, and they stay right where I can see them.

Is that what you want? You want to see your little girl exactly the way she looked when she died? Because that's how you'll see her. And no matter how hard you try, you won't be able to replace that image in your head. You'll be stuck with what she looked like dead."

"Don't talk about my daughter..."

"You don't get it, do you?" I moved closer to him, but he didn't back down. He bowed up like an angry snake. I didn't care. "This isn't some kind of super power. It sucks! It's a fucking curse! You want it so bad? Here! Take it!"

I don't know why I reached up and grabbed his head. I don't know why I shouted for him to take it. I never, even for a moment, thought such a thing was possible. But then, I should've known better. My aura raced down my arm and invaded his, blended his colors with mine and burned into him. He sucked air as if he were in physical pain, and bucked for a moment, then he opened his eyes wide and stared.

"Gods," he whispered. Tears filled his eyes and spilled down his cheeks. "I see them. Oh, Gods, I can see them!"

Kevin fell to his knees and sobbed, and I realized what an injustice I'd done him. He wanted to See, and somehow, I pushed just enough of me into him that he could. And now he could never forget what he saw.

"Get away!" he cried as he ducked his head and swung at the wraiths that surrounded us.

"They won't hurt you." I knelt next to him and put my hand on his shoulder. "They're looking for justice. They just want our help."

Kevin uncovered his face and stared.

"This is what you see?"

"Every day," I said. "They're around us all the time. Most of the time I can block them out. Sometimes I can't."

"I'm sorry," he said. "I had no idea."

"Who did this to you?" I needed to keep my mind on business. If I stopped to think about what I saw, I might crumble. The children stared at me with black eyes and blank expressions. Wraiths. The trauma of their deaths was probably too great, made them clam up. The same type of trauma damaged so many war veterans. Too much death, but to them it was much worse. It was their own.

"I want to help," I said. "But I need you to tell me what happened."

They stood, still as a photograph negative. No answer. I could've quit right then, walked out of the building and made for distant shores and hidden away, changed my name to something even less generic than Stanley Cooper, and prayed to whatever higher power would listen that it would all go away. Then maybe no one else would have to die. Maybe whoever was after me would forget about me.

I didn't really believe it either. Sure, the urge to rabbit was strong, but I couldn't look at those dead children and run. If I did, I'd never sleep again because they'd haunt my dreams.

"Okay," I said. "Idea."

The teacher's desk bore signs of Pittsburgh's finest's handiwork. Fingerprint dust smeared the drawers and little chalk marks circled things of supposed interest. I didn't care about any of them, though, so long as there was still a pencil in one of the drawers. And, as luck would have it, there was. I also found a stack of loose paper in the bottom drawer.

There comes a point in every person's life where, no matter how ridiculous a possibility sounds, it becomes a viable option. The person wants or needs something so badly that those get rich quick schemes start to sound like legitimate business ventures, and maybe Grandma's garage might hold some kind of treasure. Ninety-nine times out of a hundred, those schemes don't work. People walk away feeling battered and broken, and often worse off than before.

But then there's the one time it does work.

"What're you doing?" Kevin still stared at the apparitions, though he seemed a little less terrified than a few moments ago.

"Shush." I wasn't nearly as experienced as Maggie, or even Andi. Or even Kevin, for that matter. But I had an idea. A piece of chalk from the desk drawer helped me draw a lopsided circle on the floor, then I sat down, put the pencil in my dead hand, and closed my eyes.

"You can write through me, if you want," I said. "I can't stop this without your help. I need to know who did this, what happened. I can't help you unless you help me first."

My arm tingled. Kevin gasped. I didn't feel it move or anything, but I kept my eyes shut tight. Whatever happened, I didn't want to somehow ruin it.

In my mind's eye, the demon crept from behind a door.

"Why?" it asked. "Why you help them?"

"Quiet, Marshmallow." It shrank back a bit.

The tingling in my arm stopped, and I was left with a useless appendage again. I opened my eyes and found the room empty, save for Kevin, who stood and stared.

"What?"

"Spirit writing? How long have you been able to do that?"

"Since yesterday," I said. "Didn't know I could do it either. What'd you see?"

"One of them stepped toward you, reached out, and sank her arm into yours. Then you just started writing. Then everything faded and I couldn't see them anymore."

"Weird," I said, but it was kind of cool too. The mojo I

130

put into him must've worn off. "What'd I get?"

Of the stack of papers, about a dozen of them held markings, though they weren't any form of writing I knew. For the life of me, it all just looked like rows and rows of dots.

"Nothing," I said. "We'd better get gone before that cop wakes up."

I dropped the pages on the desk as I made my way to the doorway. Kevin picked them up and scowled, then shook his head, shot a derisive look at me, and hurried out the door. It took me a few strides to catch him in the hall.

"What's your problem now?"

"I'll show you at the car," he said. Then he ducked out the door and hot-footed across the parking lot. I followed, though not as fast as him. When I reached his car, I was out of breath.

"What's... on... the pages?"

"Look again," he said. "It's not nothing. It's Braille. That was a guide dog. The girl that talked to you was blind."

13

My father wasn't a great man in the conventional sense. He never won any Nobel prizes or stopped any wars, but he was always a great man to me. He had working-class sensibilities and a way of putting things that just made sense. Any problem in the world, brought to him, could be solved with matter-of-fact common sense that made me feel dumb for not having thought of it myself.

"It takes a brave man," he often said, "to stand up for what's right, even if he knows he's going to lose. Brave, or some would say stupid. It all depends on how a body looks at things."

He couldn't abide anyone who would hurt a child or an animal, and never hesitated to put himself between an abuser and his target. One look from those steel-grey eyes and folks usually backed down. The ones that didn't learned what pushing a shovel for thirty years gave to my father. Uncommon strength, and hands of stone.

When he died, I had to grow up fast. And every day that passed brought with it another moment that I wished I could ask him for advice.

As I drove back to the shop, I wished like hell I could talk to him one more time to get his take on things. On the one hand, whoever was killing people would keep on killing until I handed myself over to him, whoever "he" was. The fact that I didn't have clue one how to do such a thing was beside the point. Given the crowd I hung around with, I figured that if I even whispered that I was ready, he would know.

On the other hand, it was a safe bet that if I turned myself over to him, I'd die, which didn't exactly thrill me.

What advice would my father have given?

"Run," whispered the little demon inside me. "Save us. You can save us. Go somewhere safe."

"Right," I said. "You only want me alive because if I die before you find a host, you die, right?"

"I will not die!" it shouted, indignant. "I will live!"

"Then you'll be trapped inside my rotting corpse. Sounds fun."

"Run," it said again. "Hide. Before it gets worse."

"Go back to your room," I growled. The door in my mind slammed shut, and the little demon was quiet.

I pulled into the parking lot behind Maggie's shop with Kevin close behind. We got out of our respective cars and headed for the stairs. The lights in the windows still burned bright. Maggie was still awake, and if I was lucky, had Andi with her. As I crossed the threshold, Kevin stopped.

Thresholds are curious things, and one of the few things Hollywood gets right. Everywhere a person goes, a bit of that person's energy is left behind. In the case of a home or an apartment, that energy builds until it creates a sort of barrier around doorways and windows. In most cases, it's strong enough to keep out all but the biggest and baddest. Maggie's is a little stronger than most, though, because she strengthened hers with wards, spells and prayers written around the doorframe. I have the same thing in my apartment, though nowhere near as graceful or well hidden as hers. Pretty or not, they both say the same thing: "Keep Out."

"Well?" It was a challenge, one that Kevin caught and didn't appreciate. Walk in, powerless, or stay out. Evil gets roasted, good gets to come in for coffee. Simple.

He let out a loud huff of air and stepped across the threshold. No smoke, no fire, just a big bald man with a pissed-off expression in the living room. I was about to make a smart-aleck comment when something small and fuzzy nudged my leg.

"Hello, Bitsy," I said. The little cat stared at me with wide emerald eyes, then nodded. Then she turned to Kevin, then back to me.

As ridiculous as it may sound, the cat liked to be introduced to everyone who came into the house. It wasn't a game, and it wasn't just me being silly. It was actually me thinking of the safety of my shoes. The little black cat with a white crescent between her eyes might've looked like an ordinary house-cat, but in addition to her intelligence, she had a sense of humor. One slight, whether I meant it or not, meant the fuzzy monster would make my life miserable for at least a week. I learned a long time ago to not piss off the cat.

Kevin reached down to pet her before I could warn him about the possibility of digit loss, but instead of howls of pain, I heard the most unexpected sound: purring.

"Oh, come on," I said. "You just met him."

"I like this cat," said Kevin. "Good judge of character."

Maggie came out of the bedroom with her coat in her hand. She'd changed from her work clothes into blue jeans, a tight black t-shirt, and combat boots. Her normal after-work attire of yoga pants, fluffy socks and an oversized t-shirt meant relaxation. Her current outfit meant she was looking for a fight. No matter how "dressed down" she tried to be, I always found her, at the very least, cute. But the boots and jacket made her as imposing as she was beautiful.

"What'd you find out?"

"I don't know," I said as I handed her the pages. "One of the kids was blind. This was how she talked to me."

"Braille," said Maggie. Kevin flashed his best "told you so" look. Sometimes I hated that guy.

"Can you read it?"

"No," she said. "But I bet Andi can translate it."

"She reads Braille?" The kid's talents never ceased to amaze me.

"No," said Maggie. "But she's got mad Internet skills. I bet she can get it translated it in no time."

"Fine," I said. "So where is she?"

"I don't know."

Kevin and I shot each other worried looks. On any other night, her absence would've been something welcome so Maggie and I could have a little alone time. But tonight it seemed unsettling.

"Didn't you call her?" Kevin didn't bother disguising the alarm in his voice.

"Her phone went to voicemail," said Maggie. She read our expressions and sighed. "Look, she's young, got a life of her own. She's probably out with friends or at a club or something. I'm sure she's fine. But after everything that's happened, I'm going to go look."

The words were reassuring, but there was something in her eyes, in the way her smile twitched, that told me she didn't believe it either. As if to punctuate the fact, Andi's laptop, which seemed to be permanently wired to her body, sat conspicuous on the coffee table. She never went anywhere without it, and its presence gave me an uneasy feeling. To me it was less a hunk of plastic and wires and whatever else was inside a computer, and more a harbinger of something sinister. But her car wasn't in the parking lot, and finding her in a city the size of Pittsburgh would be, to say the least, difficult. Still, I wasn't about to let Maggie patrol the streets on her own.

We agreed take different paths. Maggie and I went to her favorite haunts and hangouts, while Kevin hit bars popular with kids her age. We started at her apartment, which showed no signs of foul play, then made our way to a bar in the north hills that played old movies. After the second hour of driving with no results, Maggie looked terrified.

It wasn't that she doubted Andi's abilities. In fact, she was usually the one to tell me to trust the kid more. But Andi was more than a friend, more than an apprentice. The bond the two of them shared was more akin to sisterhood, or even a mother-daughter relationship. The longer Andi stayed away, the more panicked Maggie would get.

We met up with Kevin at a club that was half dancing, half pool-hall on the west side.

"This is pointless," he said. "Even if we went to every bar in the city, we'd never find her."

"I'm not giving up," said Maggie. "She's in danger."

"You said yourself that she was capable of handing herself," said Kevin. "Go home. I'm sure she'll call, or she'll come in tomorrow morning with a great story to tell."

It made sense, even if she didn't want to admit it. But he was right. There wasn't much else we could do. Hell, she couldn't even be considered a missing person by the police until she'd been gone twenty-four hours. Maybe we were just jumping at shadows, but somehow I doubted it.

Kevin nodded as he said goodnight, and said he'd keep on the list tomorrow. But for now, he had to get some sleep. It took until that moment for me to realize how tired I was. We drove home in silence through mostly empty streets. Every pool of light looked somehow sick to me, though I couldn't put my finger on why. The whole city seemed touched by something unseemly.

When we got back to the shop, Maggie checked one more time to make sure there were no messages, no notes, that Andi wasn't waiting upstairs on her couch. But she was nowhere to be seen. After a few minutes gentle persuasion, she locked the door behind us then followed me into the bedroom. I didn't even bother getting undressed. Maggie snuggled against me, and as I closed my eyes, I heard her whisper. It made me smile. It was a spell, one of the first she worked on me. It was the spell she used that made me realize that she cared for me as much as I did her.

It kept bad dreams away.

"Stan! Wake up!"

Maggie's voice dragged me from dreamless black into harsh consciousness. I opened my eyes to blurry reality, blinked a few times, and tried really hard to hold on to the last moment before sleep turned into awake. My vision cleared to show Maggie, sitting up with a hand on my chest and worried look on her face.

"Whazzat?"

"Damn it, Stan, wake up!"

She shook me a little harder. I groaned and shook my head.

"What's the matter?"

"I've been calling all night," she said as she waved her telephone. "No answer. I can't stand this. Where could she be?"

Her hair stood in shocks and her bloodshot eyes showed puffy dark patches beneath them. While I slept, she stayed awake. While I had peaceful rest, she paced the floor, worried about Andi. I had no right.

"Okay," I said. "I'll go look for her again. You stay here and wait for her." I left out that I'd be looking at hospitals, morgues, and police stations.

"I don't think that'll help," she said. "Look."

I followed her gaze to my withered arm. In my hand was the pen I keep on the bedside table. Beneath it was the pad. The pages were covered in scribbles. My morning groggies disappeared in an ice-cold wash of dread.

What I took to be scribbles were poorly written words, a single phrase, over and over again.

Answer the phone.

We looked at each other, then to the telephone like it might leap to life and dance a jig on the nightstand. But it sat still, quiet.

"It's nothing," I said. "Doesn't mean anything. Could just be the demon messing with me again."

"Maybe," said Maggie. "I need to wake up. Listen for the phone." She climbed off the bed and headed toward the shower.

On any normal day, I would climb into the shower with her for a little happy morning wake-up. But it wasn't a normal day, and it felt like one of us should stay within earshot of the telephone at all times, just to be on the safe side.

When Maggie came out, I went in. Even the warm water down my back didn't ease the feeling that something was wrong, something serious. I hurried through my shower, dried off, and dressed quickly to meet Maggie in the shop below. When I got there, I found her sitting at the counter, eyes fixed on the back door.

"Did you try calling her?"

"She's not due in for another fifteen minutes."

"Call her anyway," I said. "Just to be sure."

She snapped up the phone and thumbed the number. A few seconds went by, then we both heard the tell-tale ring. The theme to *The Addams Family*. Andi had it programmed to play whenever the shop number called. It was her sense of humor. I hurried around the counter and followed the sound until I found Andi's phone behind a book on the bookshelf. Maybe she put it there to tell us who took her. Or maybe whoever took her left it there for the same reason. Either way, the sight of her phone without her attached made the auger in my gut rev and twist.

"No no no no no no..."

"Did you find it?" Her voice was choked with panicked tears.

"I thought you called her last night!"

"I did," she cried. "I called from upstairs. I should've called sooner! I should've..."

Andi's phone rang, the generic tune that came as a preset. *Answer the phone.*

I snatched the phone up. The number on the window was one that I recognized as coming from a throw-away phone.

"Hello?"

"S... Stan?" Her voice was raw, choked. She'd been crying. "Help me..." Her voice gave way to fresh sobs.

"Andi? Where are you? Are you alright?"

"Help me... Please help me..."

"Where are you? Who did this?"

The phone clicked and went dead. I threw it hard across the room. It shattered against the wall as I sank to the floor.

"What?" Maggie stood across the room. The look on her face said she already knew the answer, but wanted the comfort of false hope for just a moment more. "What happened?"

"They've got Andi," I said.

14

I don't have many friends. That's not a "poor me" statement, it's just the way it is. I have a hard time trusting people, and I'm pretty sure it has something to do with the way my friends ditched me after I died.

One day they were at the hospital with flowers and cards, tears and breathless well-wishes. Once I got out and told them what I saw, they laughed at me, treated me like a lunatic. I became the colossal butt of a cosmic joke to them. Hell, even my own mother tried to put me in a mental hospital. My father was a natural-born skeptic, but he wouldn't have treated me that way. But he died a long time before I did, and part of me felt cheated that I didn't get to see him again before I came back. I didn't speak to my mom for three years.

My trust and intimacy issues aside, to the few friends I do have, I'm fiercely loyal. For most of them, I'd give the shirt off my back, or at least a clean one I wasn't wearing. For a very select few, I'd lay down my life.

That number used to be three, until a person twisted with dark magic and a demonic monkey on his back murdered one of them and paraded around in his skin for a few days. I missed Taylor almost as much as I missed my father. They were very much alike. But anymore, there are only two people for whom I'd walk straight into Hell and moon the devil himself, if there is such a creature. Maggie's one. Andi's the other.

Maggie got on the phone and called everyone she knew who might be able to help, which consisted of a very short list of people from the scattered remains of Evergreen. Kevin answered, as did Bill and Brea. But the rest didn't. Kevin said he was on his way. Bill and Brea tutted and said they'd start on their end of the Burgh and work toward us. It made sense to cut the distance and meet in the middle.

But the two who didn't answer bothered me. One was Reneau, the proud militant who, as far as I could tell, hated me. The other was Blossom, who didn't seem capable of hate. We also had the rest of SPIRIT to track down and warn, or read about in the morning paper. It seemed impossible, to split our efforts.

When Kevin arrived, we filled him in.

"I'll see if I can find Blossom," he said. "No matter what happened with Evergreen, I think I can get her to at least listen to me. Reneau, I'm not so sure."

"We'll handle her," said Maggie. My gut wriggled at the prospect. I didn't like to think of myself as easily intimidated, but that woman made me want my mother. But, if she was in trouble, she might need help. If she wasn't, we might need hers. If she would give it.

We also took parts of the remainder of the list before we headed out.

I've said on numerous occasions, I'm not always the sharpest knife in the drawer. Sometimes it takes me a while to put things together.

It didn't take me any time at all to figure out that the person behind the killings was a former member of Evergreen. The way the killer signed the walls clued me in there. It also didn't take much time to guess that the killer had to be one of the core members. Why? Because none of the rest of them had the kind of power necessary to do what was being done. Which left the two big questions: Who, and what did they want with me?

There were seven core members, and while they all had the right combination of motive and ability, none of them seemed to fit the description of "cold-blooded murderer." The core membership was made up of Bill, Brea, Kevin, Trevor, Neighbor Bob, Reneau and Blossom. Trevor was still at Mercy Hospital with pudding where his brain should've been and wired into every gizmo known to man for keeping a dead husk alive. I checked in on him once every couple of weeks to make sure he was exactly where I put him. Neighbor Bob was now part of his beloved church, and I didn't think murder was on the Lord's agenda. Bill and Brea I trusted with my life, which left only three. Kevin, Blossom and Reneau. Kevin was on our side, or so he said, but I still wasn't sure I could trust him. Blossom, though powerful, didn't seem capable of the type of hatred it would take to kill innocents. Which left the one person I was certain would like to see me strung up by my ankles and fed to a tank full of rabid weasels.

And we were on our way to see her.

"You'd better do the talking," I said. "I don't think she likes me."

"What makes you say that?" asked Maggie with a smirk.

"I think it was when she said 'I don't fucking like you' that I started to get a feeling."

When we first met them, I had mental images and

expectations of the types of people who were in Evergreen. For the longest time, I believed Bill and Brea lived in a cave and Kevin lived in a torture chamber. Of course, I turned out to be wrong on every count, and the members turned out to be, more or less and mental disorders not withstanding, normal people. Reneau, I always pictured at home in a gothic mansion, surrounded by a wrought-iron fence. When Bill told Maggie where to find her, I figured we would probably wind up in some innocuous little suburb with an elementary school nearby and a white picket fence.

Imagine my surprise when, for once, my initial image turned out to be the right one.

"You're kidding."

"Nope," said Maggie as she stared up at the monstrous structure. "This is the address Bill gave me."

Okay, so there were no vultures or bats that I could see, but the old house was three stories with a "widow's walk," and surrounded by an iron fence with spikes on top. It looked like every house from every horror movie I'd ever seen, and it scared the hell out of me.

Don't go in, then. The demon. I almost forgot about him.

"Shut up, you," I said as I lifted the latch on the gate. The hinges squealed as they opened.

The yard looked overgrown, almost purposefully so. Grass encroached on the concrete path to the porch, and I half expected it to grasp at our feet. By the steps to the porch was a sign: "Beware of Dragons. Solicitors will be eaten." Then it clicked in my mind where I'd seen the type of house before. It looked like the home from an old sitcom, in which Frankenstein's monster married Dracula's granddaughter. They had a dragon that lived under the stairs.

"Cute," I said.

146

"She talks about dragons all the time," said Maggie. "I never knew if she was serious or not."

"Let's ask."

Maggie rang the doorbell. On the first chime, my stomach spasmed and my knees went weak. I fell to the porch and gasped for air.

"Stan!"

"No!" cried the little demon. "It doesn't like us! It hurts us!"

There was nothing there, no physical presence on the porch whatsoever, but, for the life of me, it felt like something *bit* me.

"What the hell was that?" I grunted. The pain subsided as the front door opened. A perplexed-looking man stood in the doorway.

"Can I help you?"

"We're looking for Reneau," said Maggie. "We were told she lives here."

The man shook his head. "There's nobody here by that name. You must be mistaken."

"Are you sure?" It was a dumb question, but it snuck out before I could think better of it. Of course the man knew who did or didn't live in his house. He looked about to give an appropriately snarky answer when a voice called him from inside the house.

"Who's at the door, hon?" The speaker appeared, and her face went ashen, then it all made sense. The whole magical name thing again. I began to doubt the man who answered the door *really* knew who lived in his house.

"They're looking for someone named... was it Reneau?"

"I know who they're looking for," she said. "Go on. I'll tell them where she lives."

147

The man shrugged and went back into the house. Reneau came out on the porch and shut the door behind you.

"What are you doing here?" she spat. "What is the point of using another name if you're just going to show up at my home?"

"He doesn't know." Maggie's confusion faded. "How long?"

"None of your business. Now what do you want?"

"Someone's killing people to try to get to me," I said. "Members of a group called SPIRIT. Heard of them?"

"Of course I've heard of them. Kevin was a member. Go bother him."

"We did. He's helping us. The killer is signing the murders with an evergreen."

"And this means what to me?" I didn't need to see her aura. Her face twitched, just at the corners of her mouth. It didn't matter how stone-faced she wanted to seem, the news hit her hard.

"We came to find out if it was you," said Maggie. "And if it wasn't, to warn you. He took Andi."

"How do you know it was a *he*?"

"Can you drop the feminist bullshit for five minutes?" I shouted because I didn't care if the neighbors to heard. I wanted the man inside to hear. I wanted everyone to know that I was tired of the crap and wanted just a little cooperation. More important, I knew Reneau *didn't* want them to hear. "Andi's very important to me, to *us*, even if you're too wrapped up in your own little better-than-everyone-else world to care."

"You should've looked after her better," she said.

"You *bitch!*" I grabbed Maggie by the arms before she got to Reneau. Pure rage poured off her in waves of heat. I didn't need to alter my perception to know what was going on. I knew

148

power when I felt Maggie draw it. She was about to burn Reneau to a crisp where she stood.

For her part, Reneau didn't move or flinch. She stood with a stony demeanor that I found unsettling.

"Get off my porch," she murmured.

The bite I felt earlier hurt, but what hit us both felt like a blunt instrument to the ribs. We both went backward off the porch and landed on our backs on either side of the path. Maggie, however, wasn't going to let a little thing like an invisible whatsit slow her down. She scrambled to her feet and bowed up.

I, on the other hand, wanted to know just what hit us. More to the point, I wanted to know if it would hit us again, and if we could avoid it. I shifted my perception and goggled at the porch.

A dragon, an honest to Godzilla dragon, stood behind Reneau. The thing's wingspan stretched the length of the porch and its tail wrapped around in front of it, ready to bat us off the porch again. But the dragon I Saw wasn't a giant lizard or some ancient dinosaur. It was a being comprised wholly of Reneau's will. Every scale crackled with energy, its eyes blazed. If it weren't for the slight shimmer and pulse of her energy, I might've sworn it was a physical being.

"People are dead!" screamed Maggie. "Our friend has been taken! Don't you care?"

"Why should I?" The cold look never left her face, but I saw what no one else could. Her energy burned with licks of yellow and brown, fear and regret. Something had her scared, but good.

"Because you could be next," I said. I locked eyes with her, felt her heart beat. The demon inside me trembled at the sight of the dragon on the porch, but I didn't want to back down. "If not for Andi, or for the other people they killed, think about your guy in there. Think about your neighbors. Think about your life. What if they come after you next?"

She let a slight, cold smile flicker across her lips.

"As you can see, Mister Cooper, we're quite well protected."

Something else flickered through her aura, so fast I almost missed it. The browns and yellow streaks were interrupted with a sudden shock of red, a tiny jolt of black. The two together meant hatred and evil, but the amounts were so small. She danced close to the edge, flirted with darkness. The potential was there. With the amount of power I saw in her, I hoped she never gave over to it.

"Let's go," I said. "We can't do anything else here."

Maggie's eyes burned, but she stormed back up the path toward the car. I hurried behind her, just in case the big energy-lizard decided I might be tasty. When the car was a good block away, I let go of the breath I didn't realize I held.

"Holy shit," I said. "Did you see that?"

"Of course I didn't," she snapped. "I'm not the one who can see dead people, remember?"

It wasn't like her to snap at me, and I knew she didn't really mean it. Stress and worry piled on her and she wore it like a heavy coat.

"It was a dragon," I said. "Made from her will."

"I don't care about that," she said. "Was she lying? Was Andi there?"

"I don't think so." The black streaks told me that she, more than any of them, was tempted by the dark side, but there wasn't enough there for me to call her our killer. Which meant Kevin was headed for trouble.

According to Bob, Blossom worked for the Pittsburgh Zoo. For some reason, her job didn't surprise me. I had a hard time with the notion that the other members had jobs, but not her. That she worked with animals seemed appropriate. I pictured her surrounded by fuzzy creatures of every size, all of them looking up at her with Disney eyes. In my mind, she whistled a merry tune and they came running with garlands of flowers between them to drape over her hair.

When we arrived at the zoo, Maggie pulled into the parking lot and drove around until we found Kevin's car. We parked a few spaces down and hurried to the gate. The ticket taker didn't buy our line about needing to speak to Blossom, mainly because he'd never heard of her. Stupid magical name thing again. It cost us the price of two full-priced adult tickets to get in. Once inside, it took us a while to find her.

The Pittsburgh Zoo isn't what most folks expect to find in the middle of Steel City. Okay, so *middle* is a bit of an exaggeration, but even off by Highland Park, most folks don't think about the more than four-*thousand* species of wild animals housed there. With so many habitats, a person might think it would be easy to get lost in the zoo. And that person would be right.

I don't like zoos very much. It isn't because I dislike animals or because I feel sorry for them. The habitats are beautiful and I can even tolerate the smell. I don't even mind the overpriced food or goodies from the gift shop. The animals, however, seem to have a problem with me. I walk through the gates and every animal in sight stops whatever they were doing to stare at me. I take a few steps, whatever creatures lay in that direction go nuts. The birds squawk and flap, the tigers growl and pace and the monkeys go... well... ape. They catch my scent and it's like they know that I shouldn't be alive.

I used to enjoy the zoo before I died. But after a few incidents, I chanced a look at their energies. In every cage, fear radiated, and it was because of me. I stopped coming to the zoo for a while. It was part of the reason I found Bitsy to be so remarkable.

As we passed the primate house, a black howler let out a shriek that set the rest of his buddies screaming. The Tamarins hid beneath a canopy while the Howlers did their best to pelt us with fresh shit. We hurried and ducked and ran while the great silverback postured and roared at us. My heart pounded. Maggie's hands shook. Past the primate cages, we hurried past the large animals of the African savanna, the Asian forest, and even to the polar exhibit. The bears didn't seem so much afraid of me as enraged by my presence, and they let us know that, were it not for a huge trench between us, they'd have no problem using my head as a chew-toy. In every area, I noted there were lots of places to hide. So many hidden cages, underground sleeping areas for the animals, feeding pits. Plenty of places to hide a hostage.

By the time we got to the far end of the compound, the children's area, I was convinced the zoo was our place, and Blossom was our traitor. We passed through the gateway to "Kid's Kingdom," however, and any negative thought about her went right out the window.

Blossom sat encircled by children with a wallaby in her lap. The smile she wore was the same one I saw over and over again, a genuine unconditional love that radiated out from her in waves of joy. The children sat enraptured as she told them about the wallaby's home and his favorite foods. Kevin leaned against a tree and scratched a goat under the chin. The smile on his face wasn't something I was used to, but it seemed to be at home.

On cue, the animals sensed my presence and ears and

tails flipped up. Blossom glanced toward me and raised her hand.

"Shhh." The animals quieted. "Stanley is a friend. Nothing to be afraid of."

The wallaby in her arms wriggled until she put him down, then he hopped over to me, sniffed my pants leg, and rubbed his head on me before bounding toward a group of shrieking and delighted children.

"How did you do that?"

"They trust me," she shrugged. "They know I'd never hurt them, just like they know you shouldn't be here."

"Kevin told you?" Maggie folded her arms, but couldn't keep her mad face pointed at Blossom. In truth, neither could I.

"Yes," she said. "It's heartbreaking. The children? Terrible. And your apprentice. I find it hard to believe anyone from Evergreen could do such a thing, but I guess I'm wrong there, aren't I?"

"I'm sorry," I said. "We had to come. We had to ask..."

"And I don't blame you," she said. "I'd want to make sure too. Go ahead. Take a good look, or whatever you're going to do. I've got nothing to hide."

I shifted my perception and looked. Blossom's aura shone almost pure silver and white. Flecks of brown floated about, along with ribbons of blue and green, but there was no sign of the evil that could've killed that room full of children. There was no sign of the malice that murdered the other members of SPIRIT. But there was something that caught my attention.

For most people, an aura is a thin corona of energy that gets bigger or smaller, depending on a thousand different factors. It takes the shape of the body it's in, or, in some cases, forms a kind of egg around them.

Blossom's aura had a definite shape, a willow tree.

"Thank you," I said as I shifted my perception back

to normal. "But you have to know that whoever it is might be coming for you next."

"Yeah," she said. "Kevin told me. I can't leave though. I have to look after my friends."

"Your friends could be in danger too," said Maggie.

A look of fury flashed across Blossom's face, a blink of rage that I never suspected she could harbor, then it was gone, replaced by her normal serene visage.

"No one will touch my friends," she said.

"You're wasting your breath," said Kevin from behind her. "I already gave her the pitch. She's not moving."

"We might need you," I said. "Please."

"Not as much as they do," she said. "I'm their guardian. I watch over all of them."

The shape of her aura made sense to me. She didn't mean her position as a metaphor or as an implied title. It was who she was. I was willing to bet the animals reacted to her in a similar, but opposite, way to how they did to me.

"I understand," I said. It was a lie, and we both knew it, but it gave her an out.

15

Our meeting with Blossom didn't go as planned. To start with, I was so sure she was the one. It was more process of elimination than any real detective work. She was the only one of the core group left. But as we walked through the iron gates, I felt lost. Ever since I got this weirdo power of mine, I believed I could make a fair lie-detector. After all, a person's aura changed when he lied. But as we went from person to person in the group, none of them fit the bill.

Kevin and Reneau were my first bets, but they both showed themselves to be more than I thought. Kevin had a soft spot for children and, of all things, the theater. Reneau, protected by her "dragons" as she was, still led a double life. In one, she was a militant hardass. In the other, a housewife whose name I still didn't know. They were the two who demanded the ancient book that raised the dead, the two who seemed most likely to throttle me for not giving it to them. But it just didn't seem possible.

Neighbor Bob, on the other hand, demonstrated enough power to send most folks screaming from the room, and only tolerated people like Maggie and me. His central focus was on love, or so he said. But, even if he wanted to do something rotten, I doubted the church would let him. He was more than human now, and less in a way. He was bonded with the church through faith in a way that most folks would never believe. The power of the faithful coursed through the church and into him. I wondered how long it would be before he burned out.

Then there was Bill and Brea. No matter what, they helped us. They bailed me out of jail and helped me put an end to the nightmare that was Trevor's twisted mind. Hell, the car in which I rode was a gift from them.

The more I thought about it, the more I realized a simple truth. I didn't know what the hell I was doing, and I was out of my element. Taylor knew police procedure, could've used his connections with Pittsburgh's finest to sweep the city or something. But he was gone and I was lost.

I'm not really good at the cat-and-mouse games, the behind the scenes shadow works. I'm more of a walk-in-with-a-baseball-bat-and-start-swinging kind of guy. Subtlety is not my strong suit, so I don't have any patience for the little games that many folks play.

The biggest problems, as I saw them, boiled down to a precious few things. First, we had no idea what the killer was doing. Sure, he was killing people to get my attention, but he got that a while ago. No contact, no instructions, no "if you ever want to see the kid again..." It seemed like the killings weren't just to get to me. It was more than a game. He had a taste for it. He enjoyed it. And it made me sick.

Second, we were out of suspects. Sure, we knew it was a former member of Evergreen, and that whoever it was had power to spare. Andi had raw power by the bucketful, which meant the bad guy either had to be stronger to subdue her, or someone she knew who took her by surprise. Either way pointed to one of the core seven members of Evergreen, all of whom seemed incapable of anything so horrible. The only one who could've done it, in my eyes, was Trevor, who now spent all his days on life support, drooling, and being fed through a tube. And even if he took her by surprise, he'd still have to be pretty powerful to contain Andi, much less hurt her.

The last problem was somewhat more pragmatic: Where would someone keep a hostage? Movies show old abandoned houses or mineshafts, soundproof cellars and places where a girl like Andi could scream herself hoarse without anyone hearing. But places like that were few and far between, especially in Pittsburgh. At least, I thought they were. A person could scream for days in the basement of the Pittsburgh Playhouse, but we were there, and the resident ghosts would've told me if Kevin hid my friend down there.

Which left me with unanswered questions and a splitting headache.

"I need to eat," I said. "I'm getting shaky." The truth was, only about half of the shakes came from hunger. The rest came from the feeling that I needed to do something, but couldn't for the life of me figure out what. Somewhere in Steel City, Andrea Bedford waited for me to save her. And I could do nothing but think about my stomach.

We pulled into the parking lot of an Eat-N-Park just at the tail end of their lunch rush. Kevin parked beside us, and we hurried in and took a booth. The waitress, a disinterested young lady with too much makeup and not enough fabric in her pants, took our order, then shambled off toward the kitchen.

"Now what?" said Kevin. "We could keep going through the list..."

"How many names do you have left?" Maggie fished her half of the list from her pocket.

"Two or three," said Kevin. "They're alive, but they've heard about the others. They're terrified. I figure the rest will be hiding, if they know what's good for them."

"We've only got a couple left too," she said. "We need to find Andi."

"How?" I didn't raise my voice or my eyes, but the room went still with the word. "Huh? How? This asshole just snatched her, and we're supposed to just find her in the middle of Pittsburgh?"

"We could..." Kevin started, but the thought died on his tongue. He didn't have any more idea than I did, or Maggie for that matter.

"Nothing," I said. "All we can do is sit here and wait for him to kill someone else, or tell us what he wants."

"We've got to do something," snapped Kevin. "Besides piss and moan about what we can't do!"

"What do you suggest?" On some level, I knew it was his frustration talking, but my own was driving my mouth, and wasn't in any mood for badgering. "You want to go out and ask person to person? Be my guest! Meanwhile, Andi's going to die! The rest of the members of SPIRIT are going to die! And when it's all said and done, I'm going to die to stop the killing. And even then, it won't stop because I figure what he wants me for won't make the world a better place! So unless you've got any real suggestions, shut your piehole and think!"

"Ahem."

I looked up at our waitress.

"Who had the chicken salad?"

"Not hungry," I growled as I stood up and pushed past her. I stormed out the door, half out of anger, but also because I didn't want Kevin to see the tears that ran down my face. Ally or not, I'd be damned if I let him see me so messed up. But I didn't know what to do about it either.

The parking lot was warmer than it should've been, heated by the sun-warmed asphalt. Still, if not cooler, it felt less stifled than inside. It did nothing to ease the tension. I wanted to scream, to tear my jacket to shreds, to bang holes in the sidewalk with my fist. But all I could do was give Maggie's car a savage kick, which twisted my ankle and set off the car alarm.

"Shut up!" I bellowed, and brought my fist down on the hood. As my hand made contact, I felt my anger and pain course down my arm. The release manifested as a bright flash, and the alarm went silent. For a moment, I was so stunned that I forgot how angry I was.

Help us...

At the far end of the parking lot stood what I first took to be people, though they stood shoulder to shoulder like a human fence. But as I watched, their forms shifted and ebbed, like sand sucked up by a vacuum cleaner. Their terrified expressions shifted to horror, then agony as something went down the line and pulled their souls apart one grain at a time. A few of the faces I recognized as victims from SPIRIT. The children from the high school held each others hands as, one by one, they joined the swirling vortex of nothing. At the end, the little blind girl clutched her dog. I didn't need to hear her voice in my head.

My heart pounded as I raced across the parking lot toward them. I had no idea what I thought I was going to do. In truth, short of reaching up and grasping at their immaterial forms, there was nothing to be done. Someone with the power of Maggie or Bill might've been able to do something, but it seemed doubtful. And even so, I was nowhere near as powerful. I was just Stanley, the guy who could see ghosts and, apparently, shut off car alarms. I reached the spot where the blind girl stood just as she and her dog joined the nothing, their frightened expressions the last I saw of them.

Help us! Their voices sang like a chorus of dry leaves in my ears. I couldn't help them in life, and now they expected me to help them in death. I couldn't look at their faces any longer. It made sense now. He had a purpose for killing them, and it wasn't just to get to me. He needed power, and his victims provided it. But if he used all their power up, his victims just poofed out of existence. No afterlife, though I wasn't convinced there was such a thing, no ghosts, just oblivion. I caught a glimpse of that great darkness when I died, and I shuddered to think of anyone else forced to endure the same experience. Or worse, just *gone*. And, if it was power he wanted, he could do a lot worse than to tap into the human battery that was Andi. Her kind of power under the control of a murderer scared the hell out of me. But it still didn't explain what he wanted with me.

I turned and hurried back into the restaurant. Maggie and Kevin still sat in the booth, though they both looked hurt and angry. And they were right to be so. I was acting like an ass. They just wanted to help, and here I was, acting like the only person in the world who mattered was me.

"I'm sorry," I said as I sat down. "I didn't mean to..."

"Forget it," said Kevin. "You want to do this on your own, be my guest." He wiped his mouth and stood.

"Please," I said. "I can't do this by myself. I don't even know where to start. But I know what he's doing now. I just don't know what he wants with me. Please. Help me."

"Help *us*, you mean," said Maggie.

Kevin let out a heavy sigh and sat back down.

"I saw them outside. All of them. They were following us."

"Who? The dead people?" Kevin looked toward the door.

"They're gone now," I said. "Sucked up. He's drawing

160

power."

"For what?"

"I don't know. If he's got Andi, he's got more power than I'll ever have, so it must be something specific about me."

"Yes," said a voice behind me. The voice was locust wings, the buzzing of flies, torn metal and hate. It was a demon. "It is."

I turned to see our waitress, all hundred-forty pounds plus makeup of her, head cocked at an unnatural angle, eyes wide, and a grin more like a gash splitting her face. Her lips bled, and bloody tears ran from her eyes. In one hand she held her order pad. In the other, a carving knife from the back room. The blade already glistened crimson.

The little demon inside me screamed, his voice a klaxon inside my head. Maggie recoiled, but Kevin seemed ready, both hands up and a scowl on his face.

"Back off!" he shouted. The sheer force of his words leaped out and struck the possessed waitress, knocked her flat. She hit the ground hard, then laughed, the sound of razors through flesh. It made my skin crawl.

The demon raised the body back to standing. Her nose was broken, and her jaw hung loose enough to see it was, at the least, dislocated. But it didn't seem to care.

"Got a bodyguard," it said. "Good. More fun that way."

The door to the kitchen opened and out stepped the rest of the waitstaff from hell, along with a cook and two dish-washers. I triggered my Sight, though I didn't need to. What I Saw was exactly what I expected, and it chilled me.

"I'm not giving myself up," I said.

"That's cute," said the server. "He thinks we're here to take him alive."

The boy in Forrest Hill's voice came back to me. *We like things just the way they are.*

"Ah... shit."

The demons howled, a horrible sound that made me want to piss my pants and run. But I knew, if I did, if I acted like a coward, I'd leave the woman I loved and the ally I didn't even know I had behind to be torn apart. And my days of cowardice were far behind me.

My shifted perception let me see the world that no one else could see. The rage that exploded from Kevin, the white-hot blast of pure anger that erupted from his core, was awesome and terrifying. Almost as much so as the swell of black and red that came from the possessed. The bright flash of white light that shone from Maggie reminded me of just how powerful, how imposing in her awesome beauty she could be. But there was another light, one that I didn't expect, and it shone from me, from my withered arm. Well, not exactly. My arm hung limp and useless at my side, but a second arm, one comprised of pure will and light, moved with blinding speed. The tattoo that exploded, the one that left my arm a burned husk of useless flesh, shone bright. But there was no time to savor what I Saw.

They attacked. Coordinated, precise, cruel, they rushed us. Three went for Kevin, three for Maggie. Only one, our server, went for me.

One might think, having seen the other side, that the thought of death doesn't scare me. But that person would be very wrong. It scares the hell out of me, and I'll fight with every last bit of will I have to stay on this side of the great black nothing.

The demon must've looked at me, with my gimpy arm, overweight physique, and general lack of all things heroic, and thought I'd be easy pickings. As I focused my will, my hate, my rage into one punch, the thing must've thought I'd hit with about as much force as a six-year-old. Hell, it's what I thought too. Until I made contact.

162

Just like the hood of the car, my fist met flesh, accompanied by a bright flash of light. This time, however, it was accompanied by the unmistakable scent of burning human skin and the sound of splintering bone. The demon-possessed waitress's head snapped back, and stayed back, neck broken, face shattered. The body fell to the floor in a heap, which left me with all kinds of emotional problems to be dealt with later.

Kevin bellowed, something between a war cry and the enraged roar of a bear, and heat poured off him into the three in front. His power was blunt, raw force, but effective. Their bodies flew backward. One slammed into the wall. Another struck the counter at mid back and snapped her spine. The third flew through the prep window. The sizzle I heard let me know it landed on the grill.

Where Kevin was a club, Maggie's power was a saber, precise hits to just the right places. No less deadly, but considerably more elegant and beautiful to watch. The level of control she showed was awesome, pinpointing targets and adjusting from defense to attack in the blink of an eye. A lance of pure white light shot out of her fingertips and pierced the forehead of one of her attackers, then snaked around and caught the others through the temples. Their bodies dropped to the floor, and I watched their lives drain out. The demons dissipated the moment their bodies went down, but the hosts themselves were left to feel the pain of dying, confused and terrified.

"Clever," came a voice from behind me, the same rustle of dry leaves. I turned to see the other patrons, families, elderly people, children, all engulfed in black flame. "Do it again."

"Run." I killed one innocent person already. Maggie and Kevin killed three each, but *I* killed one. An innocent girl. I didn't want any of us to add any more black spots to our souls.

"We can take them," growled Kevin.

"Run!" I grabbed him by the arm and took off for the door. Maggie was two steps ahead of me, and had the door open by the time I got there. When we were through, she threw the door shut.

"*Obfirmo!*" Raw power snaked from her hands and wedged into the doorframe. The first of the possessed reached the door and heaved against it. It didn't budge. I almost felt hopeful. The sound of breaking glass cured my stupid optimism as a chair flew out the window, followed by more innocents.

"We gotta go!" I shouted. Captain Obvious. That's me.

Maggie, as usual, was two steps ahead of me. She already had the car keys in her hand. A click of the button and the doors unlocked with a snap. I shoved Kevin into the car and climbed on top of him as Maggie revved the engine and threw the car into reverse. The patrons banged on the hood of the car, hammered the roof with their fists, until Maggie shifted into drive. The car lurched, took a few confused and frightened faces with it, then sped out of the parking lot. It took a few frozen moments of deep breathing to realize I still sat in Kevin's lap, then I squirmed into the back seat.

"What the hell was that?!" Kevin stared out the back window. The patrons of the restaurant collapsed like puppets with their strings cut. They'd live, but I didn't envy the headaches they'd have. More than I could say for the employees.

"That," I panted, "was the other side. They want me dead."

"What do you mean?" Maggie glared at me in the rearview mirror. "I thought you were the linchpin or something."

"Yeah," I said. "What's the easiest way to keep someone from pulling a trigger?"

"By killing him," said Kevin. There was a hint of resolution that I didn't find comforting, but, as much as I hated to admit it, he was right.

"That side likes thing just the way they are, which means they can't let whoever's responsible use me. They're just being efficient."

"So what do we do?" Kevin looked from Maggie to me. "We could run. Not to be cruel, but Andi's just one person..."

"That's not an option," I said. "Andi's family. I'm not running out on her."

"What's the plan?" Maggie's eyes met mine in the mirror. I wished I had one. There were a dozen people I could think of who had a better knack for planning than me, and the top two were dead. The only thing I could think to do was to go where I knew we'd be safe while we figured things out.

"Head to the shop," I said.

16

In the past, my apartment was what I thought of as the safest place in Pittsburgh. It had a steel fire door, wards around every entrance and exit, security cameras in the hallway, and the noxious odor of mildew and laundry that was sure to subdue any would-be intruder. But that was before I started using the space as a storage facility for unholy relics I ran across. Call it irresponsible, to keep dangerous magical items in an apartment building loaded down with families, but nothing could get in, or out. No one knew where it was except people I trusted, and the items I put there weren't the kinds of things anyone wanted left laying where curious fingers could get hold of them. Besides, who would ever think to look in someone's crappy little apartment for a cursed artifact?

The shop, on the other hand, had several advantages. First, there weren't any haunted items inside it that tended to walk around when not watched. Second, the shop had a wonderful sense of self-defense, which I figured would come in handy. It also featured simple things like groceries and the lack of pungent laundry smell. But most important, the shop was connected to

Andi. Andi was, for lack of a better term, the shop's mother. It loved her, and I hoped that connection could somehow help us locate her.

Of course, it also meant we had to deal with the equivalent of an emotionally unstable toddler the size of a city block. As we explained what happened, things went about as well as could be expected.

The walls shook so hard I was certain they'd tumble. Pipes groaned in a way that sounded way too much like an angry sob. Water ran down the walls. Shelves tipped over and lights flashed. It took nearly an hour for the shop to cry herself out, during which I questioned the intelligence of remaining inside. But after a while, the rumbling walls only trembled, the torrent of tears slowed to a trickle. The windows stayed dark and the doors locked, but at least we were no longer in danger of being buried in rubble. We sat in the back room, exhausted.

"I'll say it." Kevin stood and glanced around. "I'm hungry." Maggie and I looked at each other and nodded.

It wasn't disrespect for Andi, or disregard of our situation. It was simple physics. Energy needed fuel, and the amount of energy we had thrown around at the restaurant had depleted our reserves. Maggie once told me that she could eat anything she wanted and never gain an ounce because of how much she expelled through magic. If the gnawing ache in the pit of my stomach was any indicator, I didn't doubt her.

Maybe I could use it to get rid of the spare tire I carried around my waistline.

The refrigerator in the workroom was used for herbs of the non-cooking variety, unless the menu included deadly poisons and hallucinogens. But every now and again, Maggie stashed bag of leftovers from the Greek restaurant down the street for midday munching. And, she assured me, it was fine as long as she remembered which herbs were which, and what went well with stuffed grape leaves.

At that moment, she could've given me a handful of deadly nightshade and I would've wolfed it down. Instead, she handed me half a lamb gyro and gave Kevin the other half. She took a bowl of hummus from the refrigerator and a bag of pita chips off the shelf. For a few minutes, the only sound in the back room was the crunching of chips and the occasional sob of the pipes. But a few minute's worth of food was all there was. Two or three bites and none of us were sated, but at least we weren't starving anymore.

"You need to stay indoors," said Kevin. "Half the demonic world wants to capture and deliver you to this nutball, the other half wants to kill you."

"No," I said. "Not until we find Andi. I can't just abandon her."

"You're no good to anyone dead," he said.

"I'm going to find her."

"How? Do you even have any clues?"

"What about that Braille note?" I could've slapped myself for not having thought of it before. "Where is it?"

"I have it." Maggie pulled it out of her pocket. Beneath the dots were letters. "I started translating it, but it's slow going. I need Andi."

"We'll find her," I said as I took the note.

The dots still looked like just points on the page to me, but to the right people they had meanings. I just didn't happen to be the right person. Under each series of dots, Maggie marked the corresponding letter of the alphabet.

H. E. L. P. U. S. I. C. A. N. S. E. E. S. A. V. E. M. E.

"'Help us, I can see, Save me...' Not much useful there."

"I'll keep working on it," said Maggie. "In the meantime,

I had a thought. What about the Scats?"

Scats lived everywhere there was life energy to be had. They darted around and lived in the periphery where most folks wouldn't recognize them or even notice. Up until a year ago, I thought they were just mindless little energy bugs that zipped around. But Andi showed us different, that they moved with a singular consciousness. She figured out how to use them to send messages. Too bad she never got around to showing us how.

"What about them?"

"Maybe they can find her."

"How?" blurted Kevin.

"I'm not sure," she said. "But it's worth a try, right?"

I didn't think it would work, but I was out of ideas and willing to try anything. If Maggie could pull it off, maybe we could, at the very least, find out if Andi was still alive. Maybe we could tell her we were coming for her. Maybe she could even tell us where to look.

Yeah, and maybe I could flap my arms and fly to the moon.

"Help me," said Maggie.

We cleared off her summoning circle, a wooden platform with a pentagram inlaid in silver. Each point represented one of the major elements, air, fire, water, earth, and spirit. The circle around it bound them together. It was the place Maggie used to draw and focus power. At the easternmost point, her altar sat, a little wooden table with her ceremonial knife, two candles and a few other items on it. One was a tiny seashell, representing water, that she found when she was a little girl. There was also a feather from a red-tailed hawk to represent air. She added things that "spoke" to her.

"You know how this works," she said to me as she nodded to Kevin. "You okay with this?"

170

"Yeah," I sighed. To be honest, I wasn't. Ritual work, Maggie did skyclad. That's naked to most folks, as in "clad in only sky." It was a religious choice to her, to appear before her God and Goddess the way she'd been birthed, with no artificial coverings between her and them. But I assumed Kevin had seen a naked woman before, and I wanted nothing more than Andi back.

She nodded and killed the lights. The room pulsed with a blue glow from the walls that I never noticed before. It was the shop's life force, it's will, visible to the naked eye. As she stripped off her clothing, Kevin glanced at me. Part of me wanted to beat my chest gorilla-style and mark my territory, but there wasn't a point. Maggie chose me, and I trusted her.

The pulse of the room quickened as Maggie stepped to the center of the star and lit a match. She moved from one candle to the next, her lips moving in a quiet prayer to the Lord and Lady, then sat in the center, cross-legged, palms up on her knees.

It was a somber, holy work, but damn she looked good in candlelight.

"I call out," she said. Her voice had a strange distant quality. "Brothers and sisters, lend me your strength. Help me find her whom I seek."

The shadows shifted as the Scats stopped moving. From the look of him, Kevin noticed for the first time that the shadows never really sat still, but moved with little living things. He only noticed because their movement stopped.

"Help me," said Maggie, louder. The Scats flowed toward her. Kevin made to intercept, as if he could do anything against them, but I stopped him. He stood and stared as the Scats ran across the platform, then crawled up her bare back like ants. They passed over her until she sat obscured in living shadow, then they poured off her and shot away in every direction. When the last of them left her body, Maggie slumped in place, then righted herself. She saluted her Gods, then pinched out the candles in the reverse order in which she'd lit them.

"That was intense," she said.

"What the hell was that?" Kevin looked confused and awestruck at the same time.

"Magical instant message," I said. "Maybe they can find her."

"You need to explain that to me," said Kevin.

"It's something Andi worked out," said Maggie as she pulled her shirt on. "I'm not sure how it works, but here's hoping."

An hour went by, then two, while we waited for something, anything, to happen. Maggie busied herself with cleaning up after the shop's tantrum while Kevin and I did our best to stay out of her way. We kept ourselves occupied by trying to explain to each other what we knew about metaphysics. What Kevin knew filled buckets. What I knew filled maybe half a thimble. An outside observer might've thought we were bonding. The truth was, we were just killing time, playing the awful waiting game until we had a direction.

The very basic gist of what I knew of magic was that it was comprised almost completely of will. Will gave it shape, gave it direction, sent it out into the world to affect change. The energy was made of faith, belief, love, hate, every emotion that a person could have. But the will had to be strong. My will was strong, sure. But the energy around it I always believed to be weak. Faith wasn't my strong suit, because I had knowledge instead of blind belief.

The difference between the two is staggering. Knowledge is much weaker than faith. A person *knows* that he can't move a mountain because basic science tells him he can't. *Faith*, on the other hand, can do an insane amount of seemingly impossible things because the person's faith generates more energy and the will sends it out to affect the world. It's all very complicated, but one thing I've learned is it doesn't matter what a person believes, so long as he believes in something. All the religions have the same basic message, which I translate to "be good to each other and don't be an asshole." But the strength with which a person believes has a direct correlation to how strong that person is.

Maggie has faith in her magic, and it is formidable. I have faith in her magic, so my energies add to hers. I never had much faith in my own abilities.

But that shifted at the diner when I saw the arm. Neither Kevin nor Maggie saw it, and the only reason I did was my perception was shifted. How long I'd had it, I didn't know. But now that I knew about it, I wanted to know what I could do with it.

I sat on a stool by the workbench, a pencil in my crippled hand and a steno pad under it. Maybe another message would come through, I didn't know. But I didn't want to take the chance of missing one.

Hour three started, when we heard a loud gasp from the front room. Kevin and I ran in to find Maggie rigid in the middle of her shop, Scats climbing her like insects.

"She's... alive..." said Maggie. "Hurt... scared... but she's alive."

"Can they show you where she is?" Hope flickered for a moment. If Maggie recognized the place, we might have a clue as to who was behind everything. At the very least, we could go get her.

"I don't think so," she said. "They don't work like that. I'm getting impressions, images, but I've never seen the place before."

"Images?" Kevin moved closer, though he stopped short of touching her. "What do you see?"

"Dark," she said. "She's blindfolded. I smell copper. She's bleeding."

"Tell her we're coming," I said.

Maggie's eyes snapped open and her body jerked. The Scats on her froze, then wisped out of existence like snuffed candle flames. Her face contorted in pain as she fought for breath, then she fell to her knees as her lungs finally released and she let out a terrible scream. Kevin and I rushed to her sides as she pitched forward. We managed to catch her before her face hit the floor.

"They knew," she sobbed. "They killed them. The Scats. I don't know how, but they killed them!"

"That's not possible," said Kevin.

"I felt them die!" Her body hitched. "Thousands of them! They all just..." Her body hitched again. "Oh, Goddess."

Maggie struggled and pulled away from us, then half-ran, half staggered through the back curtain. I followed and found her in the restroom on her knees, retching into the toilet. There was nothing else to do but hold her hair back.

When there was nothing left in her stomach, she sat back against the wall while I wiped her face with a damp washcloth.

"Haven't had a guy hold my hair back like that since high school," she said with a weak smile. "You must really love me or something."

"You okay?"

Her chin shook and angry tears welled in her eyes.

"No," she said. "I'm not. I want Andi back."

"Me, too." I pulled her close and held her tight while the air around us grew warm.

17

Maggie slept. It wasn't that she wanted to, but her body just gave out on her. Exhaustion was something someone in her business had to watch for. Emotionally-draining days took their toll just as bad as the physically-demanding ones. We sat and held each other for close to fifteen minutes before I realized she'd drifted off into a fitful sleep. Kevin went home for lack of anything useful to do, after he'd helped me carry Maggie up the stairs to her apartment.

When we carried her through the door, Bitsy gave us both an accusatory glare until I explained to her that she was just asleep, and we had nothing to do with it. Then I had to explain to Kevin why I felt the need to explain myself to a cat.

I put her to bed, saw Kevin to the door, then sat down on the couch in the living room. My body felt lethargic, but my brain raced. The same questions rolled through my head, but no answers volunteered, so I sat there puzzling until my brain hurt.

Andi's laptop sat on the coffee table, conspicuous in that she wasn't attached to it. It made me miss her more. Wherever she was, I hoped she knew we wouldn't give up, and I wouldn't run.

I glanced down at my withered arm and replayed the fight from the diner. After more than a year of living as a cripple, to find out in two days that the arm still had a purpose boggled my mind. The whole automatic writing thing was gift enough, but the fight, the arm of will, that was almost too much. I let the arm hang limp in my lap and closed my eyes.

"You're not giving up, are you?" The little demon glared at me from inside my mind. "You're not going to let them kill you or change things, right?"

"Do I have a choice?" I didn't want to talk to the little monster, but I was too tired to come back with pithy sarcasm. "Whoever it is, they're going to kill my friend."

"If you give up, do you have any idea how the order will change? Where you stand now, that will become hell."

"It already is," I said.

The doors in my mind shuddered and creaked as they opened. The bricks that made up my psychic walls slid and rearranged until the pathways were clear, then I opened my eyes.

Maggie's apartment was, like anyone's living space, awash with the colors and imprints of the life that used its space. Except in Maggie's case, the energies were brighter, pulsed with the living energy of the shop. There were four distinct signatures. Maggie's, the shop, Andi's and mine. Almost like we were a family, and one I didn't want to lose.

I looked down at my withered arm and Saw only a black scab where my arm should've been. No trace of the phantom limb from earlier.

"You're going to die," whispered the little demon.

"Piss off," I said. The arm didn't show any sign of life, no energy, no movement. It didn't make sense.

"Either they'll get you," buzzed the little demon, "or we

will."

"I told you to piss off," I said. "Shut up while daddy works on grown-up stuff, okay, small fry?"

"They'll kill her to get to you."

Rage washed over me and flooded the imagined hallways of my mind with liquid fire. The little demon shrieked and ran back behind one of my mental doors.

"Shut up!" My hands tingled. Both of them. I glanced down at my dead hand and no longer Saw a black hole in space, but electric sparks danceing down the length of the ruined limb. The sparks joined into one long arc, which swelled into the phantom arm of will I'd seen earlier.

"I'll be a son of a bitch," I muttered. It looked just like my arm did before it exploded, right down to the shield tattoo on the wrist. Of course, the original wasn't blue, and the tattoo only glowed when it came into contact with something nasty, but it was unmistakable. My arm, no longer flesh, but back just the same. I bent and flexed it, stretched and wiggled the fingers. It responded just like the old one always did. When I reached to pick up a pen from the coffee table, the hand passed right through. But it was there. And it wasn't useless. I saw that in the fight, didn't I? Or maybe I was so startled at the sight of the thing that I only *thought* it was useful in the diner. Either way, I had my arm back. Sort of.

Bitsy bumped my legs and rubbed against me with her back. Without thinking, I leaned down with the phantom arm and stroked her fur. She didn't flinch, and the arm didn't pass through her. She purred, as if a real flesh-and-bone hand petted her. She even pushed against it, and I felt her push.

Then I noticed something strange. Bitsy looked at me, and I saw me, looking down at me. Just a flash, but it was unmistakable. I looked up at me through her eyes. I moved the phantom hand and once again, all I saw was the cat's giant emerald eyes staring up at me. I reached down again, and again saw myself from her vantage point, the way she would see me. More, I saw the world the way she would. The room was alive with Scats, which most of the human world wouldn't see unless they looked really hard. Every little imaginary thing at which the cat pounced made sense. She saw it all.

I also got the sense of what she felt. Not words, not images, but more impressions of emotion, feelings about her state of being. It all moved so fast, so manic, it was hard to keep a bead on what she felt at any given second. Then I got the impression she was tired of playing guinea pig, and she shot off across the room. The connection severed, I slumped back onto the couch and stared at the phantom hand.

As my sense of wonder grew, my focus waned and the hand faded. I was so surprised I couldn't refocus, and in a few seconds it was gone. I shifted my perception back to normal and my withered arm looked just like it always did, a grotesque reminder to keep my nose out of other people's business. I wished I could pay attention to it, heed the warning. But the trouble was, other people's business seemed, more often than not, to affect me and mine, so into their business went my pointy little sniffer. And every time, someone whacked it with a metaphorical newspaper. Bad dog. No biscuit.

Part of me wondered why I bothered. The other part, the large bull-headed part, knew why. Because I was one of the few who could.

"Stan?" Maggie stood in the bedroom doorway, sleep heavy on her eyelids. "What're you doing?"

"Thinking," I said. "Couldn't sleep. Too much on my mind."

She shuffled over and sat down next to me on the couch. "I had bad dreams," she said. "Then I woke up without

178

you. I don't want to wake up like that again."

"You needed sleep," I said. "You needed to recharge."

She nodded and yawned, then pulled my dead arm around her shoulder, leaned her head against my chest, and snuggled in close. Her soft hair brushed my chin, smelled of strawberries and sleep. I couldn't lose her. If they took Andi to get to me, they'd come after her too. Maggie was everything to me, savior, best friend, lover and companion.

A long time ago, she made my nightmares go away with love and magic. The magic part I couldn't do, but I hoped love would suffice. I stroked her hair with my good hand, wished I could feel the softness of her skin with the withered one, and prayed to whatever power listened that there would be no more bad dreams.

We woke up to pounding on the door.

"Maggie!" Kevin's panicked voice sounded muffled through the door, but panicked all the same. "Stan! You there? Open up!"

Maggie shifted and padded to the kitchen while I opened the door. Kevin hurried in without invitation, a newspaper clutched in his hand, his face ashen.

"They hit *eleven houses* last night!" He threw the paper down on the coffee table. "And they came for me! I heard them! Last night, they were at my door, clawing!"

"Which ones?"

"How the hell should I know?" he roared. "It doesn't matter, does it? They came after me!"

I picked up the paper. The Post-Gazette masthead looked tiny compared to the headline: "Death Toll Rises." The story gave few details, but told about eleven houses, scattered throughout

Pittsburgh and her suburbs, the inhabitants of which were all dead. All murdered, all brutal, all marked with strange messages on the walls. The police, bless them, didn't elaborate as to what the messages were, but I didn't need to be a genius to know what was coming. It was a wonder they let us sleep as long as they did.

The door rattled again, hit with urgency by a meaty fist, one I knew. I opened the door to find Detectives Menold and Appel.

"We need to talk," said Appel. Menold glared, as usual, from further back. "And it has to be official."

"Am I under arrest?"

"No," said Appel. "But we really do need to talk to you. At the station. Now."

I threw what I hoped would be a reassuring glance to Maggie. Her expression of worry didn't change, but she nodded with grim resignation.

"I'll get my coat."

It seems like I spend a lot of time at the police station. Too much time. Every time something weird happens, the Pittsburgh Bureau of Police assumes it has something to do with me. The problem is, most of the time, they're right. It's not like I cause mayhem, or go looking for trouble. Trouble just seems to know where I am all the time, and takes great pleasure in putting a big "kick me" sign on my back. I don't appreciate the attention, and I wish there was something I could do about it. But, like I said before, I'm one of a select handful of people who can help when certain types of shit hit the fan. And I'm one of an even smaller number who will. To put it another way, I've seen the back seats of many a cruiser, and know when I'm in really deep trouble.

Like now.

Menold and Appel didn't drive a black-and-white. They rode around in a police-issue unmarked car that was chosen for its ability to blend in. The back seat didn't have a cage, and I was thankful they didn't handcuff me. To anyone else, I looked like just another member of a carpool, but I still felt like what I was: A prisoner.

When they led me into the station, I was ready for the sea of ugly faces, scowls and open hatred that usually accompanied my arrival. What I wasn't prepared for were the memories that came with the building. None of them were happy, but when I saw Taylor's desk, I felt like someone hit me with a brick.

Matthew Taylor was the first cop in Pittsburgh who didn't think I was a nutjob or a con man. He was the guy who ran interference for me with the other cops, and the guy who always made sure the impound guys treated my car well. He was a friend. And no matter how many times people told me to the contrary, I still felt like his death was my fault.

I wasn't ready for the loss that hit me. I also wasn't ready for the anger I felt toward the asshole whose desk it was now. The guy didn't bother to hide his disgust when he looked at me, then went back to typing. I wanted to jerk him out of his chair and ask him if he knew anything about the man who once sat behind that desk. But Appel gently led me toward one of the interview rooms and shut the door behind us.

I lost track of time. Question after question, accusing glances from Menold, good-cop-bad-cop, and it all boiled down to the same thing. Someone wanted me, and was willing to kill to get me. I let it slip about Andi, and Appel cursed me out for not coming to the police immediately. He stormed out of the room and left me alone with my least favorite of all the cops in Steel City.

Menold, I just couldn't bring myself to use his first

name, stared at me with diamond-hard eyes. He was older than me, around Taylor's age, with grey streaks in his hair and a build that suggested he didn't intend to go quietly into middleage. The creases on his forehead revealed a face that frowned often, and a man that had anger as his natural state.

"Is this the part where you unplug the camera and beat me senseless?"

I know. It isn't wise to poke an angry tiger. I couldn't resist.

"Don't tempt me," He said. From anyone else, it might've sounded like a half-hearted joke. From him, it was a stern warning that he was a whisker away from beating the piss out of me.

"Why, exactly, do you hate me so much?"

"I don't," he said. "I don't feel about you one way or the other. To me, you're no different than any other piece of trash that blows in off the street."

"Taylor was my friend too, you know."

"You say his name in my presence again," said Menold, "and I'll forget I'm a cop and give up my pension. Got it?" There was no question as to whether or not he was serious.

Appel returned and gave Menold a questioning glance, then turned to me.

"I filed a missing persons report on Miss Bedford," he said. "We'll have people looking for her. Meanwhile, we'd like to take you into protective custody."

"No way," I said. "I'm not under arrest, and you can't keep me here."

"We could take you somewhere safe. Your lady friend too."

"There is no safe place," I said. "You put people around me, they'll die too. There's only two ways for this to end. Either the bad guy dies, or I do."

The words tumbled out of my mouth and hit the table like a dead fish. On some unconscious level, I'd known since the first message on the wall that there were only two possible outcomes to three scenarios. I just didn't want to admit to myself what they were. Scenario one, the bad guy gets me and I die to help him do whatever it was he wanted to do. Scenario two, the demons find me and thwart his plans by killing me. I didn't like either one, which left scenario three: I needed to find him first, and end him before he ended me. Three paths, only two outcomes. No matter which path, one of us had to die.

It took me a few minutes of posturing and threats of legal action, plus no small part of pants-wetting terror on my part, to get Menold and Appel to admit they had no real power over me. I did nothing wrong, as far as they knew, so they couldn't hold me against my will. They agreed, not without reservation, to let me go.

On the ride back to Maggie's shop, Appel kept trying to get me to agree to let them put us in a safe house, as if there could be such a thing. He made a few convincing arguments, but nothing that stuck.

"Look," I said. "I know you two think I'm a nut, but you don't know what you're dealing with."

"Enlighten us," said Menold. He didn't bother to hide the sardonic edge to his voice.

I wanted to explain it all. Monsters under the bed, demons, possession, the dead walking the earth, the creature in the closet, all of it. I wanted so much to pull the curtain back and watch as their world collided with mine, and show them how things really worked, just to see the look on their faces. But no matter how many times I went over it in my head, I couldn't figure out a way to explain that didn't sound like pure fantasy. Magic? Monsters? We were all told from childhood that there were no such things as monsters and magic wasn't real. The only ghosts existed in Hollywood and any demon could be cast out by a man in a penis-shaped hat.

But it was all wrong. Ghosts were real. I talked to them every day. Magic called by any other name might be a miracle. And the scars on my body were proof enough of how real monsters were. And no matter how much I wanted to tell them, there was nothing I could say to make them believe. The only way I knew to make a person believe was for that person to see it with his own eyes. And I really hoped Menold and Appel would never have to see the things I saw. Well... maybe Menold.

"Never mind," I said. "Just get me back to the shop."

"That's what I thought," said Menold with a derisive chuckle. "It's all bull... what the..?"

I craned to look through the front glass. In the middle of the street, a fire barrel sat. It wasn't quite noon, and sure, it was cold, but it was too early for the homeless to light up the barrels, and they never put them in the streets. My gut sank as the other half of my brain kicked in.

"Damn."

The force that hit the car felt like a truck at full speed. I only caught a glimpse of what really hit us, a man on foot, head down like a rhinoceros. The car skidded sideways, hit the curb and upended onto its side. Glass shattered, people screamed, and the seatbelts held. My face felt warm and sticky. I wondered which side found me, the one who wanted to kill me, or the one who wanted to take me to someone else who would.

My good arm was pinned underneath me, so I had little hope of getting the seatbelt unbuckled. I squirmed and wriggled, but couldn't seem to get my arm free. Then I heard gunshots, followed by more breaking glass.

"Cooper!" Menold's voice sounded less scared than it did angry. I wondered if he was ever anything but. "You alive back there."

"Yeah," I croaked. "Can't get free."

"Hang on!" Menold's hand snaked through between the front seats and hit the button. Without the belt, my body slumped against the side of the car. But it also allowed me to shift my weight so I could move my arm. I pushed myself up and grabbed Menold's hand.

"See if you can squeeze through!"

"You're kidding, right? Have you looked at me? No way I'm getting through there."

"It's either that or up," he said as he pointed to the driver's side door, now over my head.

I was going to make a comment about being part mountain goat or something, but Menold's hand tightened, then slid out of mine. His face contorted into surprise and he let out a yelp as something dragged him backward out of the car. More gunshots, lots of cursing. I needed to get out, and fast.

How many rounds did Menold's gun hold? Ten? Fifteen? How many did he already use? The shots kept ringing out, and I couldn't count. Did he reload? Was he that fast?

I reached up for the window, but a twisted face glared down at me and smiled. I had one option, and it wasn't good, but it was the only one I had. I worked my leg downward and pushed my foot to the handle beside the front passenger seat. If they were electric, I was screwed. But my luck held and with a flick of my toe, the seat shot forward. It was a tight fight, but enough for me to wriggle through the broken glass. On my way through, I glanced at the driver's side and saw Appel's open eyes. He was dead.

I didn't have time to say goodbye, however. As I stuck my head through the opening, a powerful hand grabbed me by the back of the jacket and hauled me to my feet. Menold stood, gun pointed at a small group. At his feet, an empty clip. On the ground in front of him, seven dead people. Well, six and one who should've been dead already.

"Give up, Cooper." The shoulda-been-dead guy's voice came out a rasp of broken bone and torn tissue. The way his head lolled, I guessed he was the one who rammed us. Three bullet holes in his chest let me know what he was. Menold stared, mouth open, with his gun trained on the guy's chest. "You're going to die, no matter what. This way, you get to die a martyr."

"Saint Stanley? I don't like the sound of it." I turned to Menold. "The head."

Menold blinked. His breaths came in shallow gulps and his hands shook. He wanted explanations. He should've been careful what he wished for.

The broken man opened his mouth and howled, a sound that never should come from a human body. Menold flinched, then pulled the trigger. The body fell face forward onto the street.

"C'mon," I said. "We have to go."

"He... he wouldn't go down."

"I know. We have to go."

"No," said Menold. "It's a crime scene. I have to... I have to write up a report. Other officers."

We didn't have time for subtlety, or for me to try to talk him into anything. I grabbed him by one of his cheap suit lapels and pushed him against the building.

"Seven dead unarmed people, your gun, your partner dead. Think anyone will believe you didn't just freak out and start shooting people?"

"But they... they were..."

"Possessed. I know. We don't want to be here."

"But..." He looked like a lost kid, like he expected me to be his park ranger. And even tired, sore and bloody, it was a role I had to play if I wanted either of us to get away from the crime scene.

"Move!" I yanked his lapel and half-dragged him between two buildings. "Now!"

He limped along behind me, gun still in hand. I only hoped we could get somewhere safe before they regrouped. The trouble was, the safest place I knew was all the way across Pittsburgh, and I doubted we would make it on foot. But there was a closer place, and although I didn't want to take Menold there, I didn't see much of a choice.

"C'mon in," I said. "It ain't much, but it's safe."

Menold followed me into my apartment, nose crinkled at the stale smell in the air.

"This place doesn't feel right."

I knew what he meant, and why the air felt charged, why there were places in my apartment that felt oppressive or just downright spooky. And I was impressed that he felt it. Maybe years of cop training gave him a sixth sense or something. Maybe he had latent abilities. Either way, he felt the cold chill that didn't hit the skin, but started at the bones and worked its way outward. It wasn't the building, though it did have a horrifically bloody history that went back to the first time I met Menold. It was because of what I stored in the spare bedroom. I treated the room like a metaphysical vault, a place to keep all the nasty things and haunted objects I ran across. The first thing I put in there, a book, was powerful enough to turn the entire population of Pennsylvania into cockroaches. Everything else in there combined didn't equal up to its power, but they were still not the sorts of things people wanted left laying around. Before we made it all the way into the apartment, I did a quick scan to see if a demon-possessed doll had gotten out again. After the day I had, the last thing I needed was some grumpy monkey in a sailor suit trying to strangle me.

"Trust me," I said. "We're as safe as we're going to get."

Menold sat down on my couch and stared at the walls. On every one, weird symbols ran together and surrounded the doors and windows, power outlets and phone line. To most people, they looked like some sort of weird acid-induced artwork. To me, they were a "keep out" sign to anything that meant to do me damage.

I hurried to the bathroom to survey the new cuts and bruises on my face. Underneath all the blood were only a couple of tiny nicks in my forehead. Amazing that they bled so much.

"You really believe in all this shit, don't you?"

I leaned out of the bathroom to see him. Menold turned his attention to me. His expression was different than the one of pure hatred he usually wore. It was almost like he just figured out that I was for real.

"Yup," I said as I wiped my face and picked pieces of glass out of my hair. "Kind of hard for me not to."

I came back into the main room and found Menold still on the couch, eyes locked on the door to the spare bedroom.

"I wouldn't," I said as I walked through to the kitchen. "You think what you saw in the street was bad?"

"I don't know what I saw," he said.

"Those? Those were just puppets. I'd be willing to bet they were dead already. Just wait until some demon-possessed innocent comes calling. You'll hate that."

My refrigerator was devoid of anything remotely resembling nourishment, and anything that may have once been "food" had long since fossilized. There were, however, two brown bottles in the back that still looked inviting.

"I don't believe in that kind of shit."

"You don't have to," I said. "Doesn't make them any less real. Beer?"

He nodded, so I opened both bottles and handed one to him. He took a long thoughtful pull. It seemed to bring him out of his dazed state.

"My God," he said. "Doug's dead."

So that was his first name.

"Yeah," I said. "I'm sorry."

He put the beer down on the side table, then slumped with his head in his hands. The way his body hitched made me feel like a voyeur, so I took my beer and went to the master bedroom to make a call.

Maggie picked up on the first ring.

"Stan? Where are you?"

"Vault. Have the police been there?"

"Yeah. They said there was an accident."

"It wasn't an accident," I said. "Puppets. One of the cops didn't make it."

"I'm coming to get you," said Maggie. "Why didn't you use your cellphone?"

"I left it on the nightstand."

"It doesn't do any good there."

The truth is, I hate cellphones. I made the mistake once of watching one with my perception shifted, and now when I see one it reminds me of a collapsing nuclear power plant. I feel the same way about hybrid cars.

"Sorry," I said. "Look... be careful, okay? They hit us while we were in the car. They could do the same to you. Chances are they're on their way here right now."

"Don't worry," she said. "Just stay inside and I'll be there as quick as I can."

We hung up and I headed back into the living room. Menold stood in the middle of the room with his beer in one hand and his cellphone in the other.

"No, sir. I can't tell you where I am. Because I don't really know. He's with me. I know. But he didn't... Yes, sir. We were attacked. You didn't see... I understand."

He flipped the phone closed and turned to look at me.

"I'm to escort you to the station, and from there we'll determine what's what."

"I'm not going to the station," I said. "And you shouldn't either. You know what'll happen to you. Seven dead civilians? You'll be lucky if all they do is fire you."

"I'll likely be prosecuted," he said, his face stony. "There'll be an investigation, but you and I already know how that'll turn out."

I thought about arguing, but the little demon in my stomach wriggled and twisted and whispered in my ear.

Coming for you.

A knock at the door made us both jump.

"Stanley Cooper! Pittsburgh PD. Open up."

Don't do it.

I went to the door and looked through the peephole. Two cops in uniforms stood on the other side.

Not what they seem.

"Better open it," said Menold.

"Not by the hair of my chinny-chin-chin," I said. I lowered the walls of my perception and looked through the peephole again. The little bastard was right. A thick black sludge covered their auras.

"We know you're in there, Cooper," said one of them.

"You'll never take me alive, copper!"

"Let us in or we'll break the door down!"

"You're welcome to try!"

I stood away from the door and waited while they decided which one was dumb enough to really try to shoulder my door open. Sure, the door was steel and strong enough to stop bullets, but that wasn't why I knew they couldn't get through. The wards that marked the inside would keep them out as long as they were possessed, but that wasn't it either. It was the threshold. Salt ran under the doorframe, as did red brick dust and a few other things from other religions used to keep nasties out. I wasn't one to discriminate.

When the first dumb-demon-possessed-cop rammed the door, a spark of power met his force, tripled it, and sent it back on him. One of Maggie's better spells. He flew backward like a ragdoll and didn't stop until his host's butt went through the sheetrock on the other side of the hallway. He hung there, limp and dazed, for a moment.

"Ha! Serves you bastards right!"

"What the hell was that?" Menold had his gun drawn and his back pressed against the far wall.

"Demons," I said. "Told you they were coming."

"Bullshit."

"See for yourself," I said.

Menold took a long look at the door.

"I'll take your word for it," he said. "Now what?"

"They can't get in here. They can try all they want, but all they'll do is hurt themselves. We're safe for the moment. But you need to make a choice. You either believe me or you don't, and I don't care which one it is. You believe me, we fight to keep me alive, find my friend, and stop the son of a bitch who's doing this. Or you don't believe me. Everything else still applies."

"Or I could take you in," he said. "Lock you up for your own protection."

"Yeah, and you'll go down for murdering your partner and seven civilians. Unless you help me. I don't care what you believe or don't. I don't care if you think I'm a whackjob. But Appel gave me the benefit of the doubt. And so did Taylor."

"And they're both dead because of you."

His words cut deep. There wasn't a day that went by that I didn't replay the events that got Taylor killed, and wondered if maybe I could've done something different. And now Appel's name was added to the list. But this time, the replay was short. It wasn't my fault. For once, I figured out that what happened wasn't because of me, but because of some asshole who wanted to use me for some reason. Maybe Menold fell back to accuse me out of defense, but it pissed me off. And as much as I wanted to throttle him, I knew it wasn't the right thing to do. So I did the only other thing that came to mind.

"I'm coming out," I shouted through the door. The demons on the other side quieted. I'm sure they knew I had something up my sleeve. But they were eager to finish their job and get back to whatever demons did when they weren't busy trying to kill me.

Before I opened the door, I scooped up a handful of salt.

"You want to see what you're up against?" Menold stared. "You want to see what you don't believe in? Fine. Have a look."

I threw the door open. Both uniformed officers stood waiting. They didn't look like demons, of course, but like a couple of rookies, straight out the academy with pressed uniforms and shiny shoes. But I knew. By the glint in their eyes, I knew.

Menold kept his gun drawn, aimed low in case he needed it. When he saw them, the color drained from his face, almost as if he could tell something wasn't right. Maybe he had a touch of the Sight on him too. All I knew was I had to move quickly if we were to get out of there alive.

"You want me?" I said to the cop in front. "Come get me."

I flung the handful of salt at his face. Wherever a grain touched, smoke billowed from the poor host's skin. The demon howled in rage and clawed at his face. His partner seized the opportunity to rush me, but I was ready. I feinted to the left and drew back with my good hand and put everything I had into one punch aimed at his face. It made contact, but it hurt my hand more than it did him. Sure, it rocked his head back, but when it came back up, the bastard smiled.

"Is that all you've got?" it sneered. "You hit like a girl."

He never saw Maggie run up behind him with a fire-extinguisher in her hand. She swung down hard and made contact with his skull and put him flat on his face on the carpet.

"Do not," I said. "Some girls hit harder than me."

The first demon got his bearings and knocked Maggie against the wall with a backhand swipe, then he leaped at me and took me down to the floor. He pinned me by the shoulders and howled, his scarred face inches from mine. It didn't matter how hard I struggled, I couldn't sit up or push him off.

He shook his head and I heard the bones in his jaw crack, then he opened his mouth wide. He was like a snake, unhinged and ready to swallow me whole. The little demon inside me screamed in panic, just like I did on the outside.

"Hey!"

The demon looked up, just for a second, and the front of his head dotted red with a thunder clap from my doorway, then the back of his head rocked back. My ears rang, but I was happy to be alive. Menold stood in the doorway, the barrel of his Glock trained on the twitching mass of blood and filth that was still on top of me. But at least it wasn't going to eat me.

"Holy shit," he said. "That was..."

"Get him off me!"

Menold shifted into action and gave the carcass a violent shove. As I scrambled to my feet, he slumped against the wall, gun still clasped in his shaking hands.

"Maggie!" I crawled over to where she slowly sat up rubbing the back of her head. "You okay?"

"Fine," she said. "You're a mess."

I looked down at my pants. Blood streaked the legs and there were little bits of I-didn't-want-to-know-what. My stomach lurched.

Movies and television shows have clever little plot devices that make clean-up a non-issue. Stake a vampire, he disintegrates into dust. Kill a demon, his body goes up in flames and leave only a big black scorch on the carpet. But real life isn't like that. It's messy. Kill a demon, the corpse of his host sits cooling and drawing flies in the middle of the hall. It isn't like there's a convenient body-disposal service, and no one ever believes the "he was possessed by a demon that tried to kill me" defense. Which presents something of a real problem.

What to do with the body.

Another thing movies and television shows never allow: Witnesses. Some cheerleader with an attitude problem can stake a thousand vampires, and no one ever calls the police because no one is ever around to see it. But Pittsburgh doesn't behave like whatever fictional California town she lives in. People in Steel City look out their peepholes when people get loud. They show concern when it sounds like there's a wild animal in the hall. And they dial the police pretty damned fast when they hear gunshots.

By my reckoning, we had about seven minutes, from the moment Menold fired his gun. Which meant we really had about five minutes to get the hell out of the building, or leave ourselves to the tender mercies of the Pittsburgh PD. Running seemed like the saner of the two options.

I ran into my apartment, grabbed a fresh pair of pants and a shirt, the pulled the door shut behind me and locked it. The combination of the steel door and the threshold would take anyone a good long while to break in, and I hoped we could figure out a way out of our mess before anyone got in and turned the things in the spare bedroom loose.

Maggie stood in front of the door and hummed, a low chant, drew power from the Earth and sky, and wove a spell over the doorway. She called it a "no-see-um" glamour. The way I understood it, it didn't actually hide anything, but it gave an irresistible urge to turn away from whatever the spell was cast on. In the case of the door, it would make anyone who came to it look the other direction. Not really invisible, but it forced the mind to not see it.

When she finished, we hurried out of the building. We decided to leave the bodies where they lay. We could've stashed them in my apartment, but that would've risked one of the unnatural objects infecting them, and the last thing I wanted was to come back and be confronted with a walking rotting corpse.

We also wanted them to be found so their next of kin could be notified.

The police arrived moments after we pulled out of the parking lot. Maggie drove slow to avoid suspicion, but the urge to scream and run like hell was almost overpowering. When she hit the freeway, and my heart stopped pounding like a spastic squirrel in my ribcage, I breathed a little easier. I took the opportunity to skin off my blood-soaked clothes and put on something a little less attention-getting. The old clothes went into a reusable grocery bag that I found in the back seat.

"What now?" Maggie's eyes in the rear-view mirror met mine.

"Shop," I said. "We need to regroup."

"I wouldn't," said Menold. "We'll have it staked out. You come within three blocks of that building, they'll be all over you like a bear on a picnic basket."

"I have to go back," I said. "It's important."

"Why?"

I scrambled to think up a convincing lie, one that sounded more plausible than the truth. I wanted to go back to tell the shop where we were going, to let her know we weren't going to just abandon her. I wanted to let her know we'd be back, and Menold didn't look like he could take any more weirdness. After the day so far, most men would do nothing but sit and drool in a corner and wait for happy-pill time. That he still remained lucid was a testament to his strength.

"I need my cellphone," I said. Maggie caught my expression in the mirror and chimed in.

"And I need ritual supplies if we're going to fight."

"Ritual? Don't tell me."

"Witch," said Maggie.

"Of course," said Menold.

18

Back in the earliest days of computer programming, hackers lived by a precious few rules. One of them, I always kind of admired: Always leave a back door. To them, it meant an embedded password that allowed them access to their programs even when the powers that be tried to lock them out. Every computer system was rumored to have one, from the electronic cash registers at the market to the main defensive computer at NORAD. The point was, gain access when access was otherwise denied.

A while ago, Maggie's shop was hit hard by people possessed by demonic rats. During repairs, we blocked the hole in the basement they made, and figured that was that. But about a year later, when the streets of Pittsburgh crawled with corpses, we figured it might be a good idea to have a hidden way out. Once we all healed and regained our bearings, Maggie and Andi and I set to work reopening, but shielding, that tunnel. Not that we expected trouble, but like my father used to tell me, it was always a good thing to be prepared. When the time came to close up the entrance, Maggie did a no-see-um spell that kept everything away. It also helped that the shop did her best to cover the entrance too. As an added precaution, Maggie warded the hell out of it and made a threshold lock that only the three of us knew how to open.

The only problem with it was also its best strength: It was damned hard to get to. The entrance was a half-dozen blocks away in a storm drain that ran beside a tattoo parlor and a nightclub. The shift-change hour hit, and traffic on the street slowed. Another hour before the club opened for business, and the tattoo shop had a breather for at least that long. Maggie parked the car across the street and we hurried to the culvert in the back parking lot of the club.

The parking lot only held a couple of cars, neither of which were parked up against the culvert. I got down on my belly and slid in, feet first. When I got to the bottom, I turned and helped guide Maggie in. Menold looked unsure, but followed anyway. His suit took a beating in the gravel parking lot, but it couldn't be helped.

The sewers and storm drains in Pittsburgh are works of engineering grace. Interlocking tunnels grid the city with junctions where water gathers and drains, and often leaves items of curious interest. Most of the time, the storm drains on Carson Street are littered with the occasional dead animal, drug needles, a lost or stolen wallet and used rubbers. But there were also people who made their livings by sifting through the refuse and pulling up treasure. A lost earring could feed a family of four for a week. A wedding ring, a month.

We hiked through the tunnels, careful of where we stepped. Because it was getting dark, we didn't want to risk any of Maggie's light spells. Even people as jaded as Yinzers tended to notice blue light coming from storm drains. I led the way with my perception shifted. About twenty yards in, we came to a ragged hole in the wall.

"Here," I said.

"How far?" whispered Menold.

"You can speak up," I said. "There's so much noise on the street that no one'll hear you. It's only a few blocks. This comes out in the basement of Maggie's shop."

"How can you see where we're going?"

"Remember how Taylor said I could see ghosts?"

"Yeah," he said. "Doug said it too."

"It's true, but I can also see energy patterns. Works like thermal vision."

"Handy," he said.

Maggie wriggled around in front of me and gestured at the hole in the wall. With my sight shifted, the opening looked like more than just a broken-out section of brick. The curtain of energy that covered it was heavy, sparked like a shock gun. A person who wasn't invited would get just enough of a shock from it to get creeped out and want to go back. But a demon, or any other malevolent entity for that matter, would be fried.

Maggie raised her hands and closed her eyes.

"*Iter Itineris.*"

The curtain parted and let us through.

"What's that?" snorted Menold. "Like 'open sesame' or something?"

"It's Latin," said Maggie. "It means 'open the way.' That, combined with a few tattoos gives me the key to get in."

"You're kidding."

"Walk back through and try it if you don't believe me."

He looked back toward the opening, considered, then shook his head.

"I'll take your word for it," he said. Smart man.

Unlike the well-crafted walls of the storm drains, the

tunnel we walked through was ragged on the sides, muddy on the bottom. It wasn't part of the city plan, but was carved out by the people possessed by rat demons. It amazed me that human fingers and teeth cut through the concrete and brick, but I saw the aftermath. We hurried through until I saw light up ahead.

"We're here," I said. Menold started to push past, but Maggie stopped him.

"Second lock," she said. "This one will hurt you, not just scare you."

The first lock may have been designed to make a person run away, but this one was more like an electric fence. Anything that got near it ran the risk of losing hair and dignity. And while the thought of Menold losing either made me smile on the inside, we didn't have time to help him recover.

Maggie drew energy from the Earth, focused her will, and placed her hands on either side of the opening. Then she pushed. Her energies bubbled out of her and created a breach in the lock, then opened at one end a tunnel through which we could get to the basement. I hurried through, followed by Menold. Maggie brought up the rear and closed the tunnel behind us.

"We're home," she said softly. The air around us warmed.

"Keep it dark, okay?" It felt weird, speaking to the building like it was a child, but after a while I got used to it. The lights dimmed as we hurried up the stairs to Maggie's workroom. The lights kept pace with us, growing brighter where we needed to step, then dimming when we passed. As we emerged from the basement, the windows in the shop darkened to opaque.

"Who are you talking to?" Menold glanced around the room like a nervous ferret.

"You wouldn't believe me if I told you," I said. I could've told him the truth, if for no other reason than to watch his brain do somersaults while he tried to figure out if I was messing with

200

him or not. But I didn't have time. I needed to get a few things, then I needed to make sure the shop knew we were coming back.

The stairs to Maggie's apartment weren't easily seen from the street, so I hurried out the side door and up. Once inside, I grabbed my cellphone, a couple of changes of clothes for Maggie and me, and made sure to fill up Bitsy's water bowl and food dish. As I picked up my bag, she gave me a reproachful look and meowed.

"I'll be back," I said. "It's not like any of this is my idea." The cat huffed, turned her back on me and swished her tail. She was mad and wanted to make sure I knew it.

I locked the door behind me and hurried back down to the shop. Menold stood with his hands in his pockets while he read the labels on Maggie's apothecary jars.

"Some of this stuff is poisonous," he said.

"None of it's illegal," said Maggie as she packed candles in her bag.

"Most of it should be. What do you do with all this crap?"

"Potions," said Maggie with a straight face. "I make oils, soaps, incense, you name it. I can make things that soothe arthritis and other things that'll cure an upset tummy."

He shook his head.

"Bunch of hippie weirdo shit," he said.

"Maybe," said Maggie. "But my hippie weirdo shit really works, and I've got the clientele to prove it."

"Look," said Menold. "You been working as a cop as long as I have, you learn that there's a sucker born every minute. Some people will believe anything you tell them."

"How about you?" Maggie cocked an eyebrow at him. "What do you believe in?"

"Me," said Menold. "And this." He patted his gun. "Only two things that've never let me down."

"That's sad," I said from across the room.

"That's life," said Menold.

Before we left, I checked my cellphone to see if there were any missed calls. When it powered up, the screen displayed eight, all from the same number. I punched in the code for my voicemail box. There was only one message.

"Stan. It's Kevin. I've been tracking down people on the list. Lots of them are dead, but a few of them are getting the hell out. Listen, I don't have much time. I think I've picked up a tail. Two guys. I don't know what they want, but I'm going to try to shake them. Meet me at the playhouse."

The drive from Carson Street to the Pittsburgh Playhouse is an easy one, or would be if not for all the construction that goes on six months out of the year. The other six, the roads are frozen and covered in salt, which makes construction difficult, to say the least. Construction means delays, which makes drivers twitch, but gives passengers time to think. On normal days, my thoughts turn ugly and depressing in about ten seconds. But every now and again, a body that's been running ragged for a few days just needs a minute or two of quiet time to let the brain focus.

I sat in the back seat. Not that I thought Maggie needed Menold to co-pilot, but I didn't trust the guy to sit behind me. Besides, it gave me a chance to stretch out. I didn't realize how tired I was until I put my head back and closed my eyes.

I saw Andi. I saw dozens of her, all seated around each other. They moved in identical motions, had the same injuries. They all wore blindfolds and gags, all their hands were tied behind their backs. Blood trickled down all their noses.

"We're coming," I said softly. "Just hang on."

The image faded, which left me to question if what I

saw was real or just some kind of worst-case scenario dreamed up by my subconscious. Either way, I sat up fast and rubbed my face. Kevin was expecting us. He had people following him, so he retreated to the safest place he knew. His home base. Realization stabbed me right above my tailbone.

"Stop the car," I said.

"What? Why?" Maggie's head snapped from side to side as she looked for attackers.

"I think it's a trap."

"What is? Kevin?"

"Think about it," I said. "He's hated me for years. He's tied to both groups. We've both seen him throw around some heavy mojo, but he's been acting like a rank amateur for the last couple of days. He wanted the book because he wanted power... It all makes sense."

"Except that you looked at his aura and said he couldn't be the one."

"I could be wrong," I said. "I couldn't see any sign of dark intent in anyone. And I wouldn't if they really believed what they were doing was right. Think about it. It can't be Neighbor Bob because he's attached to the church. Reneau has too much to lose, and I just can't believe anyone who plays with kangaroos could be evil, so that leaves Blossom out of the picture."

"Who in the hell are you talking about?" Not many people I knew could pull off angry and confused expressions at the same time, but Menold did a fine job of it.

"Members of Evergreen," said Maggie. "People like us. People you don't want to mess with."

"Neighbor Bob, kangaroos, magic, are you guys serious?"

When neither of us answered, he shuddered, pulled his gun, and checked the clip.

"So what's the plan?"

"You drop me off," I said. "Then get out of the way. Let me deal with Kevin."

It wasn't a perfect plan. In fact, as far as plans went, it sucked. To begin with, it left me little chance of survival. But I also didn't want to put Maggie in harms way again. I was lucky in that Maggie's opinion of my plan was the same as mine.

"That's a shitty plan," she said. "Here's a better one. We park, we go in, we find Andi, and we deal with Kevin."

"I don't want you in danger," I said. It was one of those moments I wished I could suck back into my mouth and pretend never happened. Maggie slammed on the brakes, put the car in park, and turned in her seat to face me.

"Don't you *dare* treat me like some weak-willed little piece of fluff," she said. "You walk in there by yourself, you're going to die and we both know it. And you also know what kind of power I have. Don't make me kick your ass."

I felt the blood drain from my face. She had a point. She'd proven time and again that she was more than capable of dealing with trouble. Why I felt the need to try and protect her was a mystery, but I put it down to my knuckle-dragging ancestors.

I glanced at Menold, who looked a little afraid.

"She's your girlfriend," he said. "My money's on her."

"Okay," I said. "Your plan works too."

19

In some of my favorite movies, the hero is willing to walk straight into a trap to retrieve someone he loves. It's the martyr complex, a willingness to sacrifice himself. And every man dreams of being that guy. Not that we're willing to sacrifice ourselves, but we want to be the movie version of the hero who not only walks into the trap, but also manages to defy the odds, rescue the girl, and get out relatively intact. We dream of getting the girl who is so impressed that we risked our lives for her that she can do nothing but love us. The problem, however, is that movies and real life are rarely ever in the same plane of existence. In the movies, a hero can turn his back on an explosion and walk away in slow motion and look really damned cool doing it. In real life, explosions carry with them things like concussive force and shrapnel, and those things hurt and make people look more like linguini than cool. In movies, the music swells as the hero kisses the girl and everyone just assumes they live happily ever after, but in real life, there's no music and relationships based on fear never last. Oh, and in movies, the hero may be bloodied and bruised, but he survives. In real life, "hero" is a euphemism for "someone who got himself and other people killed while doing something stupid."

So as we approached the Pittsburgh Playhouse entrance, the urge to run away was strong. But I couldn't just leave Andi. I had to try.

Menold went first, gun drawn, and found one of the doors unlocked. Stranger still was that there was no one inside. No security guards, no secretaries, no janitors, no lights. The place was deserted, the only sounds, the echo of our footsteps, which made it all the more spooky.

One of the main theater doors stood open, and light came from inside. Menold held his gun low, and crept to the entrance. When he got there, he pointed the gun, froze, and backed out. Maggie and I rushed to the door.

In the center of the stage sat Kevin on his stool. He wore the clown outfit. His head, painted up, sat in his lap. The crimson smile wasn't greasepaint though. Blood smeared a wicked swath across his face, and wet dark caverns marked the holes his eyes once occupied.

My legs went numb as I walked down the aisle and up the steps onto the stage. Every bad thing I said, every mistrustful thought, came back in a tidal wave of guilt. I didn't have to ask if it was my fault. I knew. They killed him to get to me.

An awful thought struck as I looked down around the stool.

"No blood. Shit."

That there was no blood around Kevin told me two things. First, he was killed somewhere else, cleaned up, dressed, and left as a message for me. Second, he was the proverbial cheese to my mouse, and like an idiot, I just stepped on the mousetrap.

Maggie stood just outside the theater doors and tried to calm Menold, who, by the sound of it, vomited in the foyer. She felt the shift in the air just before I did, because she looked up with terror on her panic-stricken face. Then the doors slammed shut in front of her, and the trap snapped shut on me.

"That was too easy." The voice came from the far side of the stage. A man in a black suit and tie stepped out from behind the curtain.

"Yeah," came another voice. "I expected a little more."

The other man, dressed just like the first, sat at the back of the auditorium. I walked right past him and didn't see because I was so focused on Kevin.

"You two look like a stereotype. You know that, right?"

I can't help it. Fear turns me into a smart aleck. It's a defense mechanism.

"Good to know," said the second.

"Which side are you on?"

"Well, we're not here to take you anywhere, if that's what you mean." The easy confidence of their voices did nothing to boost my courage. Behind them the doors rattled.

"They won't get in," said the first one. "Not until we're done and gone."

"You know, this is a lose-lose situation for you guys." I backed away from them and looked for something, anything, I could use as a weapon. "If you succeed, you killed a one-armed short fat guy. If you fail, you got beat by a one-armed short fat guy. Nothing to brag about either way, right?"

"We'll get over it," said the second. The skin on my good arm prickled. I didn't need to shift my perception to feel their power grow as they pulled it from the electrical lines and the Earth below the building. I reached the edge of the curtain and tried to find an opening without looking.

"I don't want to let him use me," I said. "You don't have to worry about that."

"You will," said the first. "Once everything is taken away from you, you'll want to. And we can't let that happen. Balance has to be maintained."

I found the edge of the curtain as they jumped at me. Overweight and out of shape I might've been, but fear motivated me to feint and spin into the curtain. The first one overshot me and crashed into something in the dark. The other one wound up tangled in the curtain for a half a second. It was all the opportunity I needed to run like hell.

The backstage area was a sea of velvet black, dotted with little strips of green, phosphorescent tape that the stage-hands used to keep from killing themselves during set changes. I ran for the first green dot I saw and shifted my perception at the same time. The room leapt into vibrant colors as the decades of passion and love lit up the stage. Snippets of productions played as I ran past, but I couldn't stop to admire them. A glance behind confirmed what I already knew: The two guys were not just inhabited by demons, they *were* demons in human form. I dodged past screens and platforms and made my way to the exit. When I got to the door, I found it chained.

"You didn't really think we wouldn't cover that, did you?" Demon number one laughed. The other gave a spine-melting smile. "Now hold still and we'll make this as painless as possible."

"He's lying," said demon number two. "This is going to hurt like hell."

They took two steps and, on instinct, I threw up my hand and screamed. Solid blue rippled down my arm and hit the first one in the chest like a battering ram. He landed hard on the floor with a wet cracking sound, and didn't move. The second one looked surprised, as, I'm sure, did I. There was a beat of a moment, a second in which we both looked at the downed man in black, then looked at each other. I shrugged, he howled, and I panicked.

The demon lunged, both clawed hands aimed at my throat. There was no time to think or to try to maneuver, only to react. The surprise came when I threw up one arm, and the other followed. My ruined arm, bolstered by the one made of pure will, took the brunt of the demon's blow. His flesh smoked where it touched mine, but all it seemed to do was make him more angry.

"He's going to kill your friends to get to you," growled the demon as he pushed me against the wall. "Let me kill you and you can save them. Don't be such a coward."

The word flipped some kind of switch in my head and all my fear mutated into bloody blue rage. The energy from my body intensified as I pushed back, and for the first time, fear flickered through the demon's eyes.

I shoved and took a step. To my surprise, I gained ground. I took another. And another. The demon floundered as I pressed the advantage. I was no coward. Sure, there was still plenty that scared me, but I didn't let my fear rule me. Not anymore.

A heavy shove and the demon stumbled backward. I didn't wait for him to right himself and connected with a hard right hook to the side of his head. For once, it hurt the target more than it did me. I made contact and light flared from under my fist where it touched his bare skin. He yelped and shrank away.

"Who's behind this?" I drew back and hit him again.

"You don't know?" He laughed and spat out a bloody tooth.

I swung and hit him again.

"Tell me!"

"You'll find out soon," he wheezed. The demon's legs went limp and he sank to the ground. The black flame around his body dissipated until all that was left was a dead husk. Two more bodies. Two more lives cut short. Two more faces to haunt my nightmares.

I staggered out from backstage as Maggie and Menold got the door open. Maggie ran to the edge of the stage, ready to fight. Menold kept his gun drawn.

"It's okay," I said. "They're gone."

"Who?" Menold checked his blind spots and pointed his gun around.

"Two of them. Demons. They wanted me dead."

"What happened?" Maggie checked the orchestra pit. "Where'd they go?"

"Dead," I said. They both stopped and stared at me. "We need to leave. There're two dead bodies backstage, and I don't think any of us wants to explain them."

Menold nodded and headed for the exit. Maggie waited for me at the edge of the stage. As I climbed down the steps, I glanced back at Kevin's body. With my perception shifted, the dead couldn't hide from me. The ghosts of the theater watched us leave. There were more than I figured; actors, patrons, a few echoes. Beside the Red Meanie and Gorgeous George, there stood a new ghost, one that would most likely never leave. The clown-man with no eyes waved at me as I walked through the theater door.

20

I'm not going to lie. We got in the car and I bawled like a baby. Forget all the manly-man stuff, and cut a corner off my tough-guy card, but I sat in the back seat with my face in my hands and didn't care that the woman I loved could see, or that a tough-as-nails cop might think less of me. I was too tired, too scared, to care.

Besides, I just went toe-to-toe with a pair of demons, and came out on top. Let's see Clint Eastwood top that.

So many people over the last few days were dead because someone thought it was a good way to get to me. And the real pisser to it all was I didn't even know why. One side wanted me to perform some unspeakable evil, the other wanted me dead to prevent said unspeakable evil, and all I wanted to do was hide in a corner and cry myself to sleep.

"It wasn't your fault," said Maggie.

"Yeah," I sniffed. "Right."

"It's not!" The car swerved a bit. "You didn't ask for any of this! You didn't..."

"If it weren't for me, Kevin would still be alive." I looked up into the rearview mirror. Maggie's tear-reddened eyes stared back. "He wouldn't have gotten involved if it weren't for me, and neither would anyone else who died. Don't tell me none of this is my fault."

"I hate to say it," said Menold. "I mean I *really* hate to say it, but she's right. This kind of stuff happens to you all the time?"

"Yeah," I said.

He let out a deep breath and sunk back into his chair. "So now what?"

"I don't know," I said.

"We can't go back to the shop," said Maggie. "The police are probably still there, though I doubt they've gotten inside yet. Your apartment's off limits too."

"They're probably looking for me at mine," said Menold. "We can't just drive around forever."

"Bill," I said. "We need to call Bill."

If there were anyone in Pittsburgh that I trusted to play straight with me, Bill and his wife Brea would be the ones. They pulled our collective butts out of the fire more times than I cared to count, and earned my respect. The trouble was, I didn't know where they lived or what they even did. At one time, it startled me to realize that Bill, one of the most powerful magical men I'd ever met, had a job. Not to mention his wife, whom I always pictured standing over a bubbling cauldron full of who-knows-what and cackling with a mad gleam in her eye. After everything they'd done for me, for us, I didn't want to call them and run the risk of them getting killed too.

But I had to.

If anyone had the know-how to get us out of the mess we were in, and to let me get out of it alive, it was them.

Maggie didn't want to call them either, but after a few minutes of gentle persuasion, she did. Bill answered on the second ring and gave her directions. About a half-hour after we passed through the Fort Pitt Tunnel, we came to our turnoff and arrived in the little town of Greentree.

"Greentree, Evergreen, does everything this guy does revolve around trees somehow?" Menold didn't bother trying to hide the amusement in his voice.

"We could drop you somewhere," said Maggie. "Maybe back in the real world?"

I was glad I was in the back seat. The front seat was getting kind of cold for me.

"No, no," he said, hands raised in mock-surrender. "I'm all in."

"Then behave yourself," she said.

We drove the rest of the way in silence. I must've checked my watch a dozen times in as many minutes because each one passed as slow as a pregnant walrus. By the time Maggie came to a stop, I was ready to chew through a window to get away from the tension.

When I first met Bill, I had all kinds of mental images of where he might live. The most prevalent of them was that he lived in a cave on the side of a mountain, lit only with burning torches and a huge fire where he sat and thought deep thoughts all day and tried to change lead into gold all night. As with everything else about Bill, those preconceived notions were almost completely wrong. He and Brea lived in what appeared to be a cabin, lit with electricity, and with a hot tub on the back deck.

On the side of a mountain.

Well, it wasn't exactly on the *side* as much as it was *in front*, but the presence of a mountain was undeniable, and it fit with my warped little version of the world. Bill met us in the driveway and directed us to the barn around the side of the house. As we passed through the gate, the little demon inside me went into spastic convulsions.

Please, it wailed in my head. *Not here! Too much! Please!*

"Cool it, junior," I muttered.

Maggie followed the gravel drive into the old wooden structure, then she killed the engine. We got out and hurried out of the barn while Bill closed the doors behind us. At the top, on the door where the hay loft would be, there was a large pentagram painted on the barn.

"It was like that when we bought the place," he said. "Pennsylvania Dutch. Don't see too many of them this far west, but near Philly, you see a lot of barns with stars on 'em."

Brea ushered us into the house and hugged Maggie and me. She gave Menold's hand a wary shake, but invited him in anyway.

As I crossed the threshold, it felt like the little demon tried to crawl out of my body by way of my spine.

"Simmer down," I said.

I'm afraid!

It was a strange thing, to hear the little beast admit to being scared, but I figured he had cause to be. Bill and Brea as individuals had enough power to cook his scrawny butt. Together, I shuddered to think of what they could do to him. And me in the process.

We made it as far as the living room before I broke down again. Maggie guided me down to the couch while I shook with gut-wrenching sobs. It seemed like my body wanted to vomit out all the pain and sadness of the last few days, and it didn't give a damn who saw. For my own part, I wanted to stop, to sit up, to be as strong and brave as my father taught me. But I couldn't. Every cathartic wave that flooded through my body brought with it a tiny measure of relief, and I was greedy for it.

"It's okay," said Brea as she waved a warm cup of tea under my nose. "You're safe now."

"Are you sure?" Menold was still on high alert. I doubted he'd ever be anything but again.

"Yes," laughed Bill. "No one knows where we live, and even if they did, our property is warded. Nothing can happen to you here."

Menold didn't seem convinced. Although he put his gun back in his shoulder rig, he didn't relax, but stayed rigid, arms crossed, near a window.

The whole story spilled out of me in a flood of wild gestures and angry shouts and bitter tears. Bill listened and nodded while Brea patted my knee. Maggie held me tight around the shoulders. Her warmth and touch gave me hope when nothing else could, but here, now, it didn't help much.

When I was done, Brea took the teacup to the kitchen. A slight gesture from Bill and Maggie took Menold out to the barn to "get a few things" from the car. Once we were alone, he leaned in, voice low.

"You're in it pretty deep," he said. "I told you, dangerous work."

"I know," I said. "I don't know what to do."

"Do you know why they want you?"

I shook my head.

"I just know that, whatever it is, it'll upset the natural balance of things. That's why the demons want me dead. Either way, I'm dead, right?"

"Probably," said Bill as he stroked his chin. "Let me do some research. I'll see what I can figure out. In the meantime, you need to unwind a little. Hot tub's out back, there's a shower upstairs. Take your pick. Guest rooms are at the top of the stairs."

"Thank you," I said. "You two've done so much for us. We'll never be able to repay..."

"Pish." He waved his hand. "That's what friends do, right? Help each other?"

"I'm going to help myself to a shower," I said.

He nodded as I made my way up the stairs.

Everyone has a vice or three. Little pleasures that trump any sin of the flesh, any other food, any other experience. For some people, it's as simple as having their back scratched. A good scratching and they'll bow up like kittens. For others, it's having their feet massaged. For me, nothing clears my head or brings back my humanity like a hot shower. As the water pours over my head, every negative thing falls away with it until I'm left with clarity and focus. Or at least I smell better. Either way works for me.

Maggie used to prefer baths until I pointed out that a bath was basically a person soaking in a warm bucket of her own filth. She didn't appreciate the image, but soon began to share my love of showers.

I stood with my eyes closed as the water pulsed down on my head. The faces of dead people replayed behind my eyelids, all there because of me. As they flashed past, a single face gained focus until it was the only one I saw: Andi.

Help me... find me... I'm scared...

I finished my shower, but I didn't feel any better. In fact, I still felt overwhelmed. Either way, one of them was going to get me. Either way, I was going to die. If I let the demons have me, they might make it quick and painless, but then what? Whoever had Andi might kill her, or worse, out of anger or spite. And if I handed myself over to him, there were no guarantees he'd let her go. And what about the rest of the world? Then there was the other little hitch that I didn't want to die. My life, while a far cry from perfect, was good. Maggie told me she needed me so often that I started to believe her a while ago.

Like it or not, I had no intention of taking the dirt nap for anyone, demon, mage or otherwise. I toweled off and wiped steam from the mirror. The eyes that looked back at me didn't seem like my own for a moment. My eyes were never that hard, that determined. So full of anger.

I dressed quickly and hurried down the stairs. Brea and Maggie sat on the couch while Menold stared out the window, his posture wooden, like he was certain that at any moment something ugly and supernatural would bust down the door.

"Bill?" I said as I reached the bottom of the stairs.

"In the study," said Brea. "Through the kitchen."

I followed the direction she pointed and found myself at a small door at the back of the kitchen. Anyone else might've thought it was a cupboard, but the hair on my arm stood up as I touched the face of the door, and I felt the familiar tingle of electric magic dance across my skin. I knocked.

"Yes." Bill's voice called from inside.

I'm not sure what I expected. Maybe I thought the door would open into a great black void like in the old comic books. Or maybe I thought the room would be a vast chamber lit with oil lamps, filled to the brim with books and other items of magical properties. Hell, half of me expected to see a unicorn nuzzling a dragon on the inside. In fact, I thought it was safe to say that nothing I saw when the door opened would have surprised me.

But again, I was wrong. It was surprising because of the sheer normalcy of the room. The converted mudroom had a couple of bookshelves, but only one was filled with books. The other one held knickknacks, candles, and a couple of boxes. On top sat an old leather journal, latched with metal clasps, and an altar similar to the one in the back of Maggie's shop. Across the room sat a battered leather easy chair with an ottoman. Close to the door sat the most unexpected thing of all, a computer. Bill sat at a rolling chair and stared into the screen.

"Good shower?"

"Yeah," I lied. "You're really killing your image here."

Bill snorted. "Blame Brea. She made me take down the torches."

"Did you find anything?"

"Maybe," he said. "A few vague references, several rituals that our friend might be trying, but nothing definite. But I think I know a way to narrow it down."

He pushed his chair out and went to the kitchen door.

"Back in a minute," he yelled, then he gestured for me to follow him out the back door.

Sometime between the time we arrived and the moment I stepped out the back door, the day died and turned to night. A chill nipped through the air, a signal that winter was fast on its way, but autumn still kicked and strained, unwilling to give up her hold on the year.

"Where're we going?"

"Up," said Bill.

I've made mention several times of my lack of athleticism. To be blunt, I'm pudgy and out of shape. I'm not old, per se, but I'm about twenty years past the point where I even think about climbing mountains. Honestly, I do well to climb a flight of stairs without gassing out.

But Bill hurried up the trail, and I felt compelled to follow. We hiked for what seemed like an eternity. By the time we stopped, I needed another shower. I was sweaty, tired, out of breath and miserable. Bill, however, looked like he might've just

218

walked across a room.

"Take a look," he said. "What a view, eh?"

The Pittsburgh skyline lit up the night sky. I always liked my city at night.

"Yeah," I gasped. "Gorgeous. What're we doing up here?"

"I need you to look at the city."

It took me a second to get his meaning, but when I did, I nodded and tried to catch my breath. A couple of minutes passed, during which time my lungs threatened to go on strike, but then I was able to slow my breathing and my heart rate returned to something resembling normal. I stood and faced the city, then closed my eyes and willed the walls in my mind to lower, the doors to open, and my perception to shift.

I've looked at Pittsburgh before with my perception shifted. The streets pulsed and the buildings glowed, even brighter than they did at night. If anyone else could see it the way I did, they'd know why I called the city a "she," and why I knew she was alive and beautiful.

What I saw when I opened my eyes stole my breath and made me want to vomit.

Over my beloved home was a cloud, large enough to cover the whole city. It wasn't rain or hail or snow, but energy. The life energy of the city, her people, the living and the dead, all fused above the highest building in a mass that looked more like a disease than energy. Cancer.

"Storm cloud," I said. "Big. All over the city."

"What kind of cloud?"

"It's green," I said. "It's sucking the city dry. Wherever it touches, the buildings are dim. The ones that aren't dim are infected with it."

"There it is," he said. "That's what he's doing."

I shifted my perception back to normal. I couldn't take

seeing my city that way.

"Come on," he said as he headed back down the trail. "We need to get back. We're not protected up here."

"What is it?" I asked.

"Not here," he said as he walked.

"Now!" I stopped on the trail.

Bill stopped and his shoulders drooped. He turned slowly.

"Think about a storm, a hurricane or a tornado or something like that. The worst one you can imagine. Now imagine that instead of wiping the land clean, it's going to do it to souls. Everyone will be wiped clean, erased, easy to control. That's what he's doing."

I stood for a moment, stunned.

"Now can we please go back to the house? I feel vulnerable out here."

At that moment, so did I.

We got back to the house and filled everyone in on Bill's theory of what the bad guy was doing. He told us I had to be there because of what I was, a person who walked halfway between life and death. I had to be there because the energy had to run through a conduit that could touch both worlds. The only trouble was that the energy would burn the conduit up from the inside, which meant that my whole body would explode like my arm did.

"There has to be a way to stop him," said Maggie. "Counter the spell, something."

"There is," said Bill with an uneasy look toward Brea. "But I don't want to use it."

"Why not?" To me there were no plans that were off the table. I'd play a magic kazoo naked in the middle of Heinz

Stadium if I thought it would help.

"Because the ritual is in the book."

Menold looked confused, but the rest of us knew what he meant, and it scared the hell out of us. "The book" he meant was one that wasn't supposed to exist, the one Trevor used a year ago to cover the city with the walking dead. The book bound in human flesh, inked in blood, and full of the most evil forms of hoodoo this side of a Lovecraft story. That the thing actually existed was a testament to man's stupidity. That anyone would want to use it was proof positive that Darwin was wrong.

"No," I said. "No way."

"You can't be serious," said Maggie.

"The ritual he's performing came from that book," said Bill. "I'm sure of it. How he got it, I don't know. But the best chance we have of fighting it is inside that book."

"There's got to be another way," said Maggie.

Bill shrugged.

"We'll find another way," I said.

"It's late," said Bill. "You're all exhausted. There are two extra rooms at the top of the stairs. You're welcome to sleep here tonight. Tomorrow, maybe we can figure something out."

Menold took the first room at the top of the stairs. Maggie and I, the second. Our room continued to fly in the face of every preconceived notion I had. The curtains on the windows were lace, and the wallpaper had a decidedly country turn to it. In fact, most of the room was done in shades of rose and pink. The queen bed had a pillow top and was covered by a quilt that looked handmade. It could've been made of stone for all I cared. I undressed and scooted between the sheets. Maggie did the same on the other side of the bed and turned out the lamp.

Moonlight filtered through the lace curtains, gave everything a blueish tint. In the relative darkness, I could just make out the shape of Maggie's head.

"I don't want to die," I whispered.

"You're not going to die," she said, though she didn't roll over to face me. Something in her voice told me she didn't quite believe it herself, but she would keep saying it until she did.

I snuggled up behind and draped my good arm around her waist. The scent of her hair, one of my favorite smells, gave me little comfort. I held her tight, almost in fear that if I let her go, my life would end right then and there.

She shifted and rolled over to face me. Moonlight glittered against her eyes, and she stroked my cheek in the darkness.

"You can't die," she said. "I need you. You always say that I saved you, that I made you a better person. That works both ways, you know. You made me a better me."

"Whatever happens tomorrow," I said, "I just want you to know that I love you. I know I say it all the time, but I mean it. I love you."

She pulled me closer and kissed me hard, lips wet with tears. We made love that night. Not animalistic sex or anything like that, but real tender lovemaking. Maybe it was her way of saying goodbye. Maybe it was mine. Maybe it was just a way for us both to hold on a little longer, to keep each other close and to feel the warmth of each other's bodies. Whatever the case, when we were spent, we drifted off into an uneasy sleep.

21

I watch a lot of movies. My favorites are horror flicks, but a close second are action thrillers, where the tough guy rattles off one-liners, looks cool while he outwits the bad guys, and he always gets the girl. Most of them end with a fade to black with the hero and the girl locked in a passionate embrace. Fade out, everyone lives happily ever after, end of story, roll credits. I love those movies because they're not realistic. They're an idealized version of what we wish would happen. Trouble is, life's not like that. In real life, a snarky comment will get a person shot. No one looks cool while running for his life. And, sure, he may get the girl, but what happens when they wake up the next day and realize that there's still garbage to take out, laundry to do, and everyone has bad breath in the morning?

I woke up before the sun hit the horizon, more clear-headed than I'd felt in a long time. Maggie was still asleep, her snores soft in the darkness. I slid out of bed quiet as I could manage, and got dressed. Everything but my shoes, which I decided to put on once I got downstairs. If she woke up, she'd insist on coming with me, so I didn't kiss her before I crept out of the room.

The house was dark, quiet. Good. I didn't want to explain myself Bill or Brea. Best if I was gone before they woke up.

"Going somewhere?"

Menold's voice scared the hell out of me. The lamp next to the couch clicked on. He was dressed. Even had his shoes on.

"What the hell are you doing sitting in the dark like that?" I whispered. "You almost gave me a heart attack, you asshole!"

"I've been awake for most of the night. Gave me time to think. I figured you'd get up and leave everyone high and dry."

"You don't know me at all." I sat down and put my shoes on. "I'm going to get the book. This is the safest place for Maggie, so I'm leaving her here. Bill says there might be something in there that can fight this thing and keep me alive? Great. More power to him. I'm just not willing to risk losing Maggie too."

Menold nodded and considered for a moment.

"I'm coming with you," he said. "You need someone to watch your back."

I thought about arguing, but the fact was, he was right. Obnoxious and a bit of a prick, but right. I might need someone good with a gun while I made a run to my apartment. No telling who or what might be waiting for me.

"Fine," I said. "But don't say I didn't warn you."

I began having second thoughts about my plan almost the moment we left Bill and Brea's house. It wasn't so much that I felt guilty about sneaking out, but that the moment we crossed the threshold, I felt eyes on me, like spiders on my arms, under my shirt, in my hair. A glance to Menold let me know he felt it too, although he probably called it his "cop sense" or something equally mundane.

"I don't like this," he said as I drove down the driveway. "Feels off. In my gut."

I didn't bother to answer. There was nothing I could say that would make him feel any better, and his jittery nature meant, I hoped, he would see attackers coming before they got to us.

"How many bullets do you have left?"

He pulled his gun and checked the clip.

"Five in the clip, one in the pipe, and one more full clip. Why?"

"We might need them."

At the edge of Bill's property, I stopped and got out to open the gate. As I walked toward the fence, a man stepped out from behind a bush. I recognized his suit as the same type the two dead guys at the playhouse wore. Maybe it was a kind of demonic uniform.

"You come on out of there," he said. "We'll make this quick."

"I'm not going to let you kill me."

He laughed, deep in his throat, and in it I heard at least three distinct voices.

"You think you can stop us?" he said. "You've got no chance. Surrender yourself to us and we'll try to rescue your friend."

"Andi?"

"Sure," he said. "Whatever. Just hand yourself over, willingly, and she'll go free."

"You're lying."

"Big talk, but you know we're going to kill you. How slow or how painful is up to you."

I turned my back on him and walked back to the car. Since he couldn't cross the property line thanks to Bill's wards, I didn't have to worry about being attacked from behind. And to turn my back on him was a grave insult. If he could've crossed the line, I'm sure he'd have ended me right there. But I let the gate swing wide.

"Me and my friend here have errands to run," I said. "Y'know, pick up the dry cleaning, loaf of bread from the market. You kids try not to get in front of the car when we go, or you might get hurt, okay?"

I didn't have to look back to feel him bristle. It stung my skin like needles. I slid back into the driver's seat and closed the door. Menold looked coiled and ready to leap out from under his hair.

"What was that?"

"Obstacle number one."

I put the car in gear and slammed my foot down on the accelerator. The wheels didn't spin out in proper tough-guy fashion, but the car did lurch as we headed through the gate. They were on us in the space of a breath. A dozen faces, twisted with rage and hatred, looked through the car's windows. Menold held his gun up, panic etched over his face.

"Calm down!" I shouted. "We'll be away from them in..."

A large rock crashed through one of the back seat windows, followed by a grinning face with wide yellow eyes. Menold didn't hesitate, but fired and sent a bullet through the man's eyeball. I felt the report from his pistol in my chest, and my ears rang in pain. The demon's head rocked, either from the impact or in surprise, before he slumped half in the window. I swerved and hit one of the possessed men, then swerved the other direction. The body dislodged and slid out the window onto the road behind us.

The back seat was washed in blood. The bullet didn't exit, but the hole it made bled plenty. We'd have a tough time explaining the damage to Maggie's insurance company, but at least we got away. As we sped down the road, a thought replayed in my head until I had to say it out loud.

"They're going to try again."

"Let 'em," said Menold. "That was easy."

"That was nothing. First wave. They won't give up."

We drove for a few minutes without incident, but the feeling of being watched wouldn't go away. I knew they were out there, watching, waiting for the perfect opportunity. As we approached the Fort Pitt Tunnel, I realized what that opportunity was.

"Ah, shit."

The Fort Pitt Tunnel is the longest one inside Pittsburgh city limits. It's a little over a half-mile's worth of two-lane pants-crapping terror. It runs under the thousand tons of rock that makes up Mount Washington, and once a car is inside, there is no way out except forward. A wreck inside the tunnel spells disaster for a number of reasons, not the least of which being the threat of carbon monoxide poisoning and death by other stupid drivers.

As we approached the tunnel, I glanced in the rear view mirror. Behind us, a pair of large trucks closed the distance.

"I see them," said Menold. "How good a driver are you?"

The thought of trying to switch drivers in motion almost made me laugh. Menold was not a small man, and there was no way he was going to get past my pudgy butt and into the driver's seat.

"I guess we'll find out," I said.

Morning rush was in full swing. Even without the trucks behind us, we were boxed in by folks on their morning commute. I couldn't speed up, couldn't veer off the road, couldn't do anything but drive straight into the big tube like a cow in a slaughterhouse chute.

"Can you maneuver with one arm?"

"I guess we'll find out," I said again.

At the tunnel's edge, both trucks gunned, twin dinosaur roars, and sped up.

"Floor it!" screamed Menold.

I did, but there was nowhere to go. The cars in front of us didn't seem in too big a hurry to get to work, and passing in the tunnel was not only illegal, it was borderline impossible. All we could do was brace for impact and hope the first hit didn't disable the car.

Steel met the recycled plastic of our bumper with a sickening crunch and enough force to snap both our heads back. It also forced us into the car in front of us. The car beside saw what happened and tried to speed up to get out of the way, but it, too, was penned in by the rest of the coffee brigade, with nowhere to go but forward.

The truck behind us sped up again and connected, which sent us into the car in front again. Instead of speeding up, the terrified driver in front of us slammed on his brakes. The airbag hit me like a prize fighter, square in the nose, and with about as much power. Tears flooded my eyes and I tasted blood. The skin on my face burned, and I couldn't breathe through my nose anymore.

"Floor it!" Menold's voice cut through the rushing wave in my head and my foot obeyed, despite my having no memory of telling it to do so. The car lurched and whined as it slammed into the guy in front of us again and pushed his car into the wall of the tunnel.

"Head for the center," screamed Menold.

I jerked the wheel blind for what I hoped would be the center, and stood on the gas pedal. Through the tears, I saw red lights as other drivers threw on their brakes, heard tires squeal and horns blare.

Over it all, I heard Menold shout. "Smile, you son of a bitch!"

The report from his gun followed. What was left of the back window of the car shattered and he fired again. My ears rang as pain rocked my head from the discharge, but I didn't let it stop me. I wiped my eyes against the acrid burn of cordite with my shirt sleeve, gritted my teeth, and plowed forward, and hoped I didn't kill anyone in the process.

The truck behind us swerved into the other lane, leaving it almost sideways in the tunnel. The second truck struck the tail end of the first and kept coming.

"We're almost through!" I shouted.

Menold turned and said something. I couldn't hear him for the damage his gunfire did to my hearing, but I thought it looked something like "Keep going."

We popped out of the end of the tunnel where the road opened up into four lanes. I took the farthest right one and exited, then got off the highway as quickly as I could. Maggie's car protested at the speed of the turn, but we managed to get down and into the grid of Pittsburgh.

It took us a few minutes to make it to my apartment because we drove around and tried to avoid both the police and the other factions that wanted me dead for whatever reason. When we were in the neighborhood, I thought about parking a couple of blocks away. If the police had my apartment staked out, the car would be a dead give-away that we were there. However, once we got what we came for, I didn't want to take the risk of walking those blocks back to the car. Being out in the open wasn't part of my plan, if one could call my loose framework of stupid ideas an actual "plan."

I parked the car and, with a nod, we both got out and ran to the entrance. We didn't stop until we got to the elevator.

"We were made," huffed Menold. "Cop in a car outside."

"You sure?"

"Judging from the look on his face, yeah, he knew who we were. We've probably got about three minutes until back-up arrives."

"Great."

As luck would have it, the elevator in my building was in a good mood and it only took us a minute and a half to get up to my apartment. We walked past the stain on the floor, still marked with flags and tape from the forensic team, and I shuddered.

"Your neighbors are probably calling the police right now," said Menold.

"I don't care," I said. "If this book is the only thing that can save Andi, then I have to get it."

I pushed the door open and glanced around. Nothing seemed out of place, nothing ready to attack. Menold followed me in and closed the door behind me.

"What the hell is so special about this book?"

"You know your Bible?" He looked pained, like he thought I might start preaching or something. "You remember who Moses was, right? He had a brother, Aaron, who basically was possessed and wrote this book under demonic possession."

"So? What's in it?"

"The keys to what you'd call Hell."

He whistled as I struggled to remember the proper words to disarm the wards on the vault room.

"Where'd you find that?"

"It found me," I said. "The damned thing isn't supposed to exist. No one'd ever seen it until it somehow wound up in my mailbox. But if Bill says there's something that can help Andi and get me out of this in one piece, I'm willing to risk it."

The door came open and I stood in the doorway for a moment. My stomach churned, as it always did when I entered the vault room. My skin itched and I felt dirty, greasy from the contact with the air. But negative feelings happened every time I walked into the room. With a room full of negative mojo, it was to be expected.

The book sat inside a steel firebox that was covered in permanent marker runes, wards, symbols, and other images designed to keep the bad thing, and all its powers, in.

"If no one else has ever seen it, how does Bill know what kind of spells are in there?" Menold's confusion caught me off guard, but it started wheels turning in my head.

It couldn't be. Just couldn't. Bill was my friend. He and Brea were the only people outside of Maggie and Andi that I trusted. He bailed me out of jail, fought alongside us, even gave Maggie his car. But then, how did he know? Kevin was dead, it couldn't be Blossom or Neighbor Bob. Reneau had too much to lose in something as overt as a bid to wipe clean all the souls on the planet. But Bill and Brea? It couldn't be. If it were, then...

"No..."

I left Maggie alone with them.

22

In action movies, there is, inevitably, a moment where the hero realizes his partner was working against him the whole time. Call it the moment of ultimate betrayal. It's that point when the good guy realizes that he left his kid with the serial killer, or when the cop figures out that the only way the bad guy could remain one step ahead of him was if he were in on the investigation. I always wondered what that felt like.

Way back, when my friends walked away from me, I thought I knew. But I was wrong. There was no preparing for the torrent of bile that washed up my throat, the panicked race to find some other solution, the utter sense of loss.

"We have to go," I said. "I know who's behind all of this."

"Who?" scoffed Menold. "The old man and his wife? They're a couple of hippies!"

Before I could argue, I got confirmation. The Scats stopped moving for a moment, then they moved, en masse, toward me. Even Menold could see them as they crawled up my legs. The moment the first one touched me, I felt a tingle of emotion, too faint to identify. The more that climbed on, the stronger it became until it was undeniable. Fear. Maggie's.

"No no no no NO!"

They sent their puppet minions after us, drove us toward them as if they were herding sheep. Then took us in to protect us from those who would stop them. All they needed was the damned book.

And now that they had Maggie, I was about to give it to them. *You'll want to give in.* Wasn't that what one of the demons said? He was right. Anything for Maggie's freedom and safety.

The Scats retreated and left me standing, tears of impotent rage streaming down my face.

"What the hell was that?"

I didn't have time to answer. Loud bangs on the door silenced any reply before I could say it.

"Stanley Cooper!" I was pretty sure this new group of cops weren't puppets or demons. They were just ordinary Pittsburgh PD doing their jobs. "We have a warrant for your arrest. Open the door!"

"Isn't there another way out of here?"

"No," I said. "The only two doors are on the ground floor, and we're four floors up."

"What about the fire escape?"

"No," I said. "I got a problem with heights."

The pounding increased in intensity.

"You'd better get over it," shouted Menold. "Or get ready to go to jail. Your lady friend needs you, right?"

I swallowed hard and moved to the window. As I slid it open, I heard the sound of something solid, most likely a battering ram, slam into my door.

Menold ducked through the window and stuck out his hand to help me through. I handed him the box containing the book.

"Come on!" he shouted. "They're not playing around!"

"Go on!" I said. "I'll meet you down there!"

"Don't be stupid!"

The ram thundered against the door again.

"Just go! I'll be there in a minute!"

Menold shook his head and cursed under his breath, but tucked the box under his arm and hurried down the fire escape. It might've made more sense for me to follow, but I couldn't. Not out there, not four stories up. It was too high. I knew what would happen. I'd get out there, look around at all the open air, and freeze up. I'd wind up sobbing like a baby as I clutched the metal support. My rational mind knew I wouldn't die, that the fire escape wasn't the same as falling from a building.

Phobias, however, aren't rational.

I slammed the window behind him, relocked it, then turned to face the door. For as long as I'd known Maggie, she practiced the art of working with energy. She called it magic. I called it energy manipulation. By whatever name it went, it amounted to the same thing: Maggie was damned good at drawing energy from within herself, and from outside sources. I watched her do it all the time, and even did a little myself when she needed it. All it took, according to her, was faith.

I closed my eyes and shifted my perception. The world around me leaped into brilliant colors, as if my apartment were made of neon. I didn't have faith on which to rely, but I did have a pretty good grasp on how the whole energy thing worked. I just hoped I could do it quickly.

With my perception shifted, it was easy to see what put off energy, where the currents ran like rivers of power, and how to tap into them. I hoped. I stuck my good arm into one of the currents, then concentrated. At first, nothing happened, but a heartbeat later the current shifted and ran up my arm, into my body. I felt energized. The hair on my arm stood at attention. I kept drawing power in until I felt like I'd had too much coffee. Then I broke contact and headed to the door.

"Alright!" I shouted. "I'm coming! Don't break the damned door down!"

The pounding stopped. I took a deep breath and unlatched the door. Before I could open it all the way, four officers, one of them plainclothes, rushed the apartment. The three uniforms had their weapons drawn. I backed across the room.

"Stanley Cooper," said the plainclothes guy. "I am placing you under arrest on suspicion of murder, destruction of public property, avoiding arrest..."

"I don't have time for this," I said.

The officers must've taken what I said as a cue, because two of them grabbed me. That's when I let go of all the energy I'd absorbed. Both of them went rigid as the wave of pure power erupted from my body. The other uniform and the plainclothes guy didn't have time to react before they both were knocked on their butts too. The two officers that had me slumped to the ground, singed, but still breathing.

For a moment, I was so surprised it actually worked that all I wanted to do was whoop and jump up and down. But then the other half of my brain kicked in. Maggie. Andi. Bill and Brea. My electric eel trick wouldn't work on them, I figured, and a toe to toe fight was a sure way to get myself barbequed. But there wasn't much choice. The only people strong enough to have a chance against them were the remaining members of Evergreen, and I didn't have time to round them up. Unless...

"Listen up!"

There was no time for one of Andi's candle rituals, and I wasn't about to get naked to talk to them, but I figured that if the Scats were as intelligent as Andi claimed, they might listen. Even if they didn't, I was no worse off for trying.

"Find me help," I said, and concentrated hard on Reneau, Neighbor Bob, and Blossom. "Track me and find me."

The Scats didn't seem to get the message or even notice. Like I said, no worse off for trying, if a little disappointed.

I hurried out the door and took the stairs down. By the time I made it out the front door of the building, I was sucking wind and it felt like my heart wanted to climb out of my chest.

I took two steps out of the front door when a dark blue sedan screeched to a halt in front of me. Menold gestured from behind the steering wheel.

"What'd you do?" I asked as I got in the passenger's side. "Hotwire a car? Adding grand theft auto to our list of offenses?"

"It's the stakeout cop's car," said Menold. "Standard procedure to leave the keys in it in case it needs to be moved or if you need to pursue a suspect. How'd you get past them?"

"Better you don't know," I said. "Head for the Strip District."

"Why?"

"I think I know where they're holding Andi."

Almost a year ago, when I lost the use of my arm and when I first came into contact with the book and all its terrible hoodoo, Bill made me believe he was my friend, that he didn't want the book. He did little things that made me take him into my confidence, treat him as someone beyond suspicion. He was my friend, or so I thought.

One of the things he did was show me something of his past, something that no one in Evergreen knew. Even Maggie didn't know about it, which made me think I could trust him. I swore I'd never tell anyone about the warehouse where his past slept.

"Through there," I said as Menold piloted the car to the security gate. He flashed his badge at the guard, who opened the gate and let us through. Once inside, it took me a few minutes to remember which warehouse was his. To be honest, they all kind of looked alike, until I shifted my perception.

Several of them lit up, glowed a bit to indicate the possessions inside were of some value, at least to their owners. As we rounded a corner, I found what I wanted. Bill's warehouse didn't just glow, it pulsed. And out of it, a weak beacon shone.

"There," I said. "She's in there."

"How do you know?"

I didn't answer, or even look at him. In fact, I didn't even wait for the car to come to a complete stop before I was out and headed for the front door. I almost didn't hear him shout.

"Look out!"

I turned too late to avoid the security guard's tackle. In the glimpse I got before I went down, I noticed he was a big fellow, the size of a linebacker. I also noticed the black flame that surrounded his body.

"Can't let you go in there," he said, a hideous smile on his face. "This could've gone so much easier for you."

"You bastards couldn't have just *told me* that it was Bill?"

"Would you have believed us?"

He had a point.

"Time to die," he said. "And it's going to hurt a lot."

He drew back clawed hands to slash me to death, but I heard two pops. The demon's head jerked and a look of surprise crossed his face, then he slumped forward, dead from Menold's gun.

"You okay?" he said as he rolled the hulking brute off me.

"No," I said.

238

The warehouse glowed, but there was no threshold, no curtain of energy around it. All the power came from the objects inside. It struck me as strange that Bill wouldn't have warded the place against intruders, or even against me for that matter. But I opened the door and nothing happened. Menold and I stepped inside, and nothing happened. In fact, nothing continued to happen until we were both a good ways inside. Then nothing stopped happening, and everything started.

The door slammed behind us.

"Damn," I said. He did ward it, only on the inside instead of the outside. It was like an old-fashioned wind-up mouse trap: Getting in was easy. Getting out, there would be the trick.

You have one chance.

Bill's voice came from every corner, echoed off every wall.

Leave now, and you won't be hurt.

"Where is he?" Menold turned in place, searched the upper levels of the warehouse for Bill or speakers, gun pointed high.

"Not here," I said. "It's a recording."

In the time I'd known Maggie, I saw her throw up some pretty nasty protection spells. Electric shocks, feelings of dread, pain illusions, all designed to keep a person out, not hurt them. I ticked off the list of spells she'd used, and wondered which one, if any or all, Bill employed, or if he had something a little meaner up his sleeve.

"I don't see anything," said Menold.

"Keep your eyes open. You go that way, I'll go this way. Shout if you find her."

"Did it ever occur to you that I don't have the slightest idea what this 'Andi' person looks like?"

"Tell you what," I said. "The first kidnapped terrified girl you come across in this warehouse? That's probably her."

"Smartass."

We split up. Sure, I knew it was a classic horror movie mistake, but we didn't have time to waste. The warehouse was huge packed to the gills with old trailers and carnival crap, and if we walked together, it would take us hours to search the place. Split up, I hoped only half as many hours.

I crept between carts and booths, shelves and stacks, Bill's threat still heavy in my ears. The further I walked, the more it made sense. He wouldn't be overt. He wouldn't go for the defense with pyrotechnics or big bad monsters. It would be subtle, subversive. Whatever he had, whatever we triggered, it would sneak up on us and take us where we were most vulnerable.

"Holy shit! The shadows!"

Menold's voice echoed across the warehouse, followed by two shots of gunfire, then screams. I looked around until I figured out what he meant. The shadows, every dark spot on the walls and floors, slid together, congealed into one mass of cold dark, a tide of blackness. It got Menold, and it was bearing down on me. I did the only thing I could think to do. I ran.

Einstein said nothing was faster than the speed of light.

He might've been right, but dark moves just as fast as light. It caught me in no time and swallowed me up in its frigid embrace. The last thing I saw as it closed around my face was the giant cloth banner of William the Magnificent staring down at me.

It was cold. So very cold. Wind snatched at my pant legs and jacket. I opened my eyes and found myself on top of the building that killed me, harness on, caulking gun in my hand. The butterflies in my stomach changed to vultures in a heartbeat. On either side, Maggie and Andi stood, both with sardonic looks on their faces.

"Little man," said Maggie.

"Loser," said Andi.

"Is this the best you got?" I shouted. I'd already been through the whole "worst fear" game with Trevor. Gone through, and come out the other side. Sure, the things that scared me then still scared me, but my fear didn't rule me. My insecurities no longer controlled my actions. At least, I liked to think they didn't.

Maggie and Andi both turned toward the gaping abyss that was the edge of the building, took each other by the hand, and jumped off.

I'd be lying if I said the sight didn't make my stomach flip, even though I knew it wasn't real. The darkness, the shadows, played on the victim's worst fears. For me, the deaths of Maggie and Andi were the worst things I could imagine, second only to my own. Which meant that the only way out of the darkness was to go *toward* the scary thing, not away. Away took the victim further into the darkness. Toward, I hoped, would bring me out into the real world. It was worth a try, anyway.

I didn't wait to see what else Bill's nasty little trap could conjure, but ran as fast as I could toward the edge of the roof. When I reached the edge, I launched myself into empty air. I flailed, and I'm sure I screamed, but when I hit the concrete, it wasn't at all as far down as it was the first time. One second, I saw the buildings rushing past on my way for a meet-and-greet with the sidewalk, the next I was face down on the concrete floor of the warehouse again. My face stung where it hit the cement, but I was otherwise uninjured. I clambered to my feet and stumbled forward.

The cart marked "House of Mirrors" stood out in that it was open. The others were still collapsed into their individual trailers, folded away for easy travel, but the house of mirrors was set up, ready to receive customers. The image from my dream, in which Andi sat surrounded by dozens of visions of herself, made sense. If she was anywhere, I bet it would be there.

The only trouble was, if she was in the house of mirrors, odds were good Bill and Brea rigged it too with some other kind of trap. There wasn't time to think about what long-legged beastie was about to chew on my head. Andi needed me.

"Andi?" I stepped over the threshold into the trailer. Mirrors covered every wall, warped in every conceivable way. Fat images, skinny images, distorted versions of myself stared back at me as I walked down the hallway. The way the trailers were set up, the hallways turned and turned again in a sort of spiral, until the patron came to the center and was then shown the way out. It made sense that the center of the thing would be where Andi waited. I glanced toward one of the mirrors and froze. In the image, I saw myself as I was a year ago. Two healthy arms, fewer lines and scars, longer hair, and a thinner waistline. Then the image shifted. The arm withered, the waist swelled. I watched what a year of my life did to me, until the image passed what I was, and moved toward what I would become. First I lost the arm, which was horrifying enough. But then I lost a leg, then an eye, then I watched as Maggie was torn to pieces by wild creatures I couldn't even name. I watched as invisible razors slashed her delicate flesh, and I was powerless to prevent it. Rot took hold as I watched, and my reflection became a shambling nightmare, a parody of life. It took me a span of a breath to see what I was to become, what would happen to those I loved, should I continue my course.

The problem was, while I didn't know what would happen if I didn't, I had a pretty good idea, and it was worse. If anyone else walked through those doors, they'd have been scared out of their minds. They'd have run if they even made it as far as the wagon. But it wasn't just anyone who walked through the door. It was me. And the only thing I feared more than the great dirt nap was being alone, being left that way because the people around me died because of my cowardice. And I wasn't about to let that happen.

I hurried down the hall, turned, turned again, until I came to the core. In the center of the room lay Andi, hands and feet bound, blindfolded and gagged. Her shirt was torn across the back, and long cuts gouged her skin. Not deep enough to kill her or put her in danger of bleeding to death, but deep enough to hurt like ever-loving hell.

"Andi!" I cradled her head in my lap as I untied the gag and blindfold.

"Stan?" She blinked, then broke into hysterical sobs. "How could they? Why? Why? They cut me!"

"Shhh," I said. "I know. We need to get you out of here. Can you walk?"

"I don't know," she sniffed. "I'll try."

The knots in the ropes around her wrists were a pain to get undone with one hand, but I managed it. Together, we worked on the knots at her ankles, then I helped her to her feet. She glanced toward the mirrors around us and let out a panicked shriek.

In the reflection, she looked skeletal, strung out and malnourished, except for the bulge at her belly. The scabs that covered her face were only slightly less horrifying than the dead look in her eyes.

"That's not me," she cried. "Not me. Not me."

"No," I said. "It isn't. Don't look. Lean on me. I'll guide you out."

We made it out of the trailer fine, but darkness surrounded us. I knew I could make it through, but Andi was weak, tired from her ordeal. I didn't know if she had enough energy to fight, but I needed her. I also needed to find Menold.

"The dark," I said. "It shows you whatever you're most afraid of."

"I don't want to go out there," she said. Fresh tears rolled down her face.

"We have to," I said. "I'm here. I'm not going to let anything happen to you again. I promise."

She sniffed and nodded. Together, we stepped off the trailer into the darkness. As it wrapped us in icy black, Andi screamed. Her grip tightened on mine.

"Don't let go!" I shouted. "It's not real! You have to fight it!"

You got her killed.

Maggie lay in a coffin in front of me.

She died saving your worthless life.

A coffin soaked in blood.

For the rest of your life, you'll be alone.

The coffin lowered into the ground.

You should've died instead.

White heat burned inside me, desperate and full of fury. As I watched the coffin slip beneath the ground, I felt something crack, a dam, a wall. My aura expanded, and heat flooded my body. The darkness cowered, pulled back away from me, retreated to the corners again.

What flooded through me was like rage, but without the hatred, without the negative aspects. It was power, determination, all the things that told me that, whatever Bill's sick little spell showed me, I could keep it from happening. I made my own choices. And there was no way in this world or any other I was going to let Maggie die.

The dam broke. Heat and light poured out of my body in an explosion of pure will. It lasted for only a moment, only a second, then it was gone, and the warehouse looked normal again.

"How..?"

"Later," I said. I hoped that when "later" came, I might have some clue as to what just happened. But at that moment, I needed to find Menold and get Andi to someplace safe.

We found him in the middle of an aisle, gun pulled, clicking on empty, slide locked. He had the wild-eyed look usually reserved for war veterans.

"Get away!" he screamed as we approached.

"It's us," I said as I made my voice as soothing as possible. "Put the gun down."

"I said get the fuck away from me!" He pointed the gun at me and pulled the trigger. It clicked, empty, but that didn't stop him from pulling the trigger over and over again. When I didn't die from a hail of bullets, he put the gun to his temple and tried again.

There wasn't time to be gentle. I snatched the gun away and, before I realized what I was doing, slapped him with my withered arm. To my surprise, it responded.

"Get up!"

He shook his head, looked at Andi, and scrambled to his feet.

"Move!" I pushed him toward the door. Outside, I guided Andi to the back seat, put Menold in the front passenger's, and I took the wheel. The keys were in the ignition.

"Good cop." I turned the key and started the car.

"Where are we going?" Andi's voice sounded tired.

"Someplace safe," I said. "And someone I know wants to see you."

245

My apartment was, in all probability, crawling with cops. If it wasn't before, there was no doubt the police would be watching it now. No see-um spell or not, the door was wide open when I left, and there was a better than one-hundred-percent chance that the vault was compromised. I shuddered to think of what would happen to the artifacts and haunted doodads, and what they might do together in police lock-up, but there wasn't time to go try to explain what happened. Besides, I'd seen enough of the inside of the Pittsburgh jail cells, thanks very much. There was only one place we could go.

The tattoo parlor was still closed when we got there, as was the club, which suited me just fine. It meant the parking lot would be empty and there would be fewer people who wanted to know what two guys and a badly injured girl were doing, climbing into a storm drain. A few tense moments passed, during which I tried to maneuver Andi down in the least painful way I could manage. Menold wasn't much better, still in shock from whatever he saw in Bill and Brea's darkness spell. He had moments of lucidity, but he kept talking to himself, kept looking like he expected to be attacked. Whatever he saw messed him up bad.

I led them through the tunnels to the first of Maggie's threshold locks. I wasn't nearly as skilled as Maggie, but I knew what to say, how to get the lock to open and let us through with our dignity intact. Once past, we made our way through the tunnel at a slower pace than I would've liked. Menold looked to be in a daze, staggering along like a zombie. Andi, on the other hand, couldn't move without considerable pain. It upset me to see her in such a state, but I had to push them both on if I was going to get them to the shop.

When we came to the final lock, I opened it, pushed the other two inside, and let it close behind us. The basement was

Scott A. Johnson

dark, uninviting, like a basement should be.

"Call her," I said. "She missed you."

"I'm home." Andi's voice was weak, but it carried throughout the basement, echoed off the concrete walls, and up the stairs. The basement light came on, and a warm breeze that smelled of lavender wafted through the air. Andi caught the scent, and fresh tears trickled down to her smile. "I missed you too," she said.

I helped her up the stairs into the work room. Menold followed, like he'd never seen the place before. Andi laid face down on the sofa while I hurried to get the first aid kit. I didn't get to see the extent of her injuries at the warehouse. Too busy trying to get all of us out in one piece. But when she lifted the back of her shirt, my throat knotted and my breath hitched at the cruelty imposed on her young flesh.

Across her back, cuts ran from side to side and from her shoulders to the small of her back. She winced as I dabbed at them with a wet washcloth.

"Salt," she sniffed. "They rubbed salt into the cuts. Said the scars would mark me, make me one of the blessed in the new order."

She lifted her torn shirt over her head. Only then did I see the cuts for what they were. An evergreen in a circle.

"I'm so sorry for this," I said. "I didn't want any of this to happen."

"You couldn't have known," said Andi. "I'm home now, so I'll be fine. Maggie'll fix me up something to help with the..."

Her voice trailed off as she scanned my face. I'm not sure how I looked, but if it was anything close to how I felt, it wouldn't take a psychic to read me.

"Where's Maggie?"

I couldn't answer. The lump in my throat wouldn't let

words past.

"We've gotta go get her!" She struggled to stand, but winced in pain and sunk back down on her stomach on the couch.

"You're not going anywhere," I said. "I think you've had enough."

As if on cue, Bitsy jumped up on the couch and sat square on Andi's butt.

"Like I can't move you," snorted Andi.

Without even shifting positions, the little cat extended the claws on both front feet and sunk them into the tender flesh of Andi's posterior. She yelped, half in surprise, half in pain.

"You're not going anywhere," I repeated. "Menold and I..."

"So much blood." Menold stood across the room, his eyes on the floor in front of him. "Didn't think one bullet would do that. Broke the back of the skull out, and he died. Didn't know. Daddy said don't play. Said we'd be in trouble, but Petey wouldn't listen. He wanted to be a cop like Daddy."

His greatest fear, the thing the darkness forced him to relive.

"Daddy's going to be mad. I put it in his hand and ran. When Daddy got home, I said he did it to himself. But it was me. I did it. It was my fault."

He broke down into tears and slid down the wall into a corner.

"My fault. My fault." With every word, he slapped himself in the forehead.

I was on my own.

23

Andi slept. For a while, Menold did nothing but sob quietly and mutter, swiped out at shadows before they could touch him. But he quieted as exhaustion dragged him down and put him to sleep. I hoped he didn't dream.

I sat in the main room in the shop in the dark. It wasn't that I was worried that someone would see in. The shop darkened her windows and no light came in or got out. In fact, I wasn't even sure what time of day it was. I sat in the dark because I wanted to. It suited my mood. Most days, I didn't like being alone or quiet because it gave me too much time to think, to brood. But I needed the time. I had to work things out in my head.

Bill and Brea wouldn't stay at their house. For starters, the cloud I saw was over Pittsburgh proper, which meant that wherever their conjuring spot was, it was somewhere downtown. I could probably drive around and find it, but then what? They weren't some second-rate conjurers or garden-variety no-goodniks. They were two of the most powerful energy benders in the state, maybe even the world for all I knew. No way they were just going to let me walk in and take Maggie without a fight.

I tossed around some serious power over the last twenty-four hours, but I didn't know how, or if it would be enough, or even if I could do it again. Any way I looked at it, I was good and hosed.

"Penny for your thoughts?" I looked up to see Andi in the doorway, a blanket draped across her shoulders.

"I don't know what to do," I said. "I'm in way over my head."

"Since when has that made any difference?"

"Since he took you and Maggie away from me."

She came over and sat next to me.

"Remember that night," she said, "when you and Taylor stuffed me in the trunk?"

"Taylor did that," I said. "I was horrified."

"Remember how no one could get me to come out? Not until you walked over?"

"Yeah."

"Know why? Because I knew then that you were a good man. You didn't try to force me out or cajole me or anything. You just talked to me. You let me know I was safe."

"So?"

"So you're a good man," she said. "Do you know the situation I was in before I met you guys?"

"Yeah," I said. "Living in a house with possessed roommates..."

"No," she said. "I mean more than that. I didn't have anyone. I didn't care about anyone or anything. Not really. I was braver than I was smart and almost got myself killed. If you hadn't stuffed me in that trunk, the rats would've killed me."

"Yeah, well, things are different now," I said. She was trying to help, but all it did was make me feel worse. A "good man" wouldn't put his friends, his lover, in danger. He'd be able to save them.

"How so?"

"I didn't know you then. Maggie and I weren't... together."

"And that makes it different, how?"

"It makes things worse!" I got up and walked across the room. There wasn't anything to the gesture, only that I couldn't stand to feel her eyes on me. "I can't think straight because all I can think about is what if she dies? What if I can't save her? What if Bill and Brea succeed? Hell, I don't even know where they are! And even if I did, what am I supposed to do about it? You and Maggie are the ones with the power, not me. Kevin's dead, you're busted up, and Maggie... And even if you weren't, you think you could go mano a mano with Bill or Brea? Much less both of them?"

"You could ask for help," she said. "What about the other Evergreens?"

"No," I said. "I don't want to drag anyone else into this. Besides, I don't think they'd help me. Bob's grafted to his church, Reneau hates my guts, and Blossom has her hands full protecting her own domain. I'm on my own."

"You should still ask," she said. "Couldn't hurt."

"No time."

"Leave that to me," she said.

Andi was the one who figured out how to use Scats as a sort of metaphysical instant messaging system. A combination of ritual and energy manipulation, she managed to get the little buggers' attention. However, like Maggie, she only worked skyclad. Also, it burned a whole lot of energy, which she didn't have at the moment.

"You can't," I said. "You're too weak."

"I can try." She stood, teetered, then slumped back down to the floor. "Maybe you're right. You'll have to do it."

"*Me?*" She was still in shock, delirious. She had to be.

She and Maggie were the magic-users, not me. Magic took faith, and I had none.

"You," she said. "I can't, so you have to."

"But..."

"I have enough faith in you for the both of us," she said. "You have an advantage over Maggie. She has to visualize magic to make it work, but you can see it. You *know* if it's working or not."

"Yeah, but..."

"Please," she said. "You need to at least try. I don't want you getting killed either. You keep saying you love us, but we love you just as much. We don't want anything to happen to you either."

Maggie had said it often enough that it sunk in. But it never occurred to me that someone like Andi could care so much for someone like me. She was, to me, like a daughter, or even a kid sister. And what was I to her? Maybe not a father figure, but someone she cared about.

"Okay," I said. "I'll try."

"Good," she said. "Take off your clothes."

"Now just a damned minute!"

She smirked. "Like I haven't seen you naked before."

Most people have an innate talent for one particular thing or another. Some folks can look at a car and tell you how it works without a day of mechanic school. Other people are good with numbers, or music, or any other thing that the powers that be decide to bless them with. It's called a knack. Everyone's got a knack for something. Maggie's knack is for magic. It seems to be something she was born to do, something that comes as naturally to her as breathing does to the rest of us. My knack, however, seems to be for getting into embarrassing or uncomfortable situations.

The floor was cold. I tried not to think about the fact that I sat naked in the middle of the main area of the shop, surrounded by candles, with a girl twenty years younger than me so close I could smell the sweat in her hair.

"I'm not comfortable," I said.

"Why?"

"I'm naked, for one thing."

"A little warmer please." The shop complied with a warm breeze. "Better?"

I nodded.

"Okay, now shift your sight so you can see them."

I did as I was told. The room sprang to life with thousands of the little creatures.

"Now focus. Concentrate on them. Make them listen to you."

"How in the hell am I supposed to do that?"

"Concentrate on them," she said. "You don't talk, you push out with your need, with what you want. Your energy into theirs. They're beings of energy, so infuse them with your will."

It all sounded like bullshit to me. Not what Andi said, but that she believed *I* could do it. But, if she believed it, I figured I could try. If not for myself, for Maggie. She was the real driving force, the real reason. It wasn't that I believed I *could* do it. I *had* to do it.

The light around my body grew, spread over the room until it radiated out from me to every wall. The Scats stopped moving and stood at attention. So far so good. For a moment, it seemed like I had them rapt, then they moved again, this time in a tide toward me. I must've flinched.

"That's good!" said Andi. "Put your will into them."

253

Before I could ask just what the hell she meant by that, I felt them all, thousands of perceptions, all joined as one hive mind. There were no words as such, but every thought, every tiny emotion echoed into infinity, every voice different but tied together. Through them, I saw Menold, still in the corner. I saw the buildings across the street, and down the block, and further than I could easily perceive. It was the strangest feeling, one of limited omnipotence. I stretched out with my mind until I found the warmth I needed, the softness that I missed.

"She's alive," I said, breathless. "They haven't hurt her yet, but she's in the dark, and alone."

"Where?"

"Can't see," I said. "They don't know the name of the place, only that it's a place of power."

"It's a start. Now, focus and send your will through them."

I did as I was told. No words, just an emotion, a feeling. *Help.* It was all I needed to say. Whoever there was in the city who could help me, I hoped the Scats would get the message through, and that the receiver would know what it meant. I pushed the feeling a few more times, then let go. The Scats retreated, and scattered. As they left, I felt my energy level drop. My perception shifted back to normal, and I was again privy to only what was around me.

"Did it work?"

"I think so," I said. "What happens now?"

"Now, you put out the candles in reverse order, then get dressed."

"About damned time."

"Then you rest and we wait," she said. "Someone's bound to answer."

"And if they don't?"

254

"We'll think of something," said Andi. She grimaced as she pushed herself up off the floor and shuffled back to the back room. "I need sleep. I feel so drained."

It was little wonder. The cuts on her back weren't the only harmful things done to her. While my perception was shifted, I had stolen a look at her aura. Where it usually radiated white and pink, more powerful than just about any other person I'd seen, it flickered, weak, with patches of brown to mark her pain and suffering. Another mark for which Bill and Brea had to answer.

The trouble was, I still didn't know how to stop them. I didn't believe anyone was coming to help me. The Scats could find anyone, but I had no guarantee anyone would understand. And even if they did, who would care? They'd be smarter to get out of the city as fast as they could, try to hide from the coming storm. If they could. A person could build a shelter from a hurricane or tornado, but could there be a shelter to shield a person from a storm that aimed at the soul? Somehow, I doubted it.

She was being held in a place of power. City Hall? Not likely. The East Liberty church? It was old enough, powerful enough, but it didn't seem like the kind of place they would use. Hell, there were buildings all over Pittsburgh's skyline that could be called "powerful," yet none of them seemed right.

The puzzle of where they were was, however, smaller than the big glaring question of what I planned to do once I got there. They'd kill her, that was certain. There could be no doubt. All the blood they'd shed, what was one more dead witch? A straight fight would be a combination of bad comedy and disaster. A mosquito had a better chance at taking down an elephant. And if I just handed myself over to them, Maggie would die anyway in the oncoming storm. Or, at least, she wouldn't be Maggie anymore.

There seemed to be only one solution, and it was one I

didn't like at all. I had to die. I had to hand myself over to them, then die before they could enact their plan. If I was alive, they'd keep coming for me, and everyone I knew would be cannon fodder. I refused to be responsible for anyone else's death.

The next question that came was how it was to be done. I didn't own a gun, Menold's was out of bullets, and I was pretty sure they'd know I had one on me anyway. It had to be something small, easily concealable, and fast.

Some of those are poisonous.

I hurried to Maggie's workshop. Andi slept sound on the couch. Good. She needed the sleep. And I didn't need her to know what I was up to. Menold lay in the corner, also asleep, though he twitched and writhed with horrible dreams. I felt bad for the guy. Therapy was expensive, and from the looks of him, he was going to need plenty.

The cabinet where Maggie kept her herbs was not locked, which was a blessing for me. Pinned to the inside of the door was a list of everything inside, complete with uses and properties. I skimmed until I found the ones marked "poisonous" with little skulls and crossbones. There were more than a dozen of them, the names of which I had only vague knowledge. Foxglove, belladonna, hellebore, they all sounded witchy and dangerous, but as I read the effects of each, I figured they'd all act too slow. When it came right down to it, I had no idea what I was looking at, so I closed my eyes and pointed. My finger landed on hemlock. I searched the cabinet until I found a small jar that contained the herb, dried and ready for use. In the drawer below, Maggie stored gelatin capsules. I took one out and filled it with the deadly herb, then I just stared at it.

Maggie's notes said hemlock was a convulsive, that it killed by respiratory failure. It also said it was fast acting. Part of me wondered why she even had it in her shop. The other part didn't care. It suited my needs.

I wrote out a note on a steno pad on Maggie's workbench, then went down into the basement. No sense in waiting. I didn't need Andi to try to talk me out of what needed to be done. Better off if she woke to find me gone. Maggie could explain later. I hated to leave her with such a burden, but it had to be done. I didn't know of any other way.

The obvious problem was still that I didn't know where they were. The cloud I saw hovered over the main part of the city, but there were dozens, hundreds even, of places where a person could set up shop. But the Scats said Maggie was being held in a place of power.

Rivers used to be revered as powerful, said Bob. *Pagans and the like still feel that rivers carry the life force of the Earth from place to place.*

The three rivers of Pittsburgh converged to a central point, which, if Bob was correct, would've been the single most powerful spot in the entire city. And there happened to be a structure right where the three came together.

"No," I said. "They wouldn't be that brassy, would they?"

24

I'm not a big fan of football. I know it's dangerous and damned near blasphemous to say so in a town like Pittsburgh, but I just never saw the appeal. Give me hockey any day of the week, but other sports just don't interest me. The rest of Pittsburgh, however, is full of lunatics when it comes to football. Every season, the streets are filled with Steelers memorabilia, people wearing their black and gold jerseys, and for good reason. They keep winning. No, they don't have a spotless record or anything of the sort, but they win more than they lose, and have an impressive collection of Super Bowl rings to prove it.

It never occurred to me before that the location of their home stomping grounds might have something to do with it, but, sure enough, Heinz Field sat right where the three rivers met. All that energy, all that power, all the hope of the fans magnified by the power of the rivers, gave the Steelers an advantage that defied luck or logic. Too bad the influence didn't carry over to PNC Park, where Pittsburgh's baseball team, the Pirates, played.

I left Andi and Menold sleeping. There was no point in waking them. Andi would only try to talk me out of what I was about to do and Menold would just drool and cry more. I didn't have time to argue. I needed to go before I lost my nerve.

The note sat on the counter where Andi would be sure to see it. I kissed the top of her head on my way out, confident that her exhaustion wouldn't allow her to be awakened, then headed to the basement. The door held fast and the knob wouldn't turn.

"Let me out," I whispered. "This has to be done."

A cold breeze hit me in the face.

"You want Maggie back, right? This is the only way."

Another breeze, accompanied by creaking pipes that sounded for the world like soft cries.

"I have to do this," I said. "She'll die if I don't. Hell, everyone will die if I don't. This way, no one dies."

I ran my hand over the doorframe.

"I'm sorry," I whispered. "I'm most likely not coming back. Take care of them for me."

The door came loose and I headed down into the basement. The box containing the book lay on the basement floor. It was as close as I wanted it to the shop. The influence it had was as contained as I could make it with the box, but some of its dark nature seeped out. If it got into the main part of the store for even a few minutes, I shuddered to think what might happen.

I scooped it up on my way out, took one last look around.

"I love you," I said to the shop. Then I headed through the tunnel.

The car idled as I stared up at the sky over Heinz Field. Worse than I imagined, the air buzzed with ethereal energies, whipped into a funnel cloud of psychic power. In the clouds, I saw faces, strained and full of pain and fear. A few I recognized, the murder victims and others. The storm held enormous potential energy. Driven by the will of the damned, powered by the dead.

For once, the streets around the stadium were empty. It was little wonder, though. The storm seared the air, prickled the flesh. Anyone could feel how wrong the air was, not just people like me. Most folks, if they were smart, were huddled in their homes with loved ones held tight.

I nudged the car forward into the empty parking lot and up to the gate. At the doors stood sentries, more puppets. No doubt the souls that once inhabited the bodies circled around above me. Not for the first time, I got the distinct impression I was in over my head. But it was too late to do anything but follow through with the plan and hope for the best, which, in this case, meant I died quickly and Maggie got away.

Also, not for the first time, I noted that any plan in which the best-case scenario included the phrase "I die quickly" was a terrible plan.

I pulled up in front of the gate where one of the puppets stood, then slowly got out of the car, box in hand.

"Cooper," he said. "I was hoping you'd be reasonable. Figured it out, did you?"

"I want to talk to you two," I said. "Face to face."

"Of course," said the puppet. "Right this way."

He gestured and I stepped through the gate. Behind me, I felt more prickles, the kind I'd felt before. Demons. More than a hundred, each inhabiting an innocent body, all in the shadows.

"You don't need to worry about them," said the puppet. "They can't get in. Not tonight. They can't interrupt our work."

"Shut up," I said. "I'm not talking through a corpse. Anything you've got to say to me, you say to my face."

"As you like."

He led me through the labyrinthine hallways, past locker rooms and trophy cases, concession stands and souvenir shops.

None of it mattered to me. In a few moments, the pill would go in my mouth and all of Bill's plans would vanish with a stomach cramp and asphyxiation.

At least, I hoped so.

The ghoul walked me out onto the field. On the center line stood Bill and Brea, dressed in ritual robes, an altar in front of them. The altar had straps on the side and a groove that looked like a place for a head. Mine. It also had two posts with straps at the top and bottom. Strapped in standing, or strapped down ready to lose my head, it seemed that neither position was a good one. Energy streamed from Bill's eyes into the puppet. When he stopped, Bill severed the connection and the corpse fell motionless at my feet.

"Stanley," said Bill.

"Hello, dear," said Brea.

"I see you've managed to get rid of your rider," said Bill. "How'd you manage it?"

I didn't know what he was talking about for a moment, then I realized what felt different. When I woke up, the demon was gone. But that was a problem for later.

"He must've gotten a better offer," I said.

"No matter," said Bill. The old man looked almost sad, but there was a grim resolve to his demeanor. Same for Brea. She knew what had to happen, and even if she wasn't completely thrilled about it, she was going to see it through to the end. "Did you bring the book?"

I held the box up.

"Give it to me," said Bill.

"Maggie goes free," I said. "I already pulled Andi out of your circus tent. I give myself over, you give me your word she goes free and neither one of them will be hurt in any way."

"Of course," said Bill. "We had no intention of hurting

them."

"Oh? Then why'd you cut on Andi's back? Fun? Shits and giggles?"

"We needed to get your attention," said Brea. "And, as anyone can tell you, pain brings a person closer to their beliefs. Even the Christian monks practiced self-flagellation."

"Why?" The question burned a hole in my brain. One word, but so many questions behind it. The murders. The purpose. The deception. Why was I so damned important to it all?

"Would you have given yourself over if we'd just asked?" Brea smiled. "You had to want to. And you're a good man. A very good man with a good soul. Your sacrifice will pave the way for a new understanding."

"Ruled by who? You two?"

"Don't think of us as rulers," said Bill. "We'll guide people toward love and peace."

"Whether they want it or not."

Bill let out a heavy sigh.

"Sometimes, people have to be told what's best for them."

"Maggie," I said. "You let her go. Now."

"Of course." Brea gestured and light leapt from her eyes into those of the corpse at my feet. It stood up and walked toward the stands.

"Neat trick," I said. "You taught that to Trevor, right?"

"Actually, he taught us," said Bill. "I'm very sorry for all this. We knew you were special when Maggie introduced you to us. That night, we knew we had a chance to end all the bigotry and prejudice in the world."

"You made me trust you." Hatred seethed inside me.

"It was necessary," said Bill. "Ah."

The puppet brought Maggie across the field. Though she wore a blindfold and a gag, and her hands were tied behind her

263

back, she still looked angry.

"You understand," said Brea. "We couldn't take any chances with her fouling the plan. She's very powerful, you know."

I removed her blindfold and pulled her close.

"Get ready to run," I whispered.

The electric eel bit wouldn't be able to hurt Bill or Brea. They were just too powerful. But they didn't know I could do such a thing, and I hoped it might take them by surprise long enough to run like hell. I had no doubt they'd catch me, but damned if I wasn't going down without a fight.

"Start walking to the gate," I said. "Don't look back."

Tears welled in Maggie's eyes. She knew what I had planned. I could see it on her face.

"Now," said Bill. "Give us the book."

"Please," I said. "Don't do this."

Brea rolled her eyes.

"Now!" she screeched. "Or Maggie dies, and the first place we go will be to finish the job on your little apprentice!"

"Alright," I said. I let the defeat in my voice hang in the air. Part of me really did hope I could reason with them, but in my heart I knew we were past the point where we could have a happy ending. Too many deaths, too much betrayal.

I held the box out to Bill, eyes turned down. He reached out and took hold of the box. Then I triggered the burst. The air between us popped like a super flash bulb, and the air became thick with the scent of burnt ozone.

"Run!"

Bill staggered back a few steps as Maggie took off for the exit. I ran right behind her, though I lost ground the whole way. Behind me, Bill roared. The force of it struck me hard and threw me to the ground. I slid on my face for a few feet before I stopped. Maggie made it to the exit. That part of the plan worked, at least.

"Why do you have to make it difficult?" shouted Brea. "We're doing this for the good of mankind!" The tiny woman grabbed me by the belt and hoisted me off the ground. Her strength was incredible, more than I would've expected from a man three times her size. She gave a heave and tossed me toward the altar.

Bill still looked a little stunned, but he crouched down by my face.

"And where'd you learn to do that?" he smiled. "Beginning to realize the extent of your power, are you?"

"What're you talking about?" My muscles screamed for mercy as I pushed myself off the ground. "Just kill me and get it over with, why don't you?"

"That's not the plan," said Brea. "You still don't know, do you? I thought you explained it to him."

"Some of it," said Bill. "Couldn't have him figuring it all out before we could finish, could we?"

I still didn't know what he was talking about, or why I was so important to their plan. And I didn't care. I didn't intend to be around long enough for it take effect.

While the two of them were occupied with each other, I reached into my pocket and pulled out the capsule. I tried to be sly, sneaky even. But before I could pop it into my mouth, a hand grabbed mine and wrenched the pill away from it.

"Couldn't have that," said the puppet. The light from his eyes went to Brea's. It walked to her and dropped the pill in her hand. "Let me guess. Hemlock, right? That's what I would use."

She tossed the pill over her shoulder into the grass. The puppet grabbed me by the withered arm while another took the good one.

"Get off!" I shouted. Another burst of energy rippled forth, nowhere near as strong as the first, but enough to make them stagger.

"We'll have no more of that, thank you," said Bill. Electric shocks hit my nervous system as he grabbed my neck. My body went rigid, then limp. The puppets dragged me toward the altar, and there was nothing I could do to stop them.

"Why're you resisting us?" Brea actually managed to sound confused. "You know us. You know we only want what's best for everyone."

"Not for you to decide." The words came out slurred because I couldn't control my mouth, but the meaning came through.

"Hush now," said Brea. "It'll all be over in a minute."

The puppets hoisted me up on the altar and strapped my wrists to the poles on either side. Bill opened the box, removed the book, and placed it on the altar. As he opened it, his expression changed. The benevolent man I knew, if he ever existed at all, was gone. What stood in his place was a dark god. Brea took his hand, and power rippled through her body.

Above me, the storm sped up, the swirl of the maelstrom increased in intensity. The wind turned into a gale, and in it echoed the howl of a thousand or more souls, trapped and held against their wills.

"Their energy will be fed through you," said Brea. "Then it'll go out to the rest of the world. Everywhere it touches, souls will be wiped clean, and the world can be reeducated into a more loving, more accepting place."

"You realize how stupid that sounds?" My facial muscles recovered enough to try to reason without sounding like a drunk. "Make everyone the same so they'll accept difference?"

"We figured, of anyone, you would understand," said Brea. "After all, look at how you've been treated by people who don't understand you."

"At least none of them wanted to kill me."

"We didn't want to," said Bill. "I hoped Dennis would be strong enough to weather the storm. He was willing, but weak. I suppose I always knew it had to be you, though. Your sacrifice will be noted. When this event is taught in schools, you'll be hailed as one of the benefactors of humankind."

He stepped in front of me and planted a metal rod into the ground.

"Hail to the Guardians of the watchtower of the east!" He had to shout to be heard over the wind and thunder. I knew what was coming. Five stakes, five points to the star, the holy symbol of his supposed faith, now perverted and warped by his ambition. Each one meant to call down the power of the growing storm, each directed to send that power through me. Just like Dennis. The amount of energy up there would kill anyone. I just hoped I wouldn't die in too much pain.

They called each of the four corners, followed by the fifth point, the one designated for spirit. They even had the audacity to call on the spirits of their brothers and sisters, the others of their same faith whose lives they were about to cut short. While they worked, I tried to block out my own fear to focus what was left of my energies on my withered arm. One part dead, one part alive, I tried to focus my will until the spectral arm appeared. When it did, it reacted just like the real arm once did. It was unshackled. I tried to use it to undo the strap that held the good one in place, but the hand kept slipping through as my concentration slipped bit by bit. Too much noise, too much pain, too tired.

"Please!" I shouted. "Don't do this! There's time to stop!"

They ignored me. When they completed the calling of the points, they both stepped out of the circle and turned toward me.

"We call forth the energies of creation itself," they said

in unison. "The power of the dead, the power of the living, the power of nature and man. Come forth! Wipe clean the slate, so we may begin anew!"

The cloud sent a wave of power down into the metal spikes. My skin prickled with the electricity in the air. In the split second before it released, realization hit me. The power would burn through me, leave my body a charred husk, and I wouldn't just die. I'd die screaming. As would the rest of the world, and they wouldn't even know. Everyone would wake up to find themselves empty, devoid of the things that made them who they were. No diversity, no differing opinions, no discourse.

The energy built, then released, fired directly into my core, into my soul. My body seized, but didn't hurt. I didn't burn, didn't feel the muscles as they tightened and tore. But there was a different sensation, one for which I wasn't prepared.

Voices. Thousands of them, all in my head, all in unison. They screamed, cried, shouted, all the dead who floated up above, all the souls inside the storm. I watched each individual life, watched their births, their experiences, their deaths. I saw them all at once, as if I just knew, experienced them all for myself. And in seeing, I was able to step back, look at all the lives together in one large tapestry, and see how they all fit together. Brothers, sisters, friends, and people who had nothing in common, all of them connected in some way or another, all of them bound by slender threads, all woven into a single fabric.

And all the threads converged on me.

"Release the power!" shouted Bill. "Purge the Earth!"

I wanted to. Really, I did. At that moment, the voices, the lives, the different perceptions, they were too much for a single mind to bear. If a person saw the entirety of his life at once, it would be hard to take. But I saw thousands, and I couldn't turn away. I wanted to release the energies and let them out of my head, send them out in a wave and let them do whatever damage they could on their way out. I wanted to be free of them, of the voices, of my own pain. I wanted to not think about Maggie, or Andi, or Taylor, or Appel, or Menold, or about anyone else. I wanted to not care. I wanted to slip away into the black, the way I should've done years ago.

But damned if I'm not a stubborn bastard.

As all the lives played before me, I noticed that each person shaped their own stream. Every energy was controlled, not by some higher power, but by the person. Sure, there did appear to be something larger, some energy that bound everything together, but the major influence of each individual life was the individual himself. Choices he made, consequences, actions and reactions. What happened next was not the will of some moldy demigod or even of Bill or Brea. What happened next was my choice, my will. The power was mine, and the mistake they made was letting me see it. I could've released it into the world. But instead, I held onto it, bottled it up.

Yes, I knew it would kill me. In fact, I knew how much it was going to hurt. But when it burned out, it wouldn't be able to affect an area larger than Pittsburgh. Everyone else would be safe.

"Release it!" screamed Brea. "Do it now!"

I felt them before I saw them. Pin pricks at my consciousness, needles on my scalp, spiders under my hair, whatever. Presences, perceptions, individual thoughts.

Hold on. We're coming.

The voice was familiar, warm and comforting like a blanket next to a radiator. There was only one person I knew, or had ever known, with a voice that could affect me so. Maggie.

I wanted to tell her to stay back, get away, run as fast as she could. No matter what she thought, she'd get along just fine without me. She didn't need to die just because I did.

Then I felt others. Andi. Menold.

Hold on, Stanley. We're coming.

No. They couldn't be. They needed to get away. Stay in the safe confines of the shop. Everything I did, I did to save them, to keep them safe, and here they were, trying to mount some suicidal rescue...

Then I felt more.

Hold on. We're coming.

I opened my eyes and lifted my head.

Maggie stood at the rail in the lowest section of seats, arms outstretched.

"Let him go." Her voice echoed off the walls of the stadium, though she didn't shout, and despite the storm.

"We're doing this for you!" shouted Bill. "We're doing this for all of us!"

"You're doing this for vanity."

Andi and Menold stepped out of the walkway and took positions beside her.

Brea laughed.

"What're you three going to do against us? You don't have the will!"

"We do." The voice came from higher up. It belonged to Reneau. Around her stood people I didn't know.

"We do." Another voice came from the other direction. Blossom stood at the second tier of seats, hands raised. More people I'd never seen before streamed past her and into the seats.

"We do." The voice came from the field, where a man in monk's robes stepped out of the shadows. "And we're stronger than you." He pulled back his hood. Neighbor Bob stared up at me and smiled.

The stadium filled. People streamed past my friends and stood in front of the seats. Men, women, children, fathers, mothers with babies in their arms.

"Now!" screamed Bob. "Strike!"

Maggie, Andi, Reneau, Blossom and Bob all raised their hands in unison, and the storm above me screamed. Or maybe that was just me. Every mind that stood beside them touched mine, in much the same way the souls in the storm did. Every person in the stadium, so many that I couldn't count, opened themselves to me, and I saw them all. Lives, fears, triumphs, pain, everything, all in a flash, all flowing into my head. They weren't Pagan or Christian, straight or gay, male or female, but were just people. Normal, everyday ordinary people who felt something wrong, and came to fight it. I knew things about them that they never told anyone, things they never wanted known. I knew them about Maggie, about Andi, about every person. And I couldn't turn them off. I couldn't block them out, just streams of hopes and dreams and fears and prayers, all thrown into my head at once.

Above them all, the warm blanket of Maggie's voice echoed.

Fight. Don't give in. Don't let yourself die.

Their collective will flooded into me and I started to burn. I felt it, like a real fire, like a wire heated by too much electricity. I had to let it go, but if I did, it might finish the job on the way out.

Then, something inside me cracked. My perception shifted a further direction than before. Not only could I see the dead and the energy patterns of the world, I saw more. I saw into every living thing, every rock, every piece of steel. I saw the girders that held the stadium together, saw the welds and knew which ones would stand the test of time and which would need to be replaced. I saw the babies in their mother's arms and knew which would go to jail and which would put them there. I saw the past to the dawn of time and the future to the end. I saw everything, and shuddered at its insignificance.

Please fight!

I latched hold of Maggie's voice, her will, and used it to guide me. The power of the storm flowed into me, but there was one thing Bill and Brea didn't count on. With the knowledge of every person in the stadium, I could direct it. I could make it do what *I* wanted. Remake the world in *my* image, if I chose. And as I sat there, with the awareness of God and the power of the living and dead, I considered it.

For a moment.

The energy erupted from me like a scream, a horrible tidal wave of pure rage and passion, that poured out and struck Bill and Brea full. They threw up their defenses, their shields, but it was like trying to stop a truck with tissue paper. My anger lifted them off their feet and threw them into a support beam, then pummeled them until flesh split and peeled away, then muscle followed. Bones pulped and organs burst until there was nothing left but a red stain on the concrete, and then not even that remained. When it was all said and done, it looked like someone sandblasted the paint right off the wall.

The energy spent, I went limp, held up only by the straps on my wrists. Everything went blurry and my mouth went dry. I think I asked for water. But then the darkness covered my eyes, and I was gone.

25

There's a long list of things I never wanted to be. Most kids think about the careers they want, like doctor or fireman. Not me. When I was a kid, I made a list of the jobs that seemed like too big of a pain in the neck to be worth a paycheck. Somewhere in the top five were gems like "adult theater janitor" and "elephant proctologist." But at the top of that list, no matter how many times I revised it over the years, one entry remained the same. God.

Lots of people feel like they could do a better job of governing the universe than the Almighty, or the Almighties, depending on what a person believes. Not me. Given the chance, I'd probably screw it up.

I didn't die. At first I thought I did, but the massive amount of pain in my limbs told me otherwise. It started at my toes and moved up to the top of my scalp without any detours along the way. My eyelids even hurt, so I didn't open them straight away. I just listened for the tell-tale signs of misfortune. I didn't hear the wind of the storm anymore. Nor did I hear any screams or cries or diabolical laughter. I also didn't hear any beeping, which told me I wasn't in a hospital. In fact, I didn't hear much of anything. I opened my eyes.

The room around me was awash in candlelight. I was, again, naked on the bed, with a tiny strip of cloth across my nethers. Only this time, I wasn't alone.

Maggie knelt in a corner, eyes closed, palms up. Her lips moved in silent prayer.

"Hey," I croaked.

Her eyes snapped open and she scrambled to my side.

"Are you okay?"

"I feel like shit," I said. "You?"

"I thought we lost you."

"How long?"

"Four days," she said. "I didn't know if you were coming out or not."

"Can't get rid of me that easy."

The door to the room flew open. Andi stood in the doorway, eyes wide and filled with tears.

"Shop told me you were awake," said Andi. "How are you?"

"Hungry, sore and tired," I said. "In that order." I tried to get up, but the pain in my muscles tied me back down to the bed.

"You're not going anywhere," said Maggie.

"I'll get you some broth," said Andi. She hurried out of the room.

"It was beautiful," I said. "Terrible, but beautiful. I saw everything."

"Can you remember it all?"

"No." Truth was, everything was all muddled together. The longer I stayed awake, the more the memories faded into nothing, like the wispy edges of a dream. Which was fine with me. I didn't want all the information. There was enough crap in

274

my head to deal with. I didn't need more from anyone. "How did you get all those people together?"

"I didn't," said Maggie. "They all showed up. Said they got a sign of some sort. I didn't figure it out until Reneau got there. She said the Scats told her where you were. That must've been some message you sent out."

"Just meant it to go out to a few people. Didn't mean to pull the whole city in."

"Well it's a good thing you did," she said. "We never could've beaten them."

"Where are they?"

"You really don't remember, do you?" She took my hand. "You... obliterated them."

Flashes of that evening popped through my mind, enough to see two bodies smashed to bits. My stomach lurched.

"Menold?"

"He's been by a few times. He acts like he doesn't remember anything, but I've caught him staring a few times. Bitsy scares the hell out of him."

"Good cat. What about the demons?"

"I think they'll leave us alone," she said. "For a while, anyway. At least they're not going to try to kill you."

"I'll call that a win."

"Most everyone else doesn't really remember anything either," she said. "We've had a few random people stop in the shop, look lost, like they've forgotten what they're doing there, and then leave. I can see it on their faces that they remembered for a moment, but then it's gone."

"Good," I said. "No one needs to remember."

"A few people do," she said. "They put up a shrine outside. I don't think most of them know why they did it, but people pass by it and put candles on it. No one's vandalized it."

"Show me," I said as I tried to sit up again.

"Shh," she put gentle pressure on my shoulders that may as well have been nailing me to the table. "You rest now. You've got to heal. I'm just thankful you're alive." She leaned in and kissed me.

One of the things they hardly ever show in movies is what happens when the bad guys are gone. The hero may be battered and bruised, but he limps away with the girl and then the credits roll. They don't show the weeks of recovery, the nightmares, the paranoia at every moving shadow. They don't show the hero when he wakes up sobbing because the images of what he did, justified or not, just won't go away. Physical healing is one thing. Psychological healing takes a good deal longer, and hurts more.

For me, the physical part took another five days of bed rest while my torn muscles decided whether or not they wanted to work for me anymore. It should've taken longer, but I couldn't stand being waited on hand and foot. Also, bed rest gave me too much time to think about unpleasant things.

You managed to get rid of your rider.

Where'd the demon go?

It'll only come out when it finds another host.

Which meant what, exactly?

I pushed myself past the pain of sore muscles and agony of hyperextended joints and got up and dressed. Every movement left me breathless, but reminded me not only that I was alive, but also how much worse it could've been.

The stairs, by the way, were pure torture. It took me a good five minutes to get down them, one step at a time. When I walked through the door of the shop, Maggie and Andi were helping customers. Their heads snapped up, as did the young man who was in the process of purchasing a grimoire.

"What are you doing out of bed?" said Maggie while Andi finished up with the customer.

"Couldn't take it anymore," I said.

The shrine was right where she said, underneath the front window outside the shop. A simple wooden box, small, was covered in candle wax as people left their well-wishes and prayers. There were no notes, no big "Get Well Stanley!" signs, but the fact that there were so many candles, and such a huge pile of melted wax, was humbling. I looked up from the shrine to see several of the Carson Street shopkeepers. They looked out their doors toward me like they'd seen a ghost. A couple waved, one even smiled. A few of the passersby on the street did the same. One little girl who was with her mother stopped and tugged at my jacket. When I leaned down to ask her what she wanted, she hugged me, then ran off.

I almost burst into tears.

Back inside, Maggie looked fit to explode with joy, as did Andi. I caught the tail end of their conversation before they realized I was there. Maybe the shop helped a little by muting the chimes over the door.

"Can I tell him?"

"No!" said Maggie. "I'll tell him at the right time."

"Tell me what?"

They both clammed up and looked like I'd caught them at something.

"C'mon," I said. "Out with it."

"Maybe you should sit down," said Maggie.

"Just tell me."

"I'm pregnant."

My smile must've faltered because the look on her face changed from impish joy to mild annoyance. "Don't act all excited."

The fact was, I was thrilled. A baby? *My* baby? It was more terrifying and exciting than anything I could've imagined.

"Are you kidding?" I stood up so fast, I think I pulled something loose, then I took her in my arms and kissed her. "I'm going to be a father!"

Her smile came back and Andi beamed.

In every dark cloud, there is a silver lining. Anyone who believes that must also believe that in every little bit of silver, there's a shadow. Every diamond has a flaw, every fortune has a measure of tragedy. We try not to go around looking for the bad things, but every so often, they just pop out and we do our best to ignore them and hope we're wrong.

Maggie carried my baby.

It will come out when it finds another host.

We made love the night before I went to rescue Andi.

It didn't take a genius to do the math. I hoped I was wrong.

I sat in the back of the shop doing the only thing I was physically capable of doing: inventory. The fact was, inventory was the single most hated duty in the shop. I figured, since the shop was alive, shouldn't she be able to count her own contents? The trouble was, she wasn't that big on counting, and occasionally just conjured, or ate, things to suit herself.

I wondered how I was going to be able to broach the subject with Maggie when I felt a presence enter the shop.

There are words that, when spoken, can reduce a grown man to tears and make even the most powerful person feel like a frightened child. The words themselves are not important, so much as how they're said. The intonation, the timbre.

I peeked through the curtain. A woman stood in a purple nylon jumpsuit with gold trim. Huge bug-eye glasses covered half her face, and her dark hair stood teased to almost statuesque proportions. I almost had time to close the curtain and run when she spoke.

"Stanley Irving Cooper!"

All the strength drained from my body and my head hung. I pushed through the curtain and faced her like a man facing a firing squad.

"Hi, Mom."

"Where's this woman who called and said she's having my grandbaby?"

Damn. Why can't things ever be simple?

ABOUT THE AUTHOR

Scott A. Johnson is the author of nine novels, three true ghost story guides, a chapbook and a short story collection. He currently lives somewhere near Austin, Texas, with his wife, daughter, four cats, a chihuahua, and a pug.

For more information, look to his website at
http://www.creepylittlebastard.com

OTHER BOOKS BY SCOTT A JOHNSON

An American Haunting

Deadlands

Cane River: A Ghost Story

The Journal of Edwin Grey

City of Demons

Deadlands: The definitive edition

Shy Grove: A Ghost Story

The Mayor's Guide: The Stately Ghosts of Augusta

The Ghosts of San Antonio

Haunted Austin, Texas

Droplets: A Short Story Collection

The Stanley Cooper Chronicles:
  Book One - **Vermin**
  Book Two - **Pages**
  Book Three - **Ectostorm**